HADES

A
CONTEMPORARY
MYTHOS NOVEL

HADES

CARLY SPADE

HADES

A CONTEMPORARY MYTHOS NOVEL

"Hateful in my eyes as the gates of Hades is that man, who, yielding to stress of poverty, tells a deceitful tale."

HOMER, *ODYSSEY*

O N E

CLICK. CLICK. SCROLL. SCROLL. As a digital forensics examiner for the Illinois State Police, my life was an endless series of mouse clicks and down arrows on the keyboard. Though a relatively large portion of my job required in-depth analysis, an even *larger* part revolved around merely sifting through a suspect's collection of files. Files pulled from devices such as computers, cell phones, and tablets. All files. Including some I'd rather not see, but could never seem to avoid. You can tell a lot about a person from their search history alone.

I peeled the glasses from my nose, rubbing my hands over my face, and giving my eyes a break from the constant blaring white light of the computer screen. One of the troopers ducked in his head. The digital forensics unit had its suite away from the other investigators. It made it easier to maintain evidence and to avoid seeing potential mind-bending images that came up on our screens. I preferred it that way. It was my own little hole in the universe where I could seclude myself and do my job.

"You have a visitor downstairs, Costas," he said, leaning on the doorknob.

After saving my case file, I grabbed a pen and brushed my bangs away from my forehead. "How many times do I have to tell you, Bruce? Call me, Steph. You trooper. Me civilian." Chuckling, I pointed between the two of us.

"Just want to make you feel like a part of the team. There are no first names here. Number one rule."

I smiled and moved into the hallway. "Who is it? Please tell me it's not Mr. Sanders. My brain is far too fried to deal with his level of crazy right now."

"Mrs. Conroy. Sound familiar?"

I pinched my eyes shut. Please tell me it wasn't *the* Mrs. Conroy. "What does she look like?"

"I'd guess early forties? Auburn hair. Sunken eyes. Looks like she hasn't slept in weeks."

Definitely sounded like her. Oh, boy.

After pushing the down button for the elevator, I removed the pen from my dress pocket. "You mind sticking around until I give the clear?" The elevator doors opened, and I clicked the pen several times as I walked in.

"Of course," he said.

When we stepped out of the elevator, the woman waiting sprinted toward me. I could picture her plain as day in the courtroom when I was on the stand, answering questions about my findings in her husband's murder case. A case that closed four years ago.

I waved at Bruce over my shoulder. "We're good."

He studied the woman's face and then looked at me. "You sure?"

"Yeah. I got it."

"I'll be in my office if you need me." He paused another beat before turning away.

"Mrs. Conroy, can I help you with something?" I placed a hand on her shoulder.

She wrung her hands together, her hair in disarray, dark bags under her eyes. Her clothes were stained with brown splotches; nails caked with something dark. She gave off a body odor that smelled like she hadn't showered in days, possibly weeks.

My great-grandma used to say I could see a person's aura. Throughout my life and in my profession, I stood firm that seeing was believing. Magic. Mysticism. Gut instinct was *my* superpower. Still, it never stopped me from seeing colors. Colors which made it possible for me to read a person without an explanation of how. Black mixed with bright yellow floated over Mrs. Conroy like vapor.

"Henry came to me from the Underworld. He came to me in a dream. There had to be more evidence, Miss Costas. There *had* to be." Her words came out frantic, rushed, and loud.

The Underworld? She was worse off than I thought. Her anxiety was rubbing off on me. It reminded me why I hated the main floor. There were always too many people. Even in their cubicles, it suffocated me. "Let's go talk over here." We moved to a quieter corner, as far away from everyone else as I could manage without leaving the building.

"Henry told me there was financial evidence. That it would

prove, Earnest Fueller bought the hammer. I'm sure the dates, the times, location…. all of it would match," She grabbed my shoulders with wild eyes.

I tensed, beads of sweat dripping down my neck. The pen. I rolled it in my palm to distract myself. It was unlikely any of what Mrs. Conroy was saying was true. Four years ago, her husband was one of a string of murders. The suspected murderer was Earnest Fueller, who'd conveniently committed suicide after the seventh murder, her husband. Without his testimony and little evidence found, he was never officially ruled as guilty. Over the years, it drove Mrs. Conroy to the brink of insanity.

"Mrs. Conroy, I understand you need closure, but there's nothing else we can do. The case was combed over and over for almost a year. There wasn't enough evidence. I personally searched devices for months on end. You know that."

"Couldn't you open it again? Take another look?" Her grip tightened, tears welling in her eyes. "Please."

With her situation and the pained look in her eyes, I'd have a hard time saying no. Then again, I couldn't remember the last time I turned down anyone's request. She needed closure. To know, with the utmost certainty, who killed her husband. Who could fault her?

"I'll take another look." Nausea boiled in my stomach, knowing it was unlikely I'd find anything. Despite it, I felt obligated to try because I didn't like letting people down if I could help it.

She let out a breath and wrapped her arms around me. Given my short stature, my face shoved against her bosom. I held my glasses to keep them from falling off.

"Thank you so much! You have no idea what this means to me." A newfound hope flickered in her eyes. A hope I put there knowing the chances were slim.

Me and my big mouth.

"I can't make any promises, but I'll try a few things between my other cases."

"I absolutely understand. I'll—I'll leave you to it. Please call me as soon as you find anything." She clapped her hands over her mouth, tears streaking her cheeks.

If I find anything. "Of course." I offered a half-smile.

She headed for the door, sniffling and bumping into desk corners.

I slipped off my glasses and pinched the bridge of my nose as I walked back to the elevator. My throat burned from the acid reflux making an unwanted visit. I fished through my pocket, pulling out a roll of Tums.

"Looks like you need to release a bit of tension there, Steph," Leo said from behind me.

After pressing the elevator button, I turned around to see his snarky grin. Every station had one. The cocky, creepy cop who loved to hit on the civilians. Was it because they didn't think we'd have as much balls as a female officer? I hadn't fallen for it yet…and wouldn't.

"Nothing a bottle of wine and a bubble bath can't cure, Leo." I regretted the words as soon as they left my mouth.

"You in nothing but suds and water…I can get behind that. Do you wear your glasses too?" His slimy grin continued as he leaned against the wall.

"Goodnight, Leo," I answered, stepping into the elevator. As the doors closed, I caught him waving at me through the crack.

I shuffled back into the digital investigation suite, and grabbed the hard drives for old cases we kept in the closet. Dragging my finger down the rows of labels on each drive, I sighed once it landed on the Fueller case. The moment I opened the file, I knew I risked becoming overly reinvested, but a promise was a promise.

Chewing another Tums, I flopped back into my desk chair, hooked up the drive, and transferred the case and evidence files to the backup drive on my computer. I plucked the stirring straw from my mug of coffee and slipped it between my teeth, feverishly chewing on it. Using two of my three monitors, I kept one case opened on one and pulled up the old case on the other with different forensic software.

Popping my earbuds in, I skipped to the next track on my playlist. Familiar images of questionable internet search histories, shopping lists, and cell phone pictures flooded the screen. I nodded to the familiar tune of *Take On Me* by A-Ha. Eighties music always leveled my head.

Something poked me in the ribs, causing me to jump from my chair. I turned around, spotting my best friend, Sara, glaring at me.

I blew my bangs out of my eyes. "You scared the crap out of me. When did you come in?"

She put her hands on her hips. "You were so focused, you didn't hear me. What if I would've been a criminal overtaking the station?"

"And said criminal somehow managed to get past several

floors of armed troopers?" I arched a brow.

Sara and I became friends once I joined the department. She was a detective, rough on the outside, but an absolute teddy bear on the inside. Her skin was umber with eyes to match, and she always kept her hair chin-length to not touch her collar.

She leaned past me, immediately drawn to the monitor with the old case pulled up. I attempted to step in front of her. She grabbed onto the back of my dress and, with little effort, pulled me away. "Is this the Fueller case? The one we closed four years ago?"

Licking Tums residue from my teeth and silence was my answer.

She stared at the roll of antacids in my hand and grabbed the mouse quicker than I could pull the cable on it. After spending a few seconds clicking through a couple of the drives, she sighed. "Why are you working on this, Steph?"

I adjusted my glasses, counting the scuff marks on my ballet flats. "Mrs. Conroy came in today. She asked me to take another look."

"Stephanie…"

Oh, that tone. I wanted to stuff my cheeks full of Tums like a hamster.

"You should've seen her, Sara. I couldn't in good conscience tell her no. I wouldn't be able to live with myself."

"When's the last time you've told *anyone*, no?"

I stuck the stirring straw back in my mouth and clicked the pen that'd never left my hand. "I didn't have the Blue Satchel software at the time. I'm going to process it through there and see if anything new comes up."

"Uh-huh. Did you look at those brochures I gave you three weeks ago?"

My gaze shifted back to the monitor. "What brochures?"

"The ones of the different resorts?" She groaned. "I asked you to look through them and give me your top two?"

Sara insisted we went on vacation, especially considering I hadn't taken a day off in over two years. Where the brochures were now would remain a mystery.

A trooper named Evans walked in with a stack of papers, brushing past Sara. He plopped the documents on my desk, sending Snickers wrappers flying in every direction.

"I've been swamped today and haven't had time to file these. Would you mind? Please?" He asked, giving his best puppy dog eyes.

"Uh…" I feverishly clicked the pen, spying Sara's death dagger stare from the corner of my eye.

"Please? My fiancé will kill me if I'm late for dinner again," he added, clutching his hands together in prayer.

I chewed on the end of the pen. "I mean…"

"Costas. Please. I'll owe you."

He'd owe me, but would never actually pay me back in any way.

"Fine. Yes. Say 'Hi' to Annie for me."

He slapped my shoulder, making my glasses slide down my nose. "You're a lifesaver."

I picked up the papers and shuffled them until they were in a perfect stack.

Sara growled under her breath, yanked the papers from my

grasp, and stormed for the door.

"Evans," she bellowed. "File your own damn paperwork. Costas isn't your secretary." She threw the papers on the ground and walked back to my desk with her arms folded.

"It really wasn't a big deal. I've got nothing else going on tonight. Just waiting on this evidence to process," I said.

"You *do* have something going on tonight."

I stopped clicking the pen. "I do?"

"Friday the thirteenth?"

"And?" I asked, dragging out the "a".

Her hand slapped over her face. "You're already distracted. Lovely. Patrick Swayze and provocative dance moves?"

My eyes fell shut. "Dirty Dancing."

"Bingo. And it's your place this time."

Dirty Dancing was one of my favorite movies of all time. Somehow Sara hadn't seen it when we met and I was quick to rectify that. It happened to be a Friday the thirteenth, and now we'd made it some bizarre ritual.

"I'll head home as soon as this is done processing in—," I peeked at the monitor and frowned. "Six hours, no wait eight hours...seven?" The estimated time for completion kept fluctuating, as it always did.

"We both know it won't finish processing until tomorrow. Come on." She wheeled my chair backward and shook it until I was forced to jump off.

"Fine. Fine. I'm going home. But if this freezes overnight and I have to start it over you're going to be...*Under Pressure*."

She narrowed her eyes. "Why'd you say it like that?"

"Under Pressure? David Bowie song?"

"You're so weird." She snorted.

"Right." I snickered. "Home I go. Meet me in thirty?"

My eyes dropped back to the progress bar as soon as Sara whisked out the door. A gust of wind blew across my desk, sending my hair into my face. Papers flew everywhere, and something landed on my keyboard with a loud *thwap*.

What in the world? Faulty vent?

Staring back at me was a colorful brochure for a resort in Corfu, Greece. One of several Sara had given me to look through. The others scattered across the floor. I shifted my eyes, shoved the brochure in my dress pocket, and left.

When I entered my apartment, Sammy, my cobalt-colored cat, greeted me by doing figure eights between my calves. I picked him up, shoving my nose into his fur, relishing the vibrations from his purrs.

My apartment was a modest studio in the suburbs with the most spartan furniture known to man. I made up for it with wall-to-wall framed posters of some of my favorite movies, including Disney's *Hercules*, *Princess Bride*, and *Dirty Dancing*. My coveted signed poster from the band Apollo's Suns hung in all its glory above my TV. It was signed by every member except Ace, the lead singer. The latest book I'd finished reading, *Korrigan*, rested on my coffee table. Scooping it up, I returned it to my bookshelf. My blessed fantasy collection. *Pitchfork*, *Rhapsodic*, Homer's *Illiad*, Homer's *Odyssey*…I yanked the *Illiad* from the shelf.

A loud knock sounded at the door.

Sara's eyeball stared back at me through the peephole. Her pearly whites beamed with an exaggerated grin once I opened the door. She held up a bottle of white merlot and ducked under my arm, heading straight for the kitchen. After shutting the door and securing the deadbolt, I followed her.

She grabbed two wine glasses from my cabinet. "Cue up your preferred streaming service, my dear. And do you have any cheese? These eyes are *hungry*," she said, somehow managing not to crack a smile.

I chuckled. "Top shelf in the door, but double-check. It's pepper jack."

"Ah, yes. Your fear that one of the peppers could be mold. How could I forget?" She snatched the cheese, shut the door with her hip, and winked. "Why do you have three pomegranates in your fridge? I don't think I've ever seen *one* in someone's fridge, let alone three."

"Uh, because I like them?" After looking for the remote control in every couch cushion crack, I was about to do the abysmal act of turning the TV on by pressing the button on the unit itself. "Besides, they have all sorts of benefits. Anti-inflammatory, natural antioxidants, cancer prevention…"

Sara gasped. "Cinnamon Bun Oreos? I thought they didn't sell these anymore." She eyed the platter of Oreos I purposely put on display and grabbed a handful.

"Randomly found some when I went to Bullseye the other day. I cleared their shelves," I said with a snicker.

I had an epiphany and dropped to the floor, peering under the couch. There, resting amidst a modest collection of dust bunnies, stale corn chips, and cat fur, was the remote.

"Doing pushups now? Good for you," Sara said, making the couch creak when she flopped onto it.

I snorted. "Me? Pushups? Maybe for my forefinger." I mimicked the motion of clicking a mouse.

Sara shook her head with a smile and popped a cheese cube in her mouth. As soon as I sat down, Sammy hopped onto the TV stand, his tail sticking straight in the air. The opening music started, and he paused right in the middle of the screen, rubbing his head against the people groping.

"He has three seconds before I start throwing cheese at him," Sara mumbled.

She wasn't kidding. Sara hated cats and never let me forget it. "Down, Sammy!" He turned and looked at us with pure boredom before continuing his head rub against the television. I sighed, stood, and yanked him into the crook of my arm. Once he was on the couch, he did several circles and curled up in a ball next to my leg.

"That cat is so spoiled." Sara sneered at him.

"If you owned more than betta fish, maybe you'd spoil a pet too." I grabbed my wine glass and curled my feet underneath me.

Sara stuck her tongue out, and we watched *Dirty Dancing* for the rest of the night. I knew the movie so well I could quote it word for word. After the second time of me doing this out loud, she requested I keep my trap shut unless it was a commentary on Swayze's glowing posterior. Instead, I resorted to "mouthing" the dialogue because I just couldn't help myself. When I zoned out during Johnny and Baby's first sex scene, my thoughts fluttering to the processing case in my office, I realized my worst fear. I was already invested.

The movie ended, but I stared into oblivion, gripping onto the remote like I'd fall through an invisible hole if I let go. Sara reached over me and yanked it from my grasp. The screen turned black.

"We're going on vacation," she blurted.

My eyes fluttered me back to reality. "I'm sorry, what?"

She flipped her phone around. A resort with mountains in the background, a pool with crystal blue water, and a swim-up bar, lit up the screen.

"Wow. That's gorgeous." It also looked *very* familiar.

She grinned and slipped the phone back in her pocket. "I'm glad you think so because it's where we're going."

"Sara." I chuckled, but it faded away when she didn't join in. "Are you serious? You know I can't afford anywhere like that."

"It's already planned and booked. Squared away our vacation time with the boss. And we leave tomorrow." She stared at me with a mischievous smirk.

A breath hitched in my throat, and I stood, pacing the length of my living room. "Tomorrow? I have so many things to do. Packing, figuring out someone to watch Sammy, get shots."

"All you have to do is pack a few dresses and a swimsuit." She gripped my arms. "The bikini. Not the one piece. I already asked my friend to watch your cat. And we're going to Greece, not a country known for malaria, Steph."

The brochure. Was Sara psychic?

I stared at her blankly. "You knew I'd try to talk you out of this, didn't you?"

"I did. Besides, this isn't out of left field. You've known about this for a month, but have been putting it off." She sighed. "You need this. *We* need this. I need a break from looking at dead bodies, and I'm sure if you find porn on one more suspect computer, you're going to scream."

Sara knew I was never one for spontaneity. Her act of prepping everything before telling me made me love her that much more. How would I ever repay her for this?

"Thank you, Sara. I—I can't give it all to you right now, but I *will* pay you back," I said, giving her my best pout.

She shook her head. "You put those big blue doe eyes away. We can argue about you paying me back later."

"How do you know my passport is current?" I narrowed my eyes.

She grinned. "Stop trying to weasel your way out of this. The department requires all employees to maintain current passports, and *you* are not the type to be out of compliance."

Son of a nutcracker. I hated how well she knew me.

I bit down on my lip with such force I tasted blood. "Well, you better go then. It'll probably take me all night to pack, unpack and re-pack again. You know me."

Her grin widened. "I'll need to wrap up a few things at work tomorrow morning. Meet me there, and we'll take a cab to the airport. Deal?"

I nodded, already dreading the thought of a crowded airport.

After she left, I stared into my closet as if it were a mysterious cave. My wardrobe wasn't what one would describe as... eclectic. Dresses with pockets were my go-to outfit for work. Comfortable and accessible. They were not, however, the type of attire you'd wear to some swanky resort. I shoved the work clothes aside, revealing skirts I hadn't worn in years and a prom dress from fifteen years ago. Why had I even kept it? Like I could still fit into it. Not that I tried or anything.

The dress stuck out like a sore thumb, nestled into a particular corner of the closet. A simple light pink dress with an a-line cut and straps. The skirt portion flared out with flowy material like a cloud when you spun in it. It was the closest I could find to the dress Baby wore in *Dirty Dancing*. Before now, I never had an excuse to wear it.

I carried the dress to my bed like it'd wither away in my hands if I weren't careful. Placing it down, I smiled, imagining myself dancing in it. By myself. Certainly not groping on some random stranger. Okay, so maybe this vacation wasn't such a bad idea after all. I continued to grab items I imagined one would need for Greece. Holding the bikini in one hand and the one-piece in the other, an internal battle ensued.

To me, a bikini suggested I was single and ready to mingle. I was single, but the mingling part? Work took most of my time. It didn't seem fair to date anyone. To be with someone meant they should be a priority. My brain never shuts off when it came to working, and there wasn't room for much else.

I groaned, throwing both suits into the bag. I'd figure it out when I got there. Who knew packing for a time in a paradise could be so stressful? Me. I knew. Sammy hopped onto my bed, kneading the top part of my suitcase before curling himself on top of it.

I slipped into the bathroom and braided my hair. It was a ritual I'd done nightly as a silent tribute to my mother, who'd shared the same chocolate hair color. Memories of the house engulfed with flames infiltrated my thoughts with each overlapping section of my hair. Holding back tears, I sniffled.

When I returned to my bedroom, Sammy slept on my suitcase, and I ran my hand down the length of his spine.

"I really do need a vacation." I furrowed my brow and fished for the dress I'd worn today from my hamper.

Removing the brochure from my pocket, I stared at it in awe. Not only did Sara pick Greece, but she chose the same resort. Coincidence. It had to be a coincidence.

TWO

I DRUMMED MY FINGERS against the mousepad on my desk. The processing was *still* going, and I wanted to make sure it finished before we left for the airport. My suitcase rested on the floor next to me, and I bounced my knee impatiently. Staring at the screen with dried eyes, I regretted my decision to wear contacts for travel.

"How long have you been here?" Sara asked from the doorway. Her hand was on her hip, the other curled around the handle of her suitcase.

"Only since 5:30. I wanted to make sure the processing finished so I could save the case file."

"I know what you're doing." She looked down at my erratic knee.

I slapped my hand over it. "What am I doing?"

"You feel guilty. You promised Mrs. Conroy you'd take another look at the evidence, and now you're going on vacation."

My eyes narrowed. "I'm simply cellophane to you, aren't I?"

"Mrs. Conroy won't know you're going on vacation and even if she did…you're doing this to clear your head. If anything, it'll help you, right? You'll come back, sit down at your desk, and have that big eureka moment." She grabbed my mouse and pulled up my playlist, using the scrolling button to search through hundreds of songs.

"You're right. You're absolutely right. I can't remember the last time I didn't think about work." I stared off into space. Imagine everything I could do non-work related.

"Vacation starts now." Her full lips spread into a grin, and she yanked my earbuds cord from the computer.

The song *Push It* by Salt n Pepa blared through the speakers. It was our anthem. I couldn't remember the last time we'd danced to it. Leaping from my chair, I pumped my hands near my chest, bumping hips with her. Our dance wasn't music video level, but it was ours. She always made exaggerated "ah" sounds before singing the words "push it," and it never failed to make me laugh uncontrollably.

Taking a moment to simply *be*, was going to be like a breath of fresh air. I'd have to figure out a way to return the favor. She'd refuse monetary compensation, so it'd need to come from the heart. We were so caught up singing the lyrics at the top of our lungs and bouncing around, we didn't hear one of the troopers come in.

"Hey! Before you go, can you *push* these papers? They're for your case that closed last week." He threw a stack of papers onto my desk.

We both froze, attempting to hold back our giggles. He

shook his head, snickering as he left.

We took a taxi to O'Hare Airport and arrived three hours before departure, as I requested. My theory was, the lines would be shorter, and I could nab a seat facing the windows at our gate.

The runway bustled with workers carting luggage across the tarmac outside. I sipped on my iced coffee, enjoying the aisle seat that Sara graciously allowed me. The straw made slurping sounds as I drained every last drop from my cup.

"How are you with airplane bathrooms?" Sara slouched in her seat to the point where her neck was resting on the back support.

I plucked the straw with my teeth. "Not a big fan. Why?"

"Just wondering. Remember, we nabbed the non-stop flight." Her gaze dropped to my empty cup.

I made a *pfft* sound. "I'll go right before we board, and I'll be fine."

"I bet you five dollars you'll have to go on the plane at least three times."

As if this woman had a personal relationship with my bladder.

"Fine." I glared at her and wiped my hand on my shirt to rid it of condensation before jutting it out to shake.

"Oh, my God. Is that who I think it is?" Sara asked, staring wide-eyed.

Women surrounded a man with long blonde hair. He wore

a tan leather jacket, ripped jeans, and boots. His bright smile flashed wide.

"Holy crud. Holy crud." I sunk in my seat like he'd somehow recognize me. "That's Ace from Apollo's Suns."

"Steph. Go talk to him. Get his autograph, a selfie, whatever. You *love* that band." She pushed my shoulders, trying to get me to stand, but I dug my heels into the carpet.

"No. He's in an airport trying to travel. Who in their right mind is ever in a good mood traveling? It'd be rude." I bit on my thumbnail, watching him drag his hand through his hair, pausing now and again to throw up the rock horns gesture for another selfie.

"All those girls don't seem to care. Judging by that smile which hasn't left his face, I'd say he doesn't either."

I shook my head, feeling my heartbeat against my chest like a jackhammer. "I can't, Sara." The moment the words left my mouth, I knew I'd regret not working up the courage to go and meet him. Mental facepalm.

"Alright, then. I will." She plucked one of the squared white napkins from my knee and reached into the front pocket of my backpack, grabbing one of seven pens I kept there and marched over.

"Oh my gosh." I sunk further in my seat.

She brushed past several women, demanding Ace's attention. They exchanged a few words before she held up the napkin and pointed in my direction. Ace looked over with a wide grin and waved.

My cheeks flushed, and I slapped my hands over my eyes. Parting my fingers enough to see Sara, she leaned forward and hugged him. She *hugged* Ace. I wouldn't have gotten out a coherent sentence, let alone brush my boobs against his chest in an embrace.

As she walked back, Ace dipped his hand behind his back for a fraction of a second. A shimmering orange glow flashed from his palm. He shoved his hand in his pocket and then removed it, showing one woman a guitar pick. What the—I stared at the ice cubes in my empty cup. I shouldn't have gotten that extra espresso shot.

"Here you go." She slapped the napkin on my leg. "Apparently, he's headed to Buffalo, New York, for a special gig."

I picked it up, and my jaw dropped. "To Stephanie. Never lose your sparkle. Love, Ace," I read out loud. "You told him I'm—sparkly?"

"No. He made it up after he looked over at you." She shrugged.

"Thanks, Sara. You gotta stop with these favors, though, or I'll never be able to make up for it." I slipped the napkin behind a cover of one of my notebooks for safekeeping.

The attendant announced our flight was getting ready to board. After going through the ritualistic process, we nestled into our seats and geared up for hours and hours of travel. It'd be worth it once the gorgeous island of Corfu came into view.

I wrapped the u-shaped pillow around my neck, secured my seat belt, and took out my iPod. After scrolling through my playlist, I settled on *You Spin Me Round* by Dead Or Alive and rested my head against the window. With any luck, I'd sleep through most of the flight and *not* have to use the restroom.

That didn't happen. Four hours in, I'd woken up in a panic, practically crawling over Sara and some stranger's lap to get to the aisle. Squeezing my knees together, I wobbled to the bathrooms only to find several people waiting in line. I'd never peed myself as an adult and didn't want to start now.

I pursed my lips and tried not to think about it. Naturally, my mind went straight to thinking about the plane flying over water.

"Miss?" The older man in front of me said. He was shorter than me by several inches, with a short gray beard, wide-rimmed glasses, and a sizeable slanted nose. "Would you like to cut in front of me? Looks like you need it more than me." His colors burst with bright blues and greens. He was as loyal as they come and beaming with spirituality. Refreshing for once.

"Really? Are you sure?" I rolled my lip under my top row of teeth, trying to hide how genuinely uncomfortable I was.

He laughed, watching my feet bounce. "Absolutely. Go for it."

"Thank you. Thank you so much," I said as I moved past him and into the next available stall. It took all I had not to moan out loud in relief.

After washing my hands twice, I stopped in front of my hero as I exited. "Thank you so much again. What was your name?"

"Pan," he answered.

I blinked. "Pan?"

"*Stan*," he repeated with a chuckle.

"Sorry. Ears must be clogged." I smiled. "Stan, I'm Stephanie, thanks again."

I shuffled back to my seat, and the stranger whipped off her seatbelt to let me in this time with an exasperated stare.

"I'm so sorry about before. It was Mission: Critical." I gave a nervous chuckle as I scooted past her and Sara to my seat.

Sara held up a single finger in my face.

"One what?" I asked, scrunching my nose.

"Two more times and you owe me five bucks."

Throughout the flight, let's just say she got her five bucks.

My eyes fluttered open, feeling Sara's elbow nudging me. After checking my face for dried drool, I peered out my window. She leaned over me, and we gawked at the gorgeous blue water, mountains, and whitewashed houses. A portion of my family was Greek, but I never considered visiting the country itself. Traveling so far as downtown Chicago was a feat, let alone overseas. Seeing its beauty staring up at me like a beacon, I regretted never considering it.

"What made you pick this place, Sara?"

"Something called to me about it. That and I remember my friend talking about it not too long ago." She rested her chin in her palm, still staring out the window. "Naturally, my mind went straight to Athens, but she told me if we're going to go, it should be Corfu. Now I see why."

"No kidding. Are there temples here?"

"Tons. Byzantine churches and Venetian fortresses too. But the *first* thing we're doing after throwing our suitcases into our room is changing into our bikinis and hitting the swim-up bar." She leaned back into her seat, shutting her eyes with a sigh.

I chuckled, pressing my forehead against the window. "Sounds like a glorious plan."

Besides the fear of our taxi cab driver killing one of several people in swimsuits swerving through traffic on four-wheelers, or them killing us, the ride was rather pleasant. Mostly the scenery. Long winding roads through hills and mountains. Vibrant green trees and shrubs as far as the eye could see. And of course, the blue water surrounding the island.

We arrived at our home away from home for the week. To say the resort was gorgeous would've been a monstrous understatement. It was two buildings nestled amongst hundreds of olive trees, seconds away from the beach. Mountains were off in the distance, and the sand was almost white.

Sara curled her arm around mine. "Amazing, right? Wait until you see our room."

"Sara, seriously, how much did this cost you? And what did I do to deserve this?"

She clamped a hand over my mouth as she pushed me toward the hallway. "You work your ass off, and I've lost count of how many favors you've done for me. Shut up and enjoy it, Steph." She didn't move her hand, so I nodded instead.

Marbled floors and Greek statues on Ionic columns lined the hall. We stepped in front of a room with a gold number seventeen. She scanned the card over the reader and bit down on her lower lip. My jaw would've hit the floor if I could've unhinged it. The room was a vast space, with one wall open to the outside. The wind whipped through, making the curtains sway. It led to a veranda complete with lounge couches and direct beach access. We could wake up and walk right outside to the beach.

"Can I stay here forever?" I mumbled, unable to tear my eyes away from the sight of sand, water, and mountains.

She hugged my shoulders from behind and let out a squeal before wheeling away her suitcase.

There were two queen-sized beds with white and pale blue striped comforters and enough throw pillows to outfit an army. Everything looked so pristine, I was afraid to touch it.

"Get that bikini on girly. There's so much more to see of this place." Sara yanked her black and white swimsuit from her case.

As I neared the beachside window, I closed my eyes, letting the wind tussle my hair. The sun was warm and inviting, like a heated blanket. The smell of salt and olives permeated the air. For the first time in a while, I felt the tension melt away like a gooey marshmallow.

"You brought the one-piece?" Sara asked.

I turned to see her holding up my swimsuits. She held the one-piece with two fingers as if it were a slimy piece of garbage. I reached for it, but she pulled it away.

"I'm not wearing that bikini. It barely covers my... essentials."

"That's kind of the point, Steph. You have a rocking bod, what are you afraid of?"

I scanned her string bikini. She frequented the gym. Between that and her profession, everything was toned, tight, and in top form. On the other hand, I spent most of my time glued to a desk, and had a bit of pudge I couldn't get rid of. Enough that it made me self-conscious.

"I'll think about wearing the bikini tomorrow. Deal?" I held my hand out for the one-piece.

She rolled her eyes before slapping it into my hand. "Fine. At least you brought it. Hurry up."

Stepping into the bathroom, my feet pressed against the coolness of white engraved tiles, all fixtures made of gray and white marble. I slipped into the suit, pausing to look at myself in the mirror. Turning my back to it, I eyed the white anchor positioned right above my butt. I didn't see anything wrong with this suit. It still clung to every curve and had a cute nautical theme.

"Stop judging yourself in the mirror, Steph. Let's go," Sara yelled at me through the door.

The resort had several pools, but only one of them had the swim-up bar she'd been going on about. In the center was the bar with a circular white roof that stretched far enough for shade. There were stools inside the water around the perimeter, all of them occupied. There were so many people in the pool, they were bumping elbows. I reached for my dress pocket and grimaced. No pockets meant no Tums.

"Hey, you go ahead, Sara. I'm going to grab a drink from the other bar."

The one with a *single* customer.

She cocked an eyebrow. "They serve the same stuff, I'm sure."

"True. This one has more…breathing room?"

She smiled. "Say no more. Come on in when you're ready. I'm sure I'll have new friends to introduce to you at that point."

She wasn't kidding. The woman's social skills were like watching a choreographed dance routine. Mine was more like a stand-up comedy headed by Ben Stein.

"Will do." I took a seat at the bar, making sure to keep several stools between the male patron and me.

"Kalimera," the bartender greeted.

I smiled. "Hello."

The bartender slapped a cocktail napkin in front of me. "What can I get you?" He asked, his voice laced with a Greek accent.

"I hadn't gotten that far yet. Hmm. Mai tai?" I tapped my finger against my lips. "No. Strawberry daiquiri. Or maybe…"

"You look like a piña colada kind of woman," the tender said with a sparkling grin that made my cheeks blush.

"Yes. Perfect. Thank you." I drummed my hands on the bar top, turning in my stool to take in the scenery.

A mysterious black cloud of fog-like smoke seeped around my feet. I furrowed my brow, following its trail. It flowed from the man sitting near me. Colors of dirty gray and varying shades of brown skirted over his arms. The overlap in hues made it hard to tell if he were gloomy, reliable, evil, or a mix of all. He had both hands wrapped around his tumbler of amber-colored liquid. His head held low, causing his chin-length dirty blonde hair to shield his face. He was dressed in head-to-toe black in a button-up short-sleeved shirt and pants, like Johnny Cash going to the beach. A hint of a tattoo peeked out from his sleeve.

He caught sight of me staring, and the fog sucked in, disappearing as if it'd never been there at all. Maybe it hadn't.

"Here you are, miss," the bartender said, snapping me back

to reality and making me jump. He snickered. "Sorry. Didn't mean to startle you."

I wrapped my hand around the tall glass and pulled it toward me. Not used to the lack of an eye shield from my glasses, I almost poked my eye with the straw. "It's no big deal. I'm just a skittish ninny."

The look he gave me was well deserved. I was sure the last time I'd heard the word "ninny" was from my great-grandma. Food needed to go in my mouth pronto to shut myself up. The glass had a decorated stick complete with an orange and pineapple slice. I opted for the pineapple, brought it to my lips, and winced when cold liquid pooled in my lap.

Lovely. A piña colada stain. Precisely what my ensemble was missing.

I stood on the rung of my stool and reached for napkins near Johnny Cash. Our hands brushed as I pulled the napkin away. A dozen indecipherable whispers flooded my ears, blocking out the sounds from the pool, the birds, everything else around me. I froze mid-sit.

His chin lifted, revealing eyes that matched the color of his whiskey, squared jawline sprinkled with a light beard, slanted straight nose, and thin lips.

"Sorry," I stuttered. "I didn't mean to disturb you."

Okay. I really was a ninny.

I sat back down and furiously dabbed at the stain.

He didn't respond and only moved so much as to finish the contents of his drink.

"Another whiskey?" The tender asked him.

"Mhm," he said, sliding the glass across the bar.

Convinced the stain would remain a stain, I balled the napkin in my palm. "So, uh, whiskey your drink of choice?" Heat flowed up my neck.

He slowly turned to look at me with a cock of his head. He smirked, and a small dimple formed at the corner of his mouth. "Listen, darlin'. I want to be left alone."

A southern accent. I was *not* expecting that.

"A resort with hundreds of people doesn't seem quite the best place to be alone." I stirred my drink, unable to take my eyes off him.

The bartender returned with his drink, and Johnny brought it to his lips, pausing before taking a sip. He peered at me through the strands of his hair that'd fallen over his gaze. "This place relaxes me," he said in a clipped tone.

His hair gave him a further sense of mystery, disguising the furrow in his brow, and the intent in his eyes.

"I hear the spa is pretty relaxing. Though I wouldn't know, considering I've never been to one." I leaned forward, resting my elbows on the bar top.

His jaw clenched, bulging at the corners. "The spa doesn't serve whiskey." He shook the glass in his hand, making the ice cubes clank, before taking a sip.

My God. Sawyer from the show *Lost*. He looked. Like. Sawyer. My stomach tightened. I concentrated my stare on my drink instead. "You seem—" I paused, watching the gray colors around him pulse. "Sad."

He turned his chin, dropping his eyes to scan over my bare legs before catching my gaze unabashedly. "I reckon I've got a lot to be sad about."

I sat up straighter, curious what a man like him would have to be sad over but didn't wish to pry.

He sighed, setting the glass down on the bar top. "My wife of over a thousand years left me for another man. A *lesser* man."

"A *thousand* years? Wow. Together so it long it felt like that, huh?"

He glared at me. "What?"

"I—you said a thousand years. I figured it was a euphemism or—"

His scowl deepened.

I tapped my finger against my thigh. "Well, I'm sorry to hear that." I should've stopped at that point, but something in my gut wouldn't let me. "What's your name?"

He took a long swig of his drink. "Hades." He said it so simply. Like he told me his name was Bob.

"Hades? You were named after the god of the Underworld?" I bit my lip to keep from laughing.

"One and only."

"Wow. Your parents were a little cruel, huh?"

A fire lit in his eyes when he looked at me, the tiniest of smirks creasing into the corner of his lips. "You have no idea."

My heart thumped against my chest, his stare turning my stomach into a series of knots.

"Are you nervous?" The smirk continued as he squinted at me over the rim of his glass.

"Nervous? What reason would I have to be nervous?"

He dragged a hand through his hair, and I bit back a whimper. "I don't know, but your chest is pink." He pointed.

Slapping my hands over my chest, I hopped off my stool.

"Well, I'll uh—leave you alone. Enjoy your whiskey."

I turned to walk away, but a string from my coverup caught on the stool, yanking me back.

Hades leaned forward with the ease of a looming predator and plucked the string free. "I didn't get your name."

"Steph. Stephanie."

He stared at me, his eyes starting at my face and scanning down to my toes. When he met my gaze again it was as if he were mentally dissecting me. Orange shades peeked through the gray, exuding the confidence that urged to break free. "I'll see you around…Stephanie." He enunciated the last part of my name with extra emphasis.

I bunched my coverup near my neck, and after one last moment of staring at him, I turned away.

The crowd in the swim-up bar had thinned out. Sara's infectious laugh echoed off the surrounding pillars. It never failed to put a smile on my face. I waded over to her with the remainder of my drink in hand.

"Well, hey there. Who was that guy you were talking to?" Sara asked, chewing on her straw.

I risked a glance over my shoulder, looking at the empty stools of the bar. He was gone. A peculiar disappointment washed over me. "Oh, just a guy who calls himself Hades."

"Hades? Is it a nickname, or does he truly think he's some kind of Greek god? I've met plenty of men with that complex."

"Does it matter? I came here to have fun and relax with my best friend. Not hook up with a random stranger."

"Oh, yeah?" She asked, right as two men walked up.

"A whiskey Coke and a gin and tonic," one man ordered.

He had blonde hair cropped short with a thin, but toned physique. Orange shadows trimmed with yellow floated around his head like a halo. The over-confidence was obvious but he could also be slightly unstable. His accent sounded American. Mid-west maybe?

"See something you like?" The blonde man said, making me choke on my drink.

Every time I was out in public, I tended to people watch, profile them. It was par for the course with my profession. I was always trying to figure out people's dirty laundry. I scanned his arms, noting a maple leaf tattoo with swirling patterns intertwined.

"I was looking at your tattoo. Any symbolic meaning?" I didn't move my eyes from his and attempted to fish for the straw with my mouth, missing it twice.

He looked down at his bicep and patted the tattoo, smiling brightly. "A patriotic symbol for my country is all."

Sara snapped her fingers. "Canadian. I thought I recognized the accent. We're close to your border. Chicago."

We lived in a town called Des Plaines, but it was easier to say Chicago. Close enough and widely known.

Sara leaned past me, extending her hand. "I'm Sara. And this here is Stephanie."

There she went being all social.

The blonde chuckled and shook her hand. "I'm Keith, and this is Guy." Guy sounded more like 'Gee'. "We're from around Ontario."

"Chicago, huh? I've always wanted to go there," Guy said, moving through the water to get closer to Sara. He was the polar opposite of Keith. Dark hair, dark eyes, and a deeply tanned complexion. His hair was long but pulled into a tight bun at the base of his neck. Like Keith however, orange hues swirled around him, sparkling here and there with flecks of gold. Prosperous? Wealthy?

"Oh? What part of the city interests you the most?" Sara turned on her stool to face him.

"Are you two here *together*?" Keith asked.

"Yup." I took a sip of my drink. "As friends. I mean, we're not—not that there's anything *wrong* with that. I just didn't want you to assume—"

He lifted his Aviator sunglasses onto his head, nestling them within the blonde spikes. "Well, good. I wanted to make sure I wasn't stepping on any toes." He smiled wide. "What are you drinking?"

"Piña colada." I rested the empty cup on the bar top while Keith flagged down the tender. My eyes betrayed me, looking at the bar for Hades again.

His smile deepened as he handed me another cup of coconut bliss. "Love the anchor on your suit there."

"The what?" Right. The anchor. I gave a nervous chuckle. "Thanks."

He bit down on his lower lip, letting his gaze rest on my nether regions longer than necessary. "So, what do you do for a living?" He breached my invisible shield, shifting himself closer.

I leaned back. "I'm a digital forensics examiner for the state police."

His brows rose. "Can't say I know what the hell that even is. Sorry." He laughed.

"It's forensics. The digital side of it. Computers and such. No stepping over dead bodies or studying blood spray patterns."

He stared at me, nodding.

I smirked. "I hack things." Hacking was not part of my job in the least, but the media had glorified it. It was the one area of cybersecurity I knew people were familiar with.

His eyes widened. "Oh, wow. That's awesome. What's been your biggest case?"

The Fueller case. I'd managed to forget about it until now. I gulped down my drink, hoping it would help flee it away from my thoughts.

"We're going to be late for scuba diving if we don't haul ass, Keith-ster." Guy slapped Keith on the back.

"Hey, it was great talking to you. We're only here all week, so I'm sure we'll run into each other again." Keith smiled, slipping his Aviators onto his face.

My knee bounced underwater, and I offered a weak grin. Mrs. Conroy's sad face loomed over me like a raincloud.

"Guy seemed nice enough," Sara said, tapping her fingernail against her cup.

"Uh, huh," I muttered.

"Hey." She turned my chin to look at her. "Time for a toast."

She always knew how to snap me out of it.

"What are we toasting?"

"To meeting the god of the Underworld."

I smiled as the mention of his name made Mrs. Conroy a distant memory. "To Hades."

We tapped our cups together.

THREE

WE WERE UP AT the crack of dawn the next day because neither of us could sleep. We could rest when we were dead. Paradise called. Sara convinced me to wear my cranberry-colored bikini, but I insisted on a swim coverup for our walk to the pool. And had every intention of wearing it the entire time. Like a passing shadow, Hades slipped onto the same stool he sat on yesterday, at the same bar, dressed in the same clothes. I couldn't look away. An older woman dressed in a resort uniform spoke to him. She flailed her hands around, her jaw quivering like she was about to cry.

He held his head low, nodding as the woman spoke. If I had a nickel for every time I wished I could read lips. She slapped her palm onto the bar top. He slid his hand over hers, and she closed her eyes. Fractals of turquoise peeked through the looming gray clouds surrounding him before the blackness consumed it. Her body relaxed, and he slipped his hand away. The woman laughed and kissed his forehead before walking away.

"Why don't you meet me by the pool?" Sara asked.

"Hm, what?"

She jutted her chin at Hades. "I'm going to go out on a limb here and say that's the guy who calls himself Hades?"

I played with one of the rhinestones on the side of my sunglasses. "I'll only be a few minutes."

"Take as much time as you want. I'll probably fall asleep by the pool anyway." She grinned and patted my shoulder.

The blackness still loomed over him, but unlike yesterday, bursts of pastel colors appeared as if trying to break through. As I got closer, the brighter colors pushed and pushed until grayness clouded them over.

I leaned next to him. We were the only ones at the bar, which wasn't surprising considering how early it was. "I didn't peg you for the older woman type."

He eyed me sidelong. "I wasn't courting that woman. And she's not older. She's an infant by comparison."

"Courting? My, my, how formal." The bartender rested a tumbler in front of him with the same brown liquid as yesterday. "An infant through wisdom or something?"

He licked his lips. "Sure."

I sniffed the tumbler. "It's five o'clock, somewhere, right?"

"What else would I be doing?" He kept his eyes trained forward.

"Oh, I don't know. Soaking up the sun by the pool? Dragging your toes through the sand on the beach? Falling into a tourist trap?"

He turned his head, moving his face near mine. "You can't

drink all day if you don't start early, sweetheart." He tipped the glass.

My stomach flipped. He smelled like burning wood and a recently extinguished flame. The scent that permeated the air after blowing out birthday candles. I flagged the bartender. "Mimosa, please."

"Mm," Hades purred. "I didn't peg you for the type to indulge in early morning sins."

"I'm on vacation. I'd never do this normally, so I figured… when in Rome, right?" I lifted the glass to my lips. "I mean—I know we're not *in* Rome."

"Why do you talk to me? There are dozens of eligible bachelors loitering the resort." He asked, turning his body to face me.

A dribble of sweet, bubbly juice escaped the corner of my mouth, and I wiped it away with my finger. "Why wouldn't I?" Noticing his close proximity made my chest tighten.

"Fair. But most people tend to steer clear of me. You on the other hand—" He dragged his thumb over his bottom lip.

"It's my job to solve mysteries. I'm drawn to them like a moth to a flame. And you—" I paused, watching his eyes scan my face as if I were as big of a mystery to him. "You're an absolute enigma." I curled my hands around my glass to keep them from shaking. "I think people just don't give you a chance. You exude this sort of brashness, but deep down… that isn't really you."

"You're wrong." His voice dropped an octave, cold, and clipped. It sent a chill down my spine. He turned away with a sneer. "Some people are inherently evil."

The black colors coiling his arms darkened as the gray settled over his chest like a cloud.

Heat traveled up my neck. "Everyone is born good. It's what happens through life, which sways them in one direction or the other. They *choose*."

He locked his gaze with mine, his pupils dilating. The glass squeaked as his hand tightened around it. "You're. Wrong. I've witnessed it firsthand."

A fuzziness clouded my brain, but I shook it away. "What is that supposed to mean?"

"You're so quick to believe in the morality of humans." He shoved his nose in his glass.

"Of course, I am." My voice was barely above a whisper.

He looked at me with a furrowed brow. The pastel colors around him pushed further through and were sucked back in by the darkness. "Then I feel sorry for you." He slid his empty tumbler across the bar.

I frowned.

An older man in a pair of tropical board shorts sat at the bar on the opposite side from us. Despite his fully rounded beer belly, he wore no shirt. A previous sunburn was evident in the shape of a tank top on his skin. The only hair he had was a small grey patch in the center of his head and a bit below his ears.

"Tell me. What do you think his story is?" Hades shifted his eyes.

Shards of red and yellow burst from him like alarming sunbeams. I looked for even a sliver of green—of guilt from him but found nothing. "Older. Mid-fifties. Alone. His company maybe had business here, and he's taking some

R&R. He's up to something. Maybe doing an underhanded deal? Selling out his own company to a higher bidder?"

Hades cocked to his head to the side with one brow raised. "Impressive and very close." He leaned over to whisper in my ear. "He's currently cheating on his wife for the fifteenth time. He takes advantage of his company's frequent travels to go outside of his marriage. He has another family on an island not far from here. Neither family knows of the other. And his wife is so aloof she hasn't a clue."

I narrowed my eyes. "How could you tell? Do you read body language or—"

"Hey, honey," the man said into his phone, his eyes blazing of a confident orange. "Yeah, they're working me like a horse over here. But I'll be home in a few days." He looked around as he spoke.

"I could tell you, but what I'm more curious about is how *you* knew those things about him." Hades tapped his finger against the tumbler.

I got a sick feeling in the pit of my stomach. My hand hit my glass, sliding it off the bar. Hades snatched it from mid-air, stopping it from crashing to the ground.

"Compassion is an admirable quality, Stephanie. But don't let it cloud your judgment. Reality is reality." Like a lunar eclipse, all other sounds faded away.

I closed my eyes, and when I opened them again, he was gone. As if he'd vanished into thin air. His empty tumbler stared back at me. I'd been so consumed by not seeing the man's colors for what they were I didn't notice Hades left. I headed for the pool.

Sara lay on one of the lounge chairs, her towel, and bag piled on the chair next to her, saving it for me. I halfway hoped she was asleep. Otherwise, she'd ask me a dozen questions about Hades. With cautious movements, I moved her bag to the ground beside my chair. I paused, eyeing her still lying there like a breathing corpse and slowly sank down.

"How'd it go?" She asked.

Fail.

"There's something about Hades, Sara. A quirk? A secret?"

"Sounds like you two were made for each other."

Grabbing the towel, I whipped it at her with a laugh. She blocked it with her forearm.

"This isn't funny. He's...different."

She lifted her sunglasses to her head. "And that makes you even more interested, doesn't it?"

I pulled at the hem of my coverup.

Sitting up on her elbows, she narrowed her eyes. "You have that look. The one you get when you're about to pour your heart and soul into a case. We're on vacation, Steph. You want to hang out with this guy, try to make his heart grow three sizes bigger, fine. But don't get wrapped up in it."

"He comes off so confused. His colors are constantly battling each other. And whenever he opens up, this brightness peeks through. It's like he needs someone truly *willing* to listen." His words replayed in my head. Compassion is an admiral quality.

"And you're invested." She flipped her sunglasses back onto her nose, nuzzling back into the comfort of her chair.

"He can profile people better than you can."

She sat straight up, whipping her sunglasses off. "Excuse me?"

"I'm not kidding. He saw all these subtle clues. I can usually read people pretty well, but he saw right past the guy's façade."

"Is he a cop?"

"I don't know. He's pretty closed off. And why does he wear so much black?"

She laughed, curling her arms around her knees. "Maybe he's grieving for his love life?"

"You're such a goober sometimes." I slunk in the chair with a snicker.

She held two fingers up, pressed together, a gesture that was uniquely hers. "Um, false. I'm a genius *all* of the time."

"Forgive me, illustrious one."

"And you have five minutes before I make you put on sunscreen."

"Yes, mother dearest."

We sunbathed by the pool for almost an hour. Sara set a repeating alarm on her phone to remind us to flip over. I put on sunscreen for fear of looking like a lobster for the rest of our vacation and rolled my cover up just enough to cover my cleavage and stomach.

"Would you mind if we used this chair?" A female British voice asked.

I lifted my head, squinting through my sunglasses. All other lounge chairs were occupied except for the one next to me. "Knock yourself out."

The woman laughed. "I bloody well hope not." She set her bag and towel down. "I'm Michelle," she said, extending her hand.

We shook. She had long, wavy auburn hair, pulled back

into a low ponytail. Her skin was ivory with patches of freckles on her arms and shoulders. She was thin, tall, and sporting a vibrant green bikini. Her colors were warm and inviting—yellow, orange, and pink. There wasn't an ounce of negativity about her.

"I'm Stephanie, and this is Sara."

Sara reached over me. "Nice to meet you. England?"

"Ah, yes. Welsh-born, but Windsor implant." She sat down, removing a bottle of sunscreen from her bag.

A man walked up with pepper-colored hair, toned physique, oiled up, and sporting a bright red speedo. "Sorry, darling, it took me a while to find a bar with tea. Fancy that." He kissed Michelle on the cheek, making sure to flex every muscle in his upper body as he leaned in. His aura was confusing, muddy yellows mixed with brownish forest greens and strokes of black. Unstable yet mysteriously showing signs of growth and jealousy.

"This is Rupert, my fiancé. We're actually here celebrating our engagement," Michelle said, curling her body toward him.

And now we were to have a conversation. I sat up on my elbows. "Congrats."

"Have you set a date yet?" Sara still leaned on my chair.

"Sometime next fall, I'd imagine. Still working out the details, right, love?" Rupert smiled, causing the creases in his cheeks to deepen. He leaned back, his gaze dropping to Sara's lap. Or it seemed to. It was hard to tell behind the shadow of his sunglasses.

Michelle playfully elbowed him in the leg. "Are you two celebrating anything?"

"Why, yes. We're celebrating *not* thinking about work," Sara replied.

We fist-bumped, following it with an explosion gesture.

"Well, that's about as good of a reason as I ever heard. Have you been here long?" Rupert sat next to Michelle, accentuating the bulge in his speedo.

I shot my eyes back up to his face. "Just since yesterday."

"Are you having a good time?" Michelle asked.

"Time of our lives," Sara snorted, elbowing me.

Michelle bounced on her seat. "We should get together at some point. We're here for the rest of the week."

"Absolutely. You two can take one of our chairs. We've been lying out here awhile, I need to take a dip to cool off," Sara said, gathering up her things.

"It was great meeting you two. Hopefully, we'll see you around," I added.

"Michelle was nice. Rupert," Sara said his name with an exaggerated English accent. "He's another story."

"You're telling me. He's the classic snake hiding his true nature with a flashy grin."

"The speedo, the subtle changes in his gaze. We'll have to watch him." She stopped in front of a bulletin board.

The board had several sign-up sheets for resort activities and a slew of advertisements for nearby restaurants, clubs, and tours. Sara grabbed the pen attached to a string and feverishly scribbled our names on pool volleyball and Greek mythology trivia.

"Woah there, Speedy Gonzalez. Do I get a say in events I'm going to embarrass myself at?" I tried to yank the pen from her grasp, but she recoiled.

"Please. Volleyball is always fun, and between the two of us, we'll kick ass at trivia." She trailed her finger over the remaining sheets, skipping over snorkeling and booze cruise.

"What? No booze cruise?" I frowned.

"You already get seasick. Can you imagine adding alcohol to the equation?"

My stomach gurgled at the thought. "Good point."

"Ooo a masquerade ball. Oh, we're *definitely* doing that." She wrote our names on the list with an extra flourish.

I poked a line on the description. "It says black tie. Did you pack a ball gown? Because I certainly didn't."

She let the pen drop, and it swung back and forth. "There are these places called stores. I don't know for sure, so hear me out, but I do believe Greece has them."

I narrowed my eyes. "You're hilarious."

"What's this all about? Did I hear you two are going to the ball?" Keith said from behind us.

He and Guy sauntered over. Keith smiled and let his eyes roam over my exposed legs. With as much subtlety as I could manage, I tugged the coverup down.

"We just signed up." Sara squared off her shoulders. "You guys going?"

Guy grinned, brushing past Sara as he grabbed the dangling pen. "We are now."

I could hardly contain my enthusiasm…

Sara grinned. "I don't know. You might have a hard time finding us with everyone wearing masks."

"How could I miss that smile of yours, eh?" Guy stepped

closer to her.

"Sorry about him. He can be pretty forthright," Keith said, smiling.

I'd give Keith one thing. He did have a sparkling smile. "Oh, she'll let him know if she no longer appreciates it. Trust me."

He chuckled. "You two playing volleyball tomorrow?"

"Apparently."

"Good deal. We'll get there early, make sure we're all on the same team."

"Full disclosure—I'm horrible at it."

"Noted." He winked. "I'll help you out."

I managed a nervous grin, which probably looked more like I passed gas.

Guy nudged him in the shoulder. "Come on, Keith. We're going to miss the last period of the Winnipeg game."

Once they were gone, I blew out a breath. I'd socialized more this week already then in the last few months. It was exhausting. "So…" I turned to Sara. "Do you like Guy?"

She shrugged, swaying her arms back and forth and snapping her fingers. "I don't know yet. He *is* pretty cute." She bit down on her lip.

"Yeah. You like him."

She tugged my ponytail. "Come on, let's get nachos and a drink at the bar. Maybe the god of the Underworld will honor us with his presence again."

It was ironic I had Keith's full attention, but the one man I wanted to figure out said just enough to keep himself a secret, but also enough to keep me nipping at the hooked bait. Perseverance is stubbornness with a purpose.

FOUR

EVERYONE PARTICIPATING IN VOLLEYBALL gathered around the biggest pool in the center of the resort. A man in a polo shirt, shoes, and socks pulled up to his knees stood near the bar, fanning himself with a clipboard. Sara and I stood in the shade, sipping on hurricane drinks while waiting for them to get the show on the road. Keith and Guy walked over to the man with the clipboard, turning to point at us.

"Glad I wore my one piece," I mumbled to myself.

Sara blew bubbles in her drink. "I'll get you in that bikini again."

"At least I can rest assured I'll have no nip slips." I plucked one of the straps.

She smiled, her eyes sparkling. "I don't know. You might have a change of heart with a certain you know who around."

"He makes me curious. Doesn't mean I want him to see me in a bikini."

She cocked her head to the side. "I was talking about Keith. Are you talking about—"

"Nope. You're right. Was talking about Keith."

"Hades? You said he was odd."

"He—intrigues me."

"Like a shiny new jigsaw puzzle?"

I furrowed my brow at her spot-on analogy. "Something like that."

Keith slapped his hands together. "You ladies ready to win this thing? It's us four and a group from Wisconsin."

Sara scrunched her nose. "Wisconsin? Please tell me one of them isn't sporting Green Bay gear."

"Is one of them that guy?" I pointed at a man in a Green Bay trucker hat wearing a tank top and floral red board shorts.

"That'd be the one," Guy said.

I playfully pinched Sara on the arm. "Play nice."

"I will, I will. We're on vacation. I can see past it this *one* time." Sara pretended to gag.

Sara and her dad had been devout Chicago sports fans since she was a kid. Her hatred for their rival, Green Bay, covered anything related to Wisconsin.

Sara cupped a hand over her mouth and yelled, "Bear down."

Two of the Wisconsinites snapped their heads in our direction, glaring.

I gave Sara a playful shove and laughed. "How is that playing nice?"

"You know I can't help myself."

"Alright, everyone! We're going to start. If everyone could get into the pool, we'll explain the rules," the man with the clipboard announced.

The resort kept every pool at the perfect temperature. Not too cold, but still cool enough to be refreshing, given the sweltering heat. A dance-y, head bobbing worthy song started to play over the loudspeaker, and I swayed my arms through the water in time.

They explained the rules of pool volleyball, but I was only half-listening, spotting Hades walking to his usual spot at the bar. He still wore the same funeral-like all-black attire, only this time, he had a tank top on, revealing his tattoo in its entirety. His arms were toned and muscular, but from this distance, the tattoo looked like a black smudge.

Fidgeting with my hands underwater, I tried to not make it obvious I stared at him.

"Stephanie, we're about to start," Keith said, his voice gruff.

"Go ahead," I mumbled, keeping my body turned from Hades' direction but looking at him sidelong through my sunglasses.

Hades ran a hand through his semi-long locks and held a finger up at the bartender. He strolled over, slipping his hands into his pockets.

Oh, dear God. He saw me.

He stepped to the edge of the pool and canted his head to one side. "Have you never heard the phrase, 'It's impolite to stare'?"

My cheeks flushed and I let out an obnoxious laugh bordering on a cackle. "Sorry. I um, was trying to make out your tattoo."

"Cerberus."

My brows shot up. "I'm sorry?"

"The tattoo."

Cerberus. The God of the Underworld's faithful canine companion.

"Cerberus. Of course, of course. How silly of me."

With a lazy lift of his gaze, he scanned the crowd readying to play volleyball.

I kicked my legs behind me, splashing water like I'd done when I was little. "Why don't you join the game?"

"Is this your way of getting my shirt off?" Still no smile.

"No. I mean—you can leave all of your clothes on if you wanted to. Not to say you'd look bad or I wouldn't—" I cut myself off, blowing out a breath, and sunk in the water until my chin rested on the edge of the pool.

He shook his head, making his hair fall over his eyes. "Water's not really my thing. I hate it. It's more my brother's deal."

"How can water not be your *thing*? More than half of the human body is comprised of water."

He bent forward. "I'm not human." His eyes darkened.

He was close enough to make out his tattoo in its entirety. The black three-headed dog with swirling smoke, fog, and symbols I didn't recognize.

I stared up at him. "Most days, I don't feel like it either, but I still have to drink water."

He stood straight, jutting his head at the game. "I'm gonna have a drink. A real drink. You have fun beating a ball back and forth over a net."

"You don't know what you're missing."

He tipped his head over his shoulder. "I'll try not to weep

over it."

This guy was about as hard to crack as a walnut. I pushed away from the wall, swimming over to Sara, my gaze glued on Hades. The volleyball collided into the side of my face, followed by Keith bashing into me. I was completely submerged underwater for several seconds before pushing to the surface, sputtering and fumbling for my sunglasses, which had gotten knocked off.

Keith gripped my shoulder. "Holy hell! Sorry. I didn't see you. You alright?"

"I don't know. How red is my face?" I laughed. My hair was in a disarray of dark tendrils over my arms and eyes.

He snickered, moving my hair away with his fingertips. "Only slightly. Red is a good color on you, though."

I tensed and looked over at Hades as if he heard Keith—or cared. He'd turned on his stool to face the pool and gazed at me with narrowed eyes as he sipped his drink.

My sunglasses couldn't get back on my face quick enough, and I gave Keith's bicep an awkward pat. Usually, I'd take the time to appreciate a shirtless man in front of me, but for some reason, Keith's nipples saluting right near my face made me uneasy. A voice, like a fainted whisper, passed over my ear. Hades still stared at me from his seat at the bar. I turned my attention back to the game before I got another ball to the face, making both cheeks match.

Between Keith and Guy, they had the game under control. One would set it up, and the other would spike. Rinse and repeat. It shouldn't have surprised me they'd try to steal the show. Not that I was complaining, considering I was about as coordinated as a toddler.

"Stephanie heads up! I'm going to set it for you," Keith said.

I shook my head so frantically my bangs fell over my sunglasses.

"It'll be fine. Just jump up and hit it as hard as you can," Guy added.

The ball flew over the net, Keith pushed it with both of his hands, and I shimmied forward, smacking it with my hand. I'd swatted mosquitos with more force. The ball hit the net on our side.

Keith's jaw tightened. "No big deal. It's only one point."

"Why did you sign us up for this again?" I tossed a glare at Sara.

She brought her drink into the water, holding it with one hand. "Figured it'd be fun. Didn't think we'd end up with two jocks on our team who can't stand losing."

The other side launched the ball, but not over the net. It zoomed off to the side, out of the pool, and rolled toward Hades' feet. He paused, drinking from his tumbler long enough to give it a sneer.

"Hey, man! You mind giving the ball a toss?" Keith yelled.

Hades didn't budge. He didn't even look in Keith's direction, turning his body further away. Keith groaned and lifted himself out of the pool.

"The view is certainly worth it, I'd say," Sara said, smiling with her straw between her teeth.

Keith's wet feet slapped against the concrete, dripping a water trail, board shorts clinging to his—legs. "Thanks for helping out," he said to Hades, scooping the ball.

Hades tipped an imaginary hat on his head. "You look like you handled it fine, kid."

"You weren't joking. That man is one big bundle of doom and gloom," Sara said, momentarily resting her chin on my shoulder.

"He has a good reason. His wife left him."

"While it does suck, excuses for behavior are distractions from facing reality. Remember what I told you my training officer always said?" She beamed at me with those pretty brown eyes.

"Results. Not excuses." I sighed, watching Hades continue to ignore everyone around him.

"He needs to suck it up. We only have one life to live. Move along, cowboy." She gave me a side-hug before backing away.

Hades set his empty glass down and slid from his stool, prowling his way toward me. He locked his gaze with mine and the wind sounded like it whispered my name.

"You guys keep playing without me," I said to no one in particular, making my way to the pool stairs.

"Then we don't have a full team," Guy said.

"You two *are* the team," Sara countered.

Hades moved toward me, crossing one foot over the other in sleek movements. He was within arm's reach when my feet slid from underneath me. There was a reason resorts put "No Running" signs up everywhere around pools. I winced, waiting for the impact of concrete, but a pair of strong arms caught me.

"You're extremely clumsy," he said.

I let my eyes roam over his arms flexing as he held onto me, supporting my weight. He wore a tank top, but it didn't stop my mind from imagining what he looked like underneath it. Did he have the 'V'? Those carved tapering abdominal muscles that led down. My gaze dropped to his cloth-covered stomach.

I stood, attempting to wipe the water beads from his arms. "Kind of you to notice."

He cocked an eyebrow, watching me squeegee his biceps. Considering my hands were also wet, it wasn't doing much good. Once I stopped, he wiped his arms on the side of his shirt.

"Are you going to the masquerade ball in a of couple nights?" I interlaced my fingers behind my back.

"Masquerade?"

"Yeah. Everyone wears masks, dresses to the nines—"

He smirked. "I know what a masquerade is, darlin'. I'm just surprised they'd have one. It seems old-fashioned."

"I figured it'd be right up your alley. You can hide your face from everyone. Pretend you're something you're not. You could even spend the whole night brooding and sulking in a corner."

He ran a hand through his hair, briefly exposing his entire face. "I'll…consider it."

"I figured you'd say th—wait, really?" I'd expected him to say no given the obvious party pooper he was.

"I said I'd consider it. But it could be refreshing to pretend I'm not the divider of souls for a change." He squinted at me, canting his head like he was gauging my reaction.

"Are you a therapist or something?

He narrowed his eyes.

When he didn't answer, I let my eyes roam over his tattoo.

His smoky scent filled the air. Why did he always smell like he'd come from a bonfire?

"Would you do something for me?" Hades cocked his head, staring down at me—studying me.

For whatever reason my mind went straight to the filthy, stinky gutter.

"I'm sorry?"

"You seem to excel at reading people. It makes me incredibly—" His eyes roamed over my hair. "Curious."

My breaths quickened. "What do you want me to do?"

His fingers grazed my skin as he turned me and pointed. "Do you see that woman there? Tell me about her."

This felt like my third-grade spelling be all over again.

The woman had bright blonde hair with a glowing smile to match. She sat with a black-haired woman at her side and several men. She kept reaching across the table and touching one man's arm, his shoulder, anything she could get away with and not seem…overzealous.

I forced my concentration on her even though I could feel Hades staring at me. Her colors took longer than most to show. Vibrant pinks and yellows floated from her like vapors.

"She's playful, energetic. A very happy person who's confident in her own skin." I snapped my gaze to Hades with raised brows.

Hades clucked his tongue against his teeth. "Are you sure there's no weakness there? Immaturity? Perhaps even a tad bit unstable?"

My mouth formed a tiny "o" at him before I looked back to the blonde.

He leaned in and dropped his lips near my ear. "Is it possible you want so badly to see the good in people you're misinterpreting their true nature? Creating these mock personalities for them all in the hopes humanity can still be saved?"

I bit down on my lower lip, concentrating so hard on the woman I made my face scowl. The colored fog around her turned to shards—jagged and mis-matched. A breath caught in my lungs and I staggered back.

Hades' hand pressed between my shoulders blade, holding me steady.

He was right.

"I don't understand. Can you read auras too? How did you—" There were only two people in my entire life who knew about my gift. My grandmother and Sara. And yet here I went blurting it to a complete stranger who thought he was a Greek god.

Hades squinted his eyes as he ran a thumb over the stubble on his chin. "So, that's how you do it. And what do you see when you look at me?" He rolled his shoulders back with a fiery glint in his gaze. "*Really* look at me."

His aura came so naturally—as if it begged to be seen. The same cloudiness wafted from him, the teal beams of light glittering just under the surface.

"You're a man with heavy burdens. It's near beaten you, worn you down, and though you try to accept it there's still a part of you that begs to be yourself." I canted my head, not fully knowing what it all meant.

His face melted into an expression resembling someone who'd been stabbed in the back.

"Did I say something wrong?"

A scowl pulled over his features, turning his face into a stone-cold gargoyle. "I've got to go."

Sara waved her arms back and forth from the pool, grabbing my attention. After holding up a single finger to her, I looked back at Hades, but he was gone.

When I reached the water, Sara smiled up at me, her eyes drooping. "I didn't want you to miss the race. Look."

They'd lined up several lounge pool floats. Keith, Guy, the Wisconsin man and Rupert, the Englishman we'd met earlier, stood at the edge outside of the water.

Though the sight was amusing, Hades' expression of shock or terror from my reading stuck in my brain. If I stayed quiet to long however, Sara would smell something was up from a mile away with her keen detective skills.

"What are they doing? And are you—drunk?" I sat down, dangling my feet in the water.

"They're going to race across the floats. Whoever gets the farthest, wins. It's Canada vs. America vs. England. Fun, huh? Oh, and I could possibly, very well be on my way to drunky-ness."

I half-grinned. "How much did you drink while I was gone?"

She held up two fingers. "Three shots."

The men sprinted across the floats. Most of them fell in after hitting the second one, but Keith managed to make it all the way across, diving into the water after the last one.

"Is there anything athletic Keith isn't good at?" I asked.

"I'm starting to think not. It explains a lot about his big—"

She pointed downward, but then moved it to her face. "Head." She giggled and burped at the same time.

"Come on, you. I need you sober so we can go shopping tomorrow." I coaxed her toward the stairs.

She gasped. "You're going to let me take you shopping for dresses? I might cry."

"As sad as it is, I don't trust my judgment. I haven't worn a gown since senior prom." I helped her up the stairs, despite her unwillingness to set her drink down.

She whined, slumping over my shoulder. "Can you carry me to our room?"

"We'd get about two feet, if that, Sara. Come on."

"Need some help there?"

A part of me wished it'd been Hades who asked, but I knew the voice didn't belong to him. Keith stood there, giving his blonde hair a toss, the sun sparkling off the water beads littering his tanned skin.

"Would you mind?" My feet were slipping, trying to hold her up.

He laughed and slipped one arm around her waist, securing the other under her legs.

It was an awkward, silent walk to our room.

"Which room?" He asked.

I contemplated ways around him knowing our room number, but came up empty. "This one right here."

I swiped the card through the reader. Would it have been impolite asking him to drop her on the floor so I could drag her in? That way, he wouldn't physically be in our room? Nah. Sara wouldn't be happy with rug burn on her back.

"If you can put her on the bed over there. I really appreciate it." I tapped the card between two of my fingers, impatiently waiting, and side shuffling to the phone on the nightstand.

After setting her down, he walked past me, rubbing the back of his neck with a snarky grin.

"Thank you! Have a good day!" I nudged him out the door.

He chuckled, stumbling forward. "Alright, alright. What are you two up to tomorrow, though?"

"We'll be off property." Thank God.

"You going to be back in time for trivia night? I hear it gets pretty crazy."

Did they stalk our names on the sign-up list or something? "Wouldn't miss it! See ya then! Bye!" I nudged him the rest of the way into the hall and slammed the door shut.

FIVE

AFTER DRINKING A GALLON of water and drowning herself in coffee last night, Sara started to act more like herself. Filling her belly with greasy food and carbs was first on today's agenda. The buffet was set up in an outside eating area with open spaces, allowing the wind to blow through, and a breathtaking view of the horizon. We sat at a table facing the beach, munching on smoked pork, toast, and brine cheese.

"How did you get me to the room yesterday?" Sara asked.

I choked on my toast and grabbed my water. "Keith."

Her forked clanked against her plate. "Keith? He carried me?"

"You wouldn't walk on your own, and you're a foot taller than me. I didn't see it going well. Don't worry. I escorted him from the premises post-haste after he dropped you off."

She groaned, dragging her hands down her face. "I'm never drinking again."

I cocked an eyebrow.

"Okay. I'm not drinking *today*."

The smell of salt, coffee, and breakfast food wafted through the air with every gust of wind. It was quiet save for the low murmurs of surrounding conversations and the tide crashing against the shore.

I wonder if the Elysian Fields looked like this.

Sara flopped her napkin on the table and scooted across the booth seat. "I've drunk so much water I feel like I'm peeing every two minutes. I'll be right back."

I chuckled and ate a piece of pork. Hades walked around a nearby corner, dressed all in black. Had the guy never heard of the color grey before? Heaven forbid he switched it up for something crazy like green or blue. He leaned against a beam, crossing his arms over his chest. Another man walked up to him with black cropped hair that transitioned to wavy in the front. He dressed like he'd gotten out of a business meeting. A full tan suit, jacket draped over his shoulder, the sleeves of his white button-down shirt rolled up to his elbows. Aura colors of blue, purple, and muddy golds eked from his pores. Cold, mysterious, and powerful.

I leaped from my seat to eavesdrop. Another pillar stood adjacent to the one they were by, and I ducked behind it.

"What I don't understand is how she worked her way around it," the dark-haired man said, rubbing a hand over the light beard on his chin.

"Well, she had a long time to figure it out, didn't she?" Hades asked.

"The clause was solid. I made sure of it."

"Oh, yeah? Tell that to Theseus."

"If you'd have been patient like I said all those years ago, maybe you wouldn't be a depressed fool all over again," the dark-haired one scoffed.

"Theseus?" I whispered to myself, so lost in my thoughts, I didn't notice their conversation had come to a screeching halt.

"Who's your friend?" The dark-haired man asked, a light flashing in his eyes.

A hand gripped my arm, and Hades yanked me from the confines of my pillar.

"Eavesdropping on me now?" He cocked a brow and let me go.

"Pfft. Don't flatter yourself. I was uh…" I eyed the smoothness of the pillar next to me and dragged my finger down it. "Admiring the resort's infrastructure. Top-notch craftsmanship."

The dark-haired man smiled, his pearly whites beaming in contrast to his olive complexion. He slipped a hand in his pocket.

"This is my brother," Hades grumbled.

His brother stepped forward and slapped Hades on the back several times. "Zane." He extended his hand.

I shifted my eyes, heat rising up my spine. "Nice to meet you, Zane. I'm Stephanie." I managed to introduce myself with only two stutters.

He cocked an eyebrow. "Stephanie? How interesting."

"It's a—pretty common name." I chuckled, and he squinted at me. "Is this the one who has a thing for water?"

Hades kept his gaze fixed on Zane. "No."

"I'm more of a fan of thunderstorms, to be honest," Zane

said, winking.

I put a hand on my hip. "Oh? Are you one of the 'getting caught in the rain' types?"

"Not so much the rain as it is the lightning. The way it crackles across the sky." He grinned, shifting his glance to Hades, who rolled his eyes.

"That's a nice suit," I said.

"Why, thank you. I'm in the middle of a big case right now, actually. I came to check in on my brother. Make sure he's relaxing like he said he would."

Hades' hands balled into fists.

"Case? Are you a lawyer?" I knew something felt off about him.

"I am. Criminal defense."

Criminal defense lawyers were the absolute, positive scum of the earth in my profession.

"And somehow, you manage to sleep every night?"

Hades arched a brow in evident surprise.

Zane's grin widened. "There's nothing quite like the challenge of defending someone you know is guilty."

My jaw dropped.

Hades stepped in front of me, casting a shadow. "Darlin', your friend's back."

Sara slid back into the booth at our table.

"I'll uh—I'll leave you to it." I took one last look at Zane, and he waved with his fingers.

Absolute. Scum.

As I walked back to Sara, I replayed the snippet of conversation I heard them having in my head. Theseus? Why did that name sound so familiar? I sat down and dug out my cell phone from my bag.

"Care to fill me in?" Sara asked.

"Eavesdropping turned into meeting Hades' brother."

"Does their entire family look like Greek gods?"

I dropped the phone long enough to give her an exasperated look.

She laughed and slapped the table. "Oh, right. That was a joke I didn't even realize I was making."

I flicked my thumbs across the screen, searching through my Google results.

"Why are you on your phone during our vacation?" She snatched it.

"Hey!" I went to grab it back but returned with nothing but air.

"Theseus? The Greek hero? Why are you randomly looking this up?

My knee bounced underneath the table. "I wanted to be prepared for trivia later tonight. I know my gods and goddesses more than heroes, and you know they'll ask both."

She narrowed her eyes. "Uh-huh." She held the phone out to me, and I yanked it back.

I could never get away with any B.S. with her.

"All I'm seeing are references to him and the minotaur."

"He was in a lot more stories than that one." She licked butter from her thumb. "Like the one about the Underworld?"

I lifted my eyes. "What about it?"

"You don't remember? Him and Pirithous ventured there to rescue Persephone. They were captured until Hercules released him. But Pirithous had to stay. Poor guy."

Hades and Zane were finishing up their conversation. Zane pointed a finger at Hades before turning to walk away. Hades dragged a hand over his face, clenched his fist, and stormed off.

"Let's get going. For some reason, this resort feels claustrophobic all of a sudden." I stood, tossing my napkin in a perfect tri-fold on the table.

"You okay? You seem spooked."

"I'm fine." I gave a reassuring smile. "Great."

We grabbed a taxi and asked the driver to take us to the nearest bazaar, or plaza, or mall...whatever they called them here. We walked through the city center with a dozen businesses. There were shops for sandals, spices, alcohol, jewelry, leather, virtually anything imaginable. The buildings were an ancient Greek style with a modern flair. Patrons of all forms made their way over the white tile walkways. You could quickly tell the locals from the tourists by the speed they walked or whether they stopped to take selfies.

We found a boutique with gowns in the window. The small width of the entrance was misleading. The place was massive. There was a high ceiling with a circular design cut into it. Wooden planks filled the circle, and every wall had racks of clothes, shoes, and purses.

A woman walked up to us, greeting us in Greek and clapping her hands together.

"Hello. We're here to find a couple of gowns," I said.

She grinned and clapped her hands again. "Wonderful. Are you from America?"

Sara gazed around the shop. Her eyes were as wide as beach balls. "We are." Even her voice sounded mesmerized.

"Splendid. Welcome, welcome! Let me show you to our dress section. Do you have any ideas in mind? Neckline? Color? Length?" She motioned to us with her finger and walked to the back. Her heels clicked against the wooden floor.

"Long length. It's for a masquerade ball," Sara answered.

The saleswoman's eyes brightened, and she smiled at us over her shoulder. "How fun!"

This woman was in full sales mode.

"Here is our selection. As you can see, we've got plenty for you to choose from. The dresses are sorted by color and vary in style from there. If you don't see your size, just ask, and we can check in the back for you. Please don't hesitate to come to me with any questions." She gave a warm smile. "Dressing room is in the back corner. And mirrors are in the center." After giving a firm nod, she walked away, approaching newly entered customers.

Sara made a beeline for the purple dresses, her favorite color. White and yellow were mine, but they only managed to drown out my already pale skin. By the time I settled on the green and blue racks, Sara had three dresses draped over her arm. I had no clue what I wanted and grabbed two at random. Sara dragged me to another stand. She feverishly pushed hangers aside until she landed on one, which made her gasp. She held the dress up, biting down on her lower lip, smiling.

It. Was. Gorgeous. A cranberry-colored dress with a

strapless bodice transitioning into a full, flowy skirt. I had no clue what the pattern was on the front or what fabric the skirt was made of, but it was perfection. "I'm not sure I'm worthy of wearing this."

She tossed it over my arm. "Stop it. It's going to look killer with that chocolate hair of yours."

We tried on all dresses, and Sara ended up going with the first dress she'd picked out. Her gut instinct dress. Dark purple, halter top style, form-fitting, and a small amount of flair at the bottom. My favorite part was the array of sparkles covering the length of it. I insisted on trying the two random dresses I'd picked out first. The green one made my boobs bulge out of the top, and the blue one didn't fit past my hips.

When I walked out in the cranberry dress, I had my hands slapped over my eyes. I hoped it looked as good as it did on the hanger. "How does it look?"

"Oh my God, Steph. You're—a vision. Take your damn hands off your face."

I peeled my fingers away, one by one. The reflection in the mirror couldn't have been me. I didn't recognize myself. An electric tingle traveled down my spine. The bodice hugged my curves, and the skirt portion made me want to twirl, but I held back. Sara stepped up behind me, gazing at the mirror over my shoulder.

"What did I tell you?" She asked with a grin.

"Care to explain what I'm wearing?"

She pointed at the bodice. "The pattern is called filigree, and the skirt is tulle."

Screw it. I twirled and twirled once more for good measure,

the skirt flowing around me like a lazy cloud. "You were right. This is perfect."

"You're welcome. Now let's get the hell out of here. We've got some last-minute quizzing to do before trivia tonight. The first-place prize is two free spa admissions. Full body massage included."

Everyone gathered in the massive atrium with a large screen and projector at the front. In the middle was a stage with a podium. Everyone sat in pairs. Predictably, Keith and Guy were there, and they'd zeroed in on us like two hounds with a fox. Sara and I did Greek mythology drills for the better part of two hours before arriving. We felt prepared and ready to win our free trip to the spa.

"King of the Gods," Guy said to Keith.

Keith bent forward, his elbows on his knees, chin resting in his hands. "Zeus."

"Goddess of Love."

"Aphrodite."

"God of the Forge."

"Hephaestus."

Guy flopped a pile of flashcards on the table. "We got this!"

Keith sat up, and they did some form of a practiced handshake.

"I certainly hope you don't think simply knowing the names of all the gods and what they're in control of is going to make you win," Sara said, her legs crossed, the top one bouncing.

Keith made a *pfft* sound. "Of course not. We were running drills."

My lips puckered, holding back a laugh. We had this in the bag. Hades appeared from the darkness in the corner of the atrium. He stayed away from everyone, folding his arms over his chest and leaning against a nearby wall. A flash glinted in his dark gaze, making his eyes look like two pieces of obsidian within the shadows.

I elbowed Sara in the arm. "Wonder why he's not joining in. You'd think he'd be great at this game being named after the god of the Underworld and all."

"Maybe he's supervising us mere mortals answering questions about his family," she replied with a sidelong grin.

Hades stood motionless, except for the idle tapping against his elbow.

"Well, this should be a lovely time, don't you agree?" Michelle asked. She and Rupert walked up to our table dressed like they'd come from an elegant dinner. At least Rupert had pants on this time.

"Fan of mythology?" I asked as they sat down.

Rupert leaned back in his chair and draped his arm over Michelle's shoulders before crossing his legs. "Not particularly, but with that grand prize, I figured we might as well bloody try, right?" He gave a light smack to Keith's shoulder.

In. The. Bag.

"Everyone, we are currently passing out buzzers for each pair. We will begin the game in a few minutes," a resort worker announced.

A woman in a white polo rested a red plastic buzzer on the

table between us. Sara couldn't help but reach forward and slap her hand on it. It made an obnoxious *boing* sound. Other sounds resonated around us: classic buzzers, cuckoo clocks, and whistles.

"Is everyone ready?" The announcer on stage asked, scanning the crowd.

I threw my fists into the air, letting out as loud of a "woo" as I could. Sara followed suit, and we were successfully the loudest duo in the bunch. *Flight of Icarus* by Iron Maiden blasted through the speakers.

Once the music died and the crowd was sufficiently pumped, the announcer held his hands up for silence.

"We will ask a series of questions regarding Greek mythology. These questions may include the gods or heroes, so be prepared for both. I will read the questions, and they will appear on the screen behind me. Ring your buzzer when you're ready to answer. Wrong answers will give you a negative point, so be sure not to buzz in prematurely."

"First question: What was the home of the Greek gods?"

I went for the buzzer, but Keith and Guy's went off first.

"Olympus," Guy yelled, and they did their stupid hour-long handshake again.

Sara shrugged. "We thought we'd give you guys that one."

I narrowed my eyes and scooted forward, hovering my hand over the buzzer.

"Correct! Next question: Who gave Pandora her infamous box?"

I slapped our buzzer and shouted, "Zeus!"

"Correct!"

"Ha!" I pointed at Keith and stuck my tongue out.

Sara chuckled. "You're really getting into this."

"What was Achilles' weak spot?"

Michelle slapped her hand down so quickly she almost knocked the buzzer off the table. "Oh, heel, heel!" She bounced in her chair.

"Correct!"

Rupert leaned over, kissing her. "Great job, love." He stared at a woman at another table.

"We practiced answering questions, but I think we should've practiced our reflexes," I said to Sara through a fake smile.

"Don't worry. There's no way they'll get the harder ones. They've been pretty easy so far," Sara reassured.

"The wand of Hermes is called what?"

Crap. I didn't know this one.

Sara pushed her hand down on top of mine, pressing the buzzer. "That would be the caduceus."

"Very good! Correct!"

Guy smiled at her. "Impressive."

"You have no idea, Canuck." She shimmied her shoulders.

Both Canadians laughed. Michelle laughed with them, then looked at Rupert, who had taken out his cell phone and was mindlessly scrolling through it.

"Who is the goddess of vengeance?"

Boing. "Nemesis!" I grinned, knowing I was right.

"Correct! Now...this next question is worth multiple points, so be prepared to answer in its entirety."

Sara and I leaned forward, ready to win.

"The story of Hades and Persephone—"

My body tensed, and my throat felt like sandpaper. I looked over at Hades, and he shifted his stance. Instead of leaning lazily against the wall, he stood rigid.

"Legend says that Hades planted a certain flower to lure her away from her guides so he could abduct her and force her to be his bride of the Underworld. What was that flower, *and* who was Persephone's mother?"

My chest tightened as I pressed the buzzer with less enthusiasm than before. "Narcissus. Demeter." I spoke my answer in Hades' direction, monotone.

"You have this *legend* as you call it…wrong," Hades said from the shadows.

The announcer shielded his eyes from the spotlight. "I'm sorry?"

Hades sauntered from his darkened corner, dressed in his long-sleeve black shirt and pants. "It was Zeus who convinced Gaia to plant the flower. He wasn't innocent in this. And you all keep using words such as kidnapping and abducting. She was *not* held prisoner. It was she who ate the food of the Underworld."

The way he spoke chilled me to the bone. Hurt and sadness laced every word. His teal colors sputtered as if almost dying out.

The announcer laughed nervously. "We have ourselves an expert here, folks! The myths are, of course, always up for interpretation, sir."

Hades' fists clenched at his sides. "Interp—"

I could see his chest heaving through his shirt from across the room. A mysterious, dark smoke started to spread across the ground near him, then disappeared. Did I imagine it?

"What the hell is his problem?" Keith asked.

"Looks like we have our winners, everyone!" The announcer ignored Hades, pointing at Sara and me.

Claps, whoops, and hollers clouded the room, but I was far too distracted to care. Hades stormed away, and I stood, gripping Sara's shoulder when I passed.

"Don't you want to at least accept our—" Sara started, but I'd already trotted off.

I made it as far as the awning-covered walkway where he stood, gazing up at the moon.

"Hades?" I approached him like one would approach a Grizzly.

He slipped his hands in his pockets and kept his back turned. "No one was there and yet they all think they *know*."

Such pain, such sadness in his words. "You should really deal with this, you know? Talk to someone. I think you might be suffering from post-traumatic stress?"

He removed one of his hands and opened his fist. "I'm not—" He turned around to face me. "You shouldn't be concerned with me, Stephanie. I'll bring nothing but bad news your way. You're far too vibrant of a being, darlin'."

I wrapped my arms around myself, feeling naked even though I was fully clothed. "I'm only trying to help you."

"I don't need, nor did I ask for your help. Walk away. You can't win every battle, and you're most certainly not going to win this one." His jaw tightened, and he shoved his hand back into his pocket.

A foreign courage zipped down my spine and I stepped in

front of him with my hands pinned to my sides. "Does this hot and cold routine work on absolutely anyone?"

"Excuse me?" He glared down at me, but there was no mistaking the pink undertones that pulsed a single time within the grayness around him.

"At one moment you're curious about me, talkative even. The next you're trying to coax me away with hurtful words like a healed wild animal. As if you know what's best for me."

He dropped his face to mine, bringing his lips centimeters from mine. "I *do* know what's best for you. And it's not me."

My knees shook but I kept my ground. "No."

"No?" He leaned back and his brows shot skyward.

"You don't get to make that decision for me. I'm going to walk away right now because I want to. Not because you told or asked me." I ground my teeth together and didn't wait for him to respond.

Tears welled in my eyes as I turned away, power-walking in any direction my feet would carry me.

There was no telling the last time I'd said no to someone. And I picked the guy claiming to be the ruler of the Underworld?

Once I was a safe distance away, I let the tears flow like the river Styx.

SIX

WE SPENT MOST OF the next day on the beach, killing time until the masquerade ball. I waded far enough into the water to let it crash against my hips, welcoming the sun warming my cheeks. Thoughts of the murder case returned and try as I might, I couldn't make it go away. There was only so much distraction that could fool my brain.

"Stephanie, what the hell is wrong with you?" Sara asked.

I didn't look at her. "What do you mean?"

"You've been uncharacteristically quiet since breakfast this morning." She counted on her fingers. "I've caught you staring into space several times. Plus, we passed Hades on our way over here, and you didn't look at him."

"Just enjoying myself, Sara. And as far as Hades goes…some people can't be helped. He made it abundantly clear."

She gave me a light shove. "Uh-huh. So, it's Hades. What did he say to you? Do I need to strong-arm him?"

"Woah there, hellion." I chuckled. "No need for violence. He just told me in a not so pleasant way to stop trying to help him. And so, I will."

"Well, forget him. We're going to have the time of our lives at the ball tonight."

"Did you purposely, sort of quote *Dirty Dancing*?" I grinned.

She looked at me, sidelong. "Maybe? Did it cheer you up?"

"Yes."

"Then, yes, I did."

I laughed and splashed her.

She grabbed her head. "What did I tell you about getting my hair wet!"

"Remind me?" I splashed her again.

She yelped and backed away, pointing at me. "Costas, I *will* handcuff you."

"Don't threaten me with a good time." I chuckled and pretended to splash her.

"I'm glad you're back to your old self. I was worried Hades was rubbing off on you with that perpetual pout."

I wrapped an arm around her waist. "Did you want me to teach you how to dance before we go to this thing?"

Her jaw dropped. "I know how to dance."

"Are you serious?" I wanted to laugh, but when she didn't crack a smile, I held back. "Sara, come on. You didn't even know how to do the chicken dance at Olson's wedding."

She rolled her eyes. "What are you going to teach me? The waltz?"

"Amongst others."

"Fine. But only because I don't want to make an ass of myself."

As we made our way back to our room, Hades sat at the same bar, and a woman sat next to him. She smiled, leaning her face near his. He didn't move and shook his head. Something he said made the woman frown and storm off.

Well, at least he's consistent.

He caught my gaze, and my feet glued to the concrete. His stare gripped my spine like a vise. He looked—defeated. The pastel colorings of his aura had almost completely faded away.

Sara snapped her fingers in front of my face. "Hey. None of that. Come on."

I blinked myself back to reality.

We spent the better part of an hour going over the most basic moves for couples dancing. I sat on a couch in our room, staring off in the distance while Sara practiced.

"You know what?" Sara blew out a breath. "All I need to do is sway during the slow songs and shake my tailfeathers during the faster ones. I'm done."

"Mmhmm," I responded.

She dipped her face in mine. "Let me guess. Hades?"

After blowing my bangs away from my eyes, I said, "You should know I'm incapable of leaving well enough alone."

"I know, sweetie." She grabbed the curling iron and sat behind me, running her fingers through my hair. "You did all you could do."

A small part of me hoped he'd inexplicably show up at the ball. The crowd would part, and he'd be standing there, beckoning me to dance with him.

Life isn't a romance novel, Stephanie.

"All done. You ready to do this?" She held up a can of hairspray. "Close your eyes." The air filled with mist and vapor, making me cough.

We slipped into our dresses. Thankfully mine was long enough I could wear flats instead of heels. Function over beauty. Besides, I could barely walk three feet in a pair of heels without spraining my ankle. The atrium had been transformed into Mount Olympus itself. Tapestries and curtains in shades of white and gold were draped over tables and hung from ceilings. Several layers of fog skirted the floor, making the walkway a hovering cloud. An array of masks lay on a front table. I selected a lacey black one with several rows of beads that hung over my cheeks.

"This looks like heaven," Sara stammered, grabbing a white mask with points on the top like horns. She snatched two flutes of champagne from a passing tray.

"Tell me about it. The resort pulled out all the stops."

There were several tables littered with finger foods, including a gelatin looking dish labeled as ambrosia. I was busy stuffing my mouth with cheese cubes when Guy walked up.

"What is this? Only one half of the dynamic duo?" Sarah asked.

Guy wore a grey suit with a dark blue necktie. "Keith got food poisoning. Been coming out of both ends since last night."

Even though I knew it was highly unlikely he'd been poisoned from cheese, I spit it out in my napkin.

"That's awful," Sara said. "What a way to ruin a vacation."

Guy nodded before giving an electric grin. "I still showed up. Specifically, to dance with you."

"That's sweet of you, but I can't leave Steph by herself."

I sputtered my champagne and shook my head. "By all means, go dance. Have fun. I've got this to keep me entertained." I held up my glass.

"You sure?" She asked, her eyes brightening.

After finishing the contents of my glass, I plopped it on a passing tray and grabbed a full one. "Absolutely. Go."

Guy took Sara's hand, and they moved to the dance floor. I shuffled my way to a table in the corner, dragging my fingertips over the burnout velvet that made up the design on my bodice. It was the perfect dress. I flopped onto a chair, sipping my champagne, and kicking my feet to make the tulle of my skirt bounce.

Sara tripped too many times to count. Guy didn't seem to mind, and they both kept laughing. It was a treasure to see her so carefree. Too many days, she spent physically chasing down bad guys and stepping around dead bodies. Seeing her spinning around in her purple gown, you'd have no clue she was a rough and gruff cop.

The song *False Kings* by Poets of the Fall blared over the loudspeakers. I closed my eyes, swaying to the rhythm and humming the melody. A chill washed over me, compelling me to open my eyes. A shadowed figure stood across the room, dressed in all black, dark blonde hair falling past his chin, face hidden by a simple black mask. Hades.

Was I hallucinating?

I sniffed my champagne.

He appeared in front of me, his hand outstretched, the other resting on his back. "No one puts Stephanie in a corner."

My lips parted. Did he know he quoted my favorite movie?

"Are you going to sit there with your mouth open, or are you going to dance with me?" He still didn't crack a smile, but his dark eyes peered down at me through the holes of his mask, almost twinkling.

I gulped and set the champagne on the table before slipping my hand into his. He led me to the dancefloor, capturing me with his stare. Once we reached the center, he tugged me to his chest, slipping an arm around my waist. A *whoosh* fluttered in my stomach.

"I didn't think you'd show up. Especially after yesterday," I said, unable to tear my eyes away from him.

He moved us around the floor as if he'd practiced for a hundred years. "I'm sorry for being so brash with you." His jaw tightened, and he lowered his voice. "It's not one of my more admirable qualities."

The anguish in his voice pulled at my heart. "Apology accepted."

"Except for my brother no one has ever—" His eyes searched my face, wandered over my hair, and landed on my lips. "Talked to me like that."

I sucked on my lower lip. "You mean call you out on your bullshit?"

He pulled me tighter against him and his nose grazed near my earlobe. "Precisely."

We continued to float across the floor, weaving through other couples. "You've done this before," I said.

"I've been to a few balls in my time, yes. They're normally not so—" He paused, looking around with a grimace. "Bright."

"How else would you see your dance partner?"

He kept my gaze. "You'd be surprised what can be accomplished by candlelight."

Stomach Whoosh.

He pushed on my hip, spinning me outward, keeping his grip on my hand. "You really don't believe I'm who I say I am, do you?" He twirled me back in, and I tripped on my dress, falling against him.

"Can you blame me? It's a pretty outrageous claim." I trailed my gaze from his chest up to his face, eyeing the light beard over his chin.

"Just remember when you reach that epiphany," he dipped his face closer to mine. "I told you the truth from the very beginning."

My eyes fluttered, lashes hitting the mask. He was serious, deadly serious.

He tightened his grip around my waist, my chest pressing into his ribs, and he glided across the floor again. "That dress suits you."

"Think so? Sara said cranberry is my color."

"Funny. I would call that color more—" He dipped me, our eyes locking from behind the shields of our masks. "Pomegranate."

My heart thumped against my chest. His face was so close to mine I could feel his breath against my lips. He yanked me back to standing.

"I quite like pomegranates." I gulped.

"Do you?" A fire roared in his eyes. "I'll have to remember that."

My lips parted, and I sucked in a breath through my nose. Persephone.

He dropped his mouth to my ear, whispering. "Don't worry. If I ever chose to pursue you, I'd do it the old-fashioned way, darlin'."

I couldn't stop my eyes from widening, my heartbeat feeling like a jackhammer inside my chest. When he leaned back, his eyes bore into mine. A swirl of black fog started to float around us.

"They must've really pumped up those machines," I said.

The fog wrapped itself around my legs, cascading over my body. No one else on the dancefloor batted an eyelash.

"What color fog do these machines normally produce?" He asked.

I furrowed my brow. "Gray-ish?"

"Hm." He dipped me.

He searched my face, his eyes brightening. "You're truly not afraid of me." A fractal of turquoise punched through the blackness.

My brow creased and I shook my head, letting my fingertip trail over the corner of his mask.

The fog cascaded back down, gradually disappearing.

He stood me upright. "I've not once met a mortal who hasn't feared my presence."

"Well, maybe if you smiled once and awhile." I concentrated on what I could of his face from behind his mask as if it hid a new side to him I had yet to see.

81

His gaze dropped to the floor. He took my hands and placed them on his shoulders. His arms wrapped around my waist, and we swayed.

"Read me again. What do you see? Anything different from yesterday?"

I gazed up at him, watching those beautiful pastel shreds of light trying to squeeze past the shadows. "Hurt. You've been hurt deeply, but yearn to feel free again."

He pulled me closer, my chest pressing against him. His cheek rested against the side of my head. "Continually impressive. But I can't be free. Not in the way I want."

I peeled away to look at him. "Why?"

"If I were to explain, it'd be wasted on deaf ears." His eyes glinted behind his mask. "For whatever reason, I want nothing more than for you to believe, and it frustrates me." His lips thinned.

My heart fluttered and I pushed a strand of hair that'd fallen over his mask away from his eyes. His fingers drummed against my spine to the beat of the music.

"I've done some wicked things in my time, Stephanie." He kneaded my lower back and his gaze locked to mine.

I slipped the lapel of his black suit jacket between two fingers. "And do these things define you?"

He traced his fingers over my collarbone, curled his hand lightly around my neck, and cupped my chin. "No."

"Then why let it?" I found myself leaning further into him, relishing in the ash smell wafting from his skin.

He stared down at me, trailing his finger under my jaw, letting the tip catch on my lower lip.

The song faded to a close, and we stepped away from each other, but he didn't let go of my hand. After bowing, he placed a kiss against my knuckles. I blinked, and he was gone. The crowd danced and twirled around me, smiling and laughing. The urge to find him coursed through my veins. I pushed myself into the sea of people, forgetting I was claustrophobic. I needed to see him. Mirages of his face would appear, but once I thought I'd reached him, he'd fade away. I backed myself into a corner, wondering if I'd officially gone insane, chasing after nothing. The feeling of the mysterious smoke fog coiling around me like a caress burnt itself into my skin.

"Was that Hades you were dancing with?" Sara asked.

Hades. God of the Underworld. How could I believe it? I couldn't. Gods didn't exist, let alone show up at a resort on vacation and dance at a masquerade ball.

"Yes," I clipped, absently dragging a finger across the exposed skin of my collar bone.

Her eyes dropped to my hand, practically groping myself, and I dropped it to my side.

"That good, huh?" She asked.

Guy walked up with two drinks in hand, looking between us.

She narrowed her eyes at me, staring into space. "Guy, I'm going to dance with Steph for a few minutes."

"And I will gladly watch," Guy said.

Sara pursed her lips. "Real mature."

She tugged my arm, but it took several tries before I let her pull me to the center of the floor. She gripped my shoulders, shaking me.

"You look like you've seen a ghost, Steph."

I nodded, swaying back and forth with her, offbeat with the music. The first encounters with Hades kept replaying in my head. Wife of a thousand years? A divider of souls?

I locked eyes with her. "Earlier, did you see this swirly black smoke on the dancefloor?"

"No?" The skin between her eyes creased.

"I think Hades did it."

"I'll tell you what's happening," she said, poking my shoulder. "He's dragging you into his delusions. And you're diving right in because you want to help him. What good is it going to do if you're both stranded with no life jacket? Someone needs to stay in the boat."

I snorted. Hades would most certainly be the one in the boat. "Quite the analogy."

"Did you like that?"

"I do want to help him. But I'm just not sure how."

"I'm going to have to talk with this guy. I've interrogated plenty of people who tried to manipulate me. If he's trying that on you—I'll break one of his ribs."

"I don't think he's trying to manipulate me. Why would he have tried to push me away?"

A man with dark hair, a dark beard, and a metallic gold mask stepped up to Sara, tapping her on the shoulder. "Mind if I cut in?"

Sara folded her arms. "I do, actually. We're in the middle of an important conversation."

"Oh, are you? My mistake." The man pushed a fingertip against her forehead.

Her arms fell slack at her sides, and she shrugged. "On

second thought, be my guest."

My hands went numb, watching Sara walk off like a zombie. I moved to follow her, but his arm slipped around my waist, pinning me against him.

"I'll scream," I said, trying to pull away, but his grip tightened, holding me captive.

His pearly grin spread wide, eyes beaming with mischief even behind the guise of his mask.

He dipped his lips to my ear, and I grimaced. "My brother has taken quite the liking to you."

Zane. I knew I recognized that slimy grin.

"How would you know? Judging from the last time I saw you two together, he doesn't seem to like you very much."

He chuckled, the whiskers from his beard scraping against my cheek. "I don't need him to like me."

"Is there a point to all of this?"

"I need you to make sure he's happy."

"I don't *need* to do anything."

He smiled against my chin. "You've no idea the forces you've become intertwined with, Stephanie."

I forced my head back, peering up at him. "Are you threatening me?"

"That's for you to decide."

He backed away, letting the dozens of dancing bodies swallow him like quicksand until he disappeared. The hair on my arms stood at attention like after an electric shock. I wrapped my arms around myself, looking for Hades one last time amongst the slew of guests. The room was far from empty, but strangely, without him there, it felt hollow.

SEVEN

CONSIDERING THE NIGHT I'D had, sipping fruity drinks by the pool was the last thing on my mind. I convinced Sara I felt under the weather from too much champagne. Between the mind games of swirling smoke, the disappearing act, and Zane's cryptic threat, I needed a distraction. Today was for me.

The resort's computer lab was a short walk from our room. I found a station in a hidden corner and patched myself through to my work computer back home. Forcing my brain back into work-mode was my only real form of distraction. I expected Sara to walk around the corner at any given moment, scolding me. I looked for her so many times one might think I was hacking the NSA database.

I went to work, scrolling through the gallery of images with the processing finished from the new software. Satisfied Sara wasn't going to sneak up on me I slipped one of my earbuds in. *(I Just) Died in Your Arms* by Cutting Crew fueled my endless mouse clicking.

Several hours flew by, and I was unable to find any new evidence. Backed into a corner—again. I rubbed my eyes. If there were any hope of continuing my investigation, I'd need caffeine and vitamin B injected into my veins, stat.

"I may be no expert at relaxing, but this doesn't seem like a good way to go about doing it," Hades muttered behind me.

I jumped. "How did you find me?"

"Do you really want me to tell you?" His tone dropped an octave.

He peered at me like he had last night from across the room, and my heart raced. "Your brother stopped by to see me last night."

"What?" He growled.

"He's an asshole, by the way."

"On that, we can agree. What did he say?"

To lie or not to lie. "He said I needed to make you happy. Almost sounded like a threat."

He crossed the room. "He won't hurt you. I won't let him."

"Hurt me? Who *are* you guys? Are you with the mafia or something? Just tell me. Maybe I can help you." I stood, making the earbud pop from my ear.

His eyes searched mine, and his lips parted as if to speak. After a beat, he said, "Will you go somewhere with me?"

"Depends on what you had in mind?"

If he said a guided tour of the Underworld, I was out of here.

"There's an old temple not too far from here. I'd like to show it to you."

Considering the beach, pool, and alcohol was all I'd

experienced in Greece thus far, I loved the idea. "Alright." I grabbed the mouse. "Let me just finish up here."

He leaned forward, eyeing the monitor. "What are you doing?"

"Work I shouldn't be doing, but can't seem to stop thinking about. I'm a digital forensics examiner."

"*Digital* forensics? Oh, how times have changed," he scratched his chin.

"Who are you kidding?"

"Why can't you stop thinking about it?"

I sighed, shutting down the computer. "It's an old murder case. The suspect committed suicide, which left a lot of things unanswered. Because there wasn't enough evidence, he was never convicted. You can imagine the pain it's caused the families of the victims."

"A murderer who committed suicide? We could—have a chat with him?" He said it so matter-of-fact I couldn't help but laugh.

I slapped his shoulder. "Very funny."

He stared at me, not finding *me* funny.

Sara walked past and did a double-take. She marched in, glaring daggers into Hades' skull. "What are you doing in here?"

Lie. You can do this. Just…lie. I opened my mouth to answer but snapped it shut when no words followed.

"I'm taking her on a tour. Considering I'm horrible with technology, I asked her to help me book a boat ride online. Isn't that right, Stephanie?"

When I didn't answer, he nudged me.

I forced a smile and snapped my attention to Sara. "Yes! Yes, absolutely. And online, that's right."

Sara looked between us before standing toe-to-toe with Hades. "Let me make this perfectly clear. That woman is like a sister to me. If you hurt her, I'll permanently damage something of yours and make it look like an accident." She poked his chest.

After glaring at her finger, he took her hand, keeping her gaze, and lowered it. "Noted."

She stared at him for a moment and shook her head like clearing cobwebs. "Glad we're on the same page." She slid her sunglasses on.

Hades held out his hand. "Darlin'?"

Sara grabbed my elbow. "Don't let him take you anywhere that's not public and watch for signs like I taught you."

"Thank you. I'll be fine, promise." I patted her hand.

A part of me, a *very* small part, wanted to believe I hadn't dreamt up everything. I loved Sara, but I couldn't talk to her about it. It sounded crazy, even to me. I needed proof.

"So, where are you taking me?" I asked.

"A small island off the coastline."

Off the coastline? That didn't sound very public.

"Uh, how far off the coastline?"

He whipped around to face me and folded his arms over his chest. I tried not to get distracted by the tautness of his bicep. "Tell me, what do you think the role of the god of the Underworld is?"

"I always assumed he was like the devil."

He leaned forward, bits of his hair falling over his eyes. "Not even close. And if you're worried about something happening to you during our little excursion, you can rest assured there'll be plenty of tourists on the island." He turned back around and continued walking.

How could I be wrong? Hades was in control of the bad people and chose their punishments accordingly. How was that not like the job bestowed on Lucifer himself? I trotted to his side and tugged on his shirt sleeve.

"Are you going to tell me where I'm wrong with that comparison, or let me guess?"

"When you're ready, I'll tell you."

He led us to a ticket booth. A sign with a cartoon boat and the words "Roundtrip Rides" in both English and Greek hung from the window. He dug in his back pocket, removing a black leather wallet. When he opened it, hundreds of Euros sprouted out, and I tried not to stare. He slid several to the attendant, giving an absent nod as he handed him two tickets.

"What makes you think I'm not ready to hear it now?"

He cocked an eyebrow. "You don't believe."

"Are you Santa Claus now?"

"Oh? Don't believe he's real, either?" He graced me with a small smirk.

I narrowed my eyes. "Don't patronize me."

We walked across a wooden dock, leading to a small white boat with two levels. The attendant greeted him in Greek, and the two had a quick conversation I couldn't understand. Hades stepped up, holding his hand out to me. I stared, knowing there was a grand possibility of me getting sick.

"How long is this ride?" I asked.

"Twenty minutes. Why?"

I fidgeted with the hem of my shorts. "I get seasick."

"I'll put in a word for calm seas. Will that help?"

"Oh, is one of your supposed powers persuasion?" I snorted as he helped me into the boat. I waved a hand at the water like Obi-Wan Kenobi. "You will be calm for the duration of the trip."

He looked off in the distance. "Something like that."

I followed him to the second level; the wind whipping through my hair. When the boat shoved off, Hades leaned on the railing, closing his eyes, letting the bright sun warm his cheeks.

It was hard not to ogle him with how serene he looked. "You don't get out much, do you?"

"No. I can count on one hand the number of times I've been able to let the sun kiss my face. Or smell sea spray." He opened his eyes, and his jaw clenched.

Greek mythology rolled through my head. Brothers, Zeus and Poseidon, gained control of Olympus and the seas while Hades received the Underworld. I tapped the railing. "Demanding job?"

The wind tousled his hair in the most majestic of ways. "Very."

He said everything with such conviction. My rational brain said this was crazy, but he had a way of making crazy sound convincing.

"You don't get vacation days?"

He looked at the water. "It's not that simple."

"Then how'd you manage this one?"

"Very rarely, with catastrophic occurrences, I'm granted—a break."

Blood rushed to my ears. "To keep you—happy."

I didn't look at him, my eyes fixed on fish leaping from the water.

He turned to face me, leaning on the railing with one elbow. "In a manner of speaking."

"Do you work for your brother?"

"Partners."

Why were all his answers cryptic enough to reel me right back in?

"How's your stomach?" He asked.

I pressed a hand over my abdomen. "I feel—fine. I haven't felt the boat rock at all. How is that possible?"

"The—" A corner of his mouth twitched. "—captain and I are on good terms."

"I don't care how good of a captain he is; it still doesn't explain how the water doesn't make the boat bob up and down. Even a little."

"Fine. You want the truth?"

He stared at me, waiting for an answer. A small squeak escaped my throat, but no words followed. The boat slowed down, pulling to a rickety dock leading to a tiny island.

"We're here," he grumbled.

I guess my silence wasn't the answer he was looking for.

Every few planks were missing on the dock, and I took baby steps across. Hades strode over it without a care in the world. He didn't so much as look down. The sight of the boat pulling away, leaving us stranded on the island, made a knot form in my stomach. Sara was going to kill me. No, she'd kill Hades first, *then* me.

"Are they coming back?" I asked.

"Of course, they are," he answered, making his way to a deeply wooded area.

After pushing past several tree branches, palm fronds, and vines, we reached a clearing with hundreds of squared rocks—wall remnants of an old building.

I traced my fingers over the rubble. "Is this a temple?"

"What's left of it."

Part of a column still stood. In my opinion, the staple of ancient Greek architecture. "Was it dedicated to someone?"

He crouched down, pressing his hand against a crumbled slab. "Artemis."

"I imagine it was beautiful when it was standing, but I have to ask, why is this one of significance to you?"

He stood, looking around at the rubble as if picturing in his mind what it used to look like. "The Greeks built these temples to honor their gods. At first, they were made of wood, but this is the first with stone. It wasn't an easy task considering you had to have the proper distribution of weight, or it'd crumble."

"Really? And here in Corfu?"

He nodded. "Their dedication to their gods knew no bounds, including the lengths they went to develop temples in their honor. Much like these ruins, however, the dedication crumbled through the ages."

"I'm sure there are those who still believe in them."

"Like you?" He peered at me from across the foundation of the fallen temple.

A sharp prick of guilt stung me in the chest. I picked up a

rock, rolling it between my fingers. "Was there one for Hades?"

"They called it Nekromanteion. It's not so much of a temple as it is a door, however. It's in Epirus, once known as Ephyra. They thought it was the gateway to the Underworld."

Intrigue traveled down my spine like a burning wick. "Thought it was?"

"There are only so many ways to get to the Underworld, and it's most certainly not through a gateway made of stone."

"A chariot ride with the King himself?" I wrapped my hand around the stone, pushing an imprint into my palm.

"That's one way. Or—" His gaze locked onto my very soul. "Death."

We stared at each other.

"There's another reason I enjoy this particular temple." He motioned for me to follow him out of the woods.

Cerulean water and mountains in the distance greeted me. Several branches from the trees dipped in front of us, framing the scene like a painting. He leaned forward on the railing and took a deep breath.

"This is one of my favorite spots in all of Greece," he said, sighing.

"I can see why. It's breathtaking." I eyed him sidelong. "Why me?"

"What do you mean?"

"This is your favorite spot, and you're sharing it with me. Why?"

His eyes remained on the water. "I've never had anyone invested in me. At first, I thought you might just be infatuated with me. With the idea of this so-called 'bad boy image,' but no…" His gaze lifted to me. "You're real."

How ironic he questioned *my* reality.

I frowned and hovered my hand over his forearm. Never in my life had I as much confidence as I felt around him. I rested my hand on his arm after staring at it for a second or two. "What's really going on with you, Hades? You seem so…"

His eyes focused on my fingers wrapped around his arm.

"…broken," I finished.

His gaze snapped to mine, and he turned away. "I want to prove to you who I am, but only if that's what you want, Stephanie."

My heart skipped a beat. "I want to believe you. I do. I just—need more."

He faced me and pulled his shoulders back. "Do you *want* to see proof? Yes or no."

I blinked with the speed of a hummingbird and wrung my hands together.

He slipped a hand on my shoulder and lowered his head, so we were face-to-face. "I need to hear it, Stephanie. I made poor decisions in my past, and I'm not doing it again."

"Your decisions couldn't have been that bad. I've seen some monstrous deeds I would've never thought someone was capable of."

He leaned back. "In your profession, you mean?"

"Not only my profession. My mom —there was a house fire, and she was inside sleeping. We found out later it was arson. Someone trying to kill my dad, but he was working a beat. And I was at a sleepover."

"I'm sorry." His face softened.

"It was a long time ago, but I guess I shared it with you because there's a lot of things I'd have said I wouldn't believe were possible—but was proven wrong."

A gust of wind flew between us, making our hair flutter.

"What would you show me? The chariot? A three-headed dog?"

"Definitely *not* Cerberus. He's far too big." A corner of his lip lifted.

Was I really about to say this?

"Show me," I whispered.

His eyebrows drew together, staring at me like a chessboard. He held out his hand. "Have you had anything to drink today?"

"No?" I elongated the 'o', taking his hand.

He led me into the thick of the woods, taking me into his arms like we'd done the previous night amidst the magic and glamour of the ball.

"Why did you ask me that?"

"Because it means you have no excuse to believe it isn't real." His eyebrow quirked and the same tendrils of smoke from last night swirled around us.

It started at his feet, spreading to mine like dancing on a rain cloud. It made its way over our bodies, swirling around us in a spiral. I gasped once it reached my neck, a caress teasing itself through my hair. His eyes turned white, devoid of an iris or pupil, and the sight made me recoil.

He held his palms up, facing me, and the smoke faded away. His eyes morphed back to normal, and I had to blink several times to make sure my vision hadn't blurred.

"You—you're—"

"Hades. Yes, Stephanie." He didn't try to approach me.

Dozens of images flew through my mind of fire, death, and—what if this wasn't his true form? It couldn't be. Shivers consumed me, and I threw a hand out when he got within arm's reach.

"Don't. Please don't come any further," I said through a shaky breath.

He stopped with a heavy sigh. "You told me before you weren't afraid of me. God of the Underworld or not, you still have no reason to fear me."

Was it the fear of him hurting me? Or was it the fear of realizing Greek mythology was all true?

Cerberus. The Underworld. It. Was. All. Real.

I slapped my hands on my head. "I don't know how to process this."

"Stephanie, you look like you're going to—" he started as he took a step forward.

I dragged my hands down my face, my finger catching on my bottom lip, staring at him. "I feel like I'm going to pass out." The numb feeling traveled down my arms, followed by the tunnel vision eking its way in.

"Please don't do—" Was all I heard from him before I did just that.

EIGHT

THE SUN PEEKED THROUGH the window. My fingertips grazed over the smooth stripes of the comforter of my hotel room bed. I groaned and sat up, shoving a palm in my eye socket.

"What time is it?" I asked, hoping someone was in the room.

Sara leaned forward. "Almost noon. You passed out and then didn't wake up all night. Scared me half to death."

"I had the strangest dream." At least I thought it was a dream. I slid off the bed, the coolness of the wood floor shocking my bare feet. "Hades conjured this—smoke. It was like it had a life of its own."

She cocked an eyebrow. "Animated smoke? Like the smoke monster in *Lost*? The one that sounded like a typewriter?"

Was that where I'd seen it before? Was it my subconscious? But it felt *so* real. "Yeah. I guess so."

"Well, there you go. You already said Hades looks a little

like Sawyer. It's your mind playing tricks on you, associating things. And he was the last person you saw before clocking out. He carried you in here."

I widened my eyes. "Oh, God. Please tell me you didn't give him a black eye or something."

"It was close." She smirked. "But we had a civilized conversation, and he explained to me you got seasick and passed out on the boat."

No, I didn't. I specifically remember being in the woods when it happened.

I dragged my hands over my face and blew out a breath. "Can we agree on not having to get someone to carry either of us back to our room for the rest of this trip?"

She laughed, wrapping her arms around me in a tight hug. Her hugs were the best in the world, and I'd kick anyone in the shin who disagreed. She peeled back, still holding my shoulders. "You're going to try and avoid him, aren't you?"

"Pfft, no." I couldn't make direct eye contact with her. She was like a viper with a penetrating gaze. "Why do you say that?"

She squished my face with one hand, making my lips pucker like a fish. "Because you're embarrassed. And a small part of you is still wondering what the dream was all about."

"I really need to pick friends with occupations like veterinarian or ranch worker or something." The words distorted, given the situation of my face.

"I'd like to talk to him some more, you know. You should talk to him about hanging out with us tomorrow. Maybe rope him into an excursion." She grinned mischievously.

"I'll see what I can do, but the man's insistent on saving his spot at the bar." I half-smiled.

"Come on. You could use a Lemondrop." She grabbed my hand.

"Shouldn't I change first?" Considering I was still in the same clothes as yesterday.

"We're at a resort. You're wearing shorts, a tank top, and a bikini underneath. Standard attire. Let's go."

We returned to the swim-up bar. Michelle and Rupert were there, sipping on drinks with pink and yellow swirly straws. I slipped into the water, continually glancing at Hades' usual spot at the bar. Empty.

"Well, hello there. We were just saying how strange it was we hadn't run into you two again yet," Michelle said, tossing her hair over her shoulder.

"Is this your first time at the swim-up bar?" Sara asked, taking a stool next to Michelle.

Michelle took a sip from her drink, glaring at Rupert before smiling. "It is."

"Well, there's your answer," Sara replied, grinning and waving the bartender over.

The bartender was the same one we'd had since the day we arrived. He smiled wide, patting his hands on the concrete bar top. "What'll it be today, Miss Sara?"

"Hugo, what did I tell you, just Sara." She giggled. "Two Lemondrops to start, please."

"Oh, we're doing shots? We'll get in on that too, barkeep," Rupert said, shoving his sunglasses onto his head.

Michelle placed her hand on his forearm, dipping her

mouth to his ear. "Love, shouldn't you take it easy after the—incident yesterday?"

Rupert yanked his arm away. "I'm on bloody holiday, Shelly."

She frowned, recoiling her hand.

Sara and I exchanged a quick glance.

Hugo set four shots in front of us with a smile and said, "Yamas."

I held mine in the air. Michelle's frown continued, but she grabbed her and Rupert's, hesitantly handing his over. He grabbed it with such force, he almost knocked it out of her hand.

"To Greece!" I toasted.

We tapped our plastic cups together and tossed back the sweet, lemony goodness.

Rupert winced, holding his hand at his side.

"Love?" Michelle touched his shoulder.

He shook his head, sliding his shot glass across the bar top. "I'm fine. I'm fine. Just a little heartburn." He pointed at his empty glass, getting Hugo's attention. "Another shot, but something a little harder, eh, mate?"

Sara nudged my forearm. "Look lively."

Hades stood between the pool and the outside bar, scanning the area. I dropped into the water, my sunglasses floating to the surface as my head submerged. Peeking my head above the surface just enough to breathe, I sputtered. Sara made a suitable shield between Hades and me. Once he walked away, I stood up, plopping my arms on the bar top.

"You're a nut," Sara said, taking a sip from her pink drink.

I ran a hand over my face, ridding it of water droplets. "Is my make-up completely ruined?"

"What make-up?"

I stuck my bottom lip out. "I'm going to go—freshen up."

"You're not going back to hide in the room, are you?" She blocked me with her arm.

With vigor, I shook my head. "Nope." It was the truth, but I left out the small detail of where I really planned to go.

She narrowed her eyes before lowering her arm. "Alright. But don't make me come looking for you."

"I'll be right back," I said, wading to the stairs.

My wet bathing suit seeped through my clothes as I whisked off to the nearest gift shop. I plucked a pair of pink binoculars from a turn style. Halfway to the register, I stopped. Bright pink probably wasn't the most inconspicuous color choice for spying. I traded them out for a black pair, grabbed a roll of Tums, and hurriedly paid. A fierce need to know if Hades was *the* Hades ate at me like a festering wound.

Now to find him. I sniffed the air for the smell of burning wood like I was a bloodhound. Nothing, but was worth a shot. After checking every bar on the property and turning up empty, I started to lose hope. Maybe he went back to his room? I passed the lobby area and did a double-take. There he was, plain as day, sitting at the bar inside. A quaint bar compared to all the others.

I ducked behind a nearby bush, raising the binoculars. After going cross-eyed several times, I managed to focus through both eyepieces. Wait. How was I supposed to hear anything this far away? There was another bush a few feet closer, and I scampered behind it, sputtering when several of the leaves slapped me in the face.

"What'll it be?" The bartender asked.

"A Backdraft."

The bartender nodded and returned with a shot glass full of brown liquid, sliding it in front of him.

Hades looked down and then back up at the tender. "Aren't you gonna light it on fire?"

"New liability regulations, I'm afraid. No open flames." The bartender shrugged.

Hades sighed, scratching his beard. "Kind of defeats the purpose of this particular drink, doesn't it?"

"Rules are rules, sir. Sorry." The bartender held his hands up and walked away.

Hades stared at his drink before looking around. Besides the bartender who'd left and me behind a friggin' bush, there was no one in sight. He snapped his fingers over the shot glass, igniting the contents into a raging flame. My jaw dropped, and I fumbled with the binoculars, struggling to get them back to my eyes. Did he have a lighter hidden in his hand? He blew the flame out and lifted the glass to his lips, knocking it back.

I lowered the binoculars, blinked, and shoved them back over my eyes so harshly it gave me a headache. There was definitely no lighter in his hand or anywhere to be seen. My heart thudded against my chest.

More. I needed more. This could *not* be happening.

He threw some Euros on the bar top and left. He went for the opposite door from my makeshift coverage. Thank God because half of my body stuck out from the bush.

He stopped at one of the twenty-four-hour food stands.

There weren't any nearby bushes, so I made do with a trash can.

"A gyro, please," he ordered.

They handed one to him wrapped in parchment paper and foil.

"Do you have ketchup?" He asked.

Ketchup on a gyro? Gross.

"Sorry, sir, we're out."

He was hitting zero for two tonight. As if the guy needed any other excuse to be depressed.

"That's fine. I'll make do," Hades said, clutching the gyro in his hand and heading further down the tiled walkway.

The smell of curdled tzatziki sauce made me gag. The trashcan was a horrible hiding spot, but to move now would be spying suicide. He shifted his eyes and twirled his free hand in a circle toward the ground. A small hole with a glowing orange hue opened in the grass beside the walkway, and a pale hand holding a bottle of ketchup emerged from it. Hades grabbed the bottle, popped the top off, squirted some ketchup on his gyro, and handed it back to the—hand. The hand didn't disappear immediately, and he batted it a few times before it slipped away. The hole sealed up as if it were never there in the first place.

Oh. My. God.

I fell back. Hades really *was* Hades. How could I possibly look him in the face, let alone hold a conversation? I *danced* with a Greek god. Bile made its way up my throat, and I kept it back. No. No. I refused to believe it. He was dragging me straight into his metaphorical Underworld. That or this Greek vacation had gotten entirely too interactive.

I made my way back to the swim-up bar, munching on Tums, but couldn't remember how I got there.

Sara waved her hand in front of my face. "You walked into the pool like a zombie. Are you okay?"

The image of the hand appearing inexplicably from the ground played on a constant loop in my head. "Oh, yeah. A little sleepy is all."

"You slept for fourteen hours."

I braided my hair and tossed it over my shoulder. "There is such a thing as *too* much sleep."

Michelle and Rupert were gone.

"You missed a hell of a show. Rupert had six shots before Michelle asked him to stop. He didn't take it too lightly, and they started arguing until it turned into all-out yelling."

"What's going on with those two?"

She crossed her legs. "I could guess, but I told you from the beginning, Rupert was a bad egg."

"How are the two prettiest women in the resort today?" Guy asked, wiggling his way in between us, a can of beer in hand.

Sara snorted. "What do *you* want?"

"Do I need a reason to dote on beauty?" He grinned.

I held back an eye roll.

Guy snapped his fingers. "Oh, Steph, do I remember hearing you like *Dirty Dancing*?"

"The movie, yes. Why?"

"They put up a flyer in the lobby. Looks like some contest or something."

I stood straighter. "What? Really?"

His brow rose over the top of his sunglasses. "Pretty sure I read it right, but you should go check it out."

Water splashed as I clamored out of the pool, slipping on the stairs. I made a beeline for the lobby, not willing to stop for anything or anyone. The hanging pen on the bulletin board couldn't get in my hand fast enough, and I dragged my finger across the typed-out details.

"Special Valentine's Day Event: Dirty Dancing contest for *the* dance. You know the one. First prize: VIP access to a special event. Note: For couples only (it is Valentine's Day after all)," I read aloud, my excitement deflating with the last part.

"You've been avoiding me," Hades said from behind me.

I turned around, re-positioning the pen in my hand like a knife, trying to hold it above my head, but the string halted my effort. "Do *not* appear out of thin air like that, please."

"Actually, I walked around the corner. You were too preoccupied with reading out loud." His eyes dropped to my bikini-clad form before dragging their way back to my face.

My cheeks warmed.

"By the way, sweetheart, when you want to spy on someone, it's usually best to be further away. That's the idea behind binoculars."

My face fell, arms dropping back to my sides. "You knew I was there?"

"The entire time. I have to say I was impressed you didn't pass out again." He brushed past me, eyeing the flyer.

I couldn't form words. He was Hades. *Hades.*

He flicked a finger at the paper. "Are you entering this?"

I took a step away from him, worried he'd randomly light something on fire again. "Thinking about it."

"I'll enter with you."

I laughed. "You?"

"Why not?" He narrowed his eyes.

"You're—" I referenced him from head to toe. "You."

"Who else would you enter with? Keith?" The corners of his jaw bobbed.

Green mist fell over his grey cloud.

"Hades, did you…have anything to do with Keith's food poisoning?"

"Did he die from it?"

I shifted my eyes. "No."

"Then I'd say no. Look—"

He'd *say* no?

He stepped forward, and I grabbed the dangling pen again. He sighed and ran a hand through his hair. "You'd be giving me another opportunity to be human."

"No. Absolutely not. I can't enter a contest with the—" I looked around for anyone else within earshot. "—god of the Underworld," I whispered.

He leaned in. "Why not?"

"Because you're the god of the Underworld!" I clapped my hands over my mouth.

"You've already danced with me once. How is this any different?"

"It just is."

He glared. "You think I can't handle filthy dancing?"

"It's dirty dancing," I mumbled, undoing my braid, and re-doing it. "Fine."

On the inside, I was jumping up and down like a twelve-year-old me at a Backstreet Boys concert. I've wanted to try *the* dance since I was a little girl. *Especially* the lift.

He cupped a hand over his ear. "What was that?"

"I said fine. I'll enter with you."

He picked up the pen and scrolled our names with the flourish of ancient calligraphy. "I'll make sure we win."

"Wait—what do you mean? You don't plan on setting people on fire or trapping them in Tartarus if we're losing or something, are you?"

He cocked one eyebrow. "No. I was going to suggest we practice." His arms bulged as he folded them over his chest, glowering down at me. "When you read me, is darkness the only thing you see?"

The teal color burst from behind him like ethereal rays.

"No," I whispered.

He leaned forward and paused, testing to see if I'd cower away this time. I didn't. He lifted a hand and delicately traced a finger over my chin like he'd done at the masquerade.

Stifling a whimper, I batted my eyelashes at him. "People always think of you like the one in the *Hercules* cartoon. Ruthless. Erratic."

He stared at me. "The *Disney* cartoon?"

"Yes."

His gaze dropped to my lips and his finger trailed to the other side of my face. "I can assure you my true form doesn't have flaming blue hair."

A true form. Now all I could do was think about what that might look like. Horns? Pointy teeth?

I undid my braid and did it over again. "Are there times you have to be?"

His hand fell away and he lifted his brow.

"Ruthless?" I focused on the darkness of his eyes, remembering the way they looked glowing white.

His gaze dropped to the floor, narrowing. "I am when I need to be. I don't take pleasure in punishing people, but those who deserve it…I don't go lightly." He lifted his eyes, locking with mine.

Such burdens.

"I have so many questions."

"And I'll tell you anything. *Anything,* Stephanie."

I rested my hand on his arm. "I went somewhere with you yesterday. Tomorrow, will you go somewhere with me? And Sara?"

He squinted. "Sure. But where are we going?"

"You'll see." I raised to the balls of my feet and flopped back onto my heels. "I should get going. I'll see you tomorrow."

"Stephanie," he beckoned. "Would you like to know what I see when I look at you?"

I turned back to face him, playing with my braid. "What do you see?"

"Hope." His jaw tightened before he bowed his head and turned away, leaving me standing there staring at the back of the King of the Underworld too shocked to move.

NINE

![decorative greek key border]

"DID YOU TELL HADES what time to meet us out here?" Sara asked, glancing at the clock hanging in the lobby.

"Did we decide on an actual time? I told him to meet us in the lobby in the morning."

She crossed her arms. "Oh, great. Considering his love of all things dark, he's probably a night owl and won't show up until eleven."

"Who won't show up until eleven?" Hades asked after rounding the corner.

He had his same black ensemble on with the tank top and a flowy, undone button-up short-sleeved shirt. The sight of him made my heart race.

"There you are. That's what you're wearing? You might regret that choice. Let me get them to hail us a taxi," Sara said, trotting over to the attendant desk.

I started to follow her, but Hades caught me by the crook of my elbow. "What's wrong with what I'm wearing?"

"It might be…" I bit my lip. "Too many clothes for where we're going?"

He cocked an eyebrow before narrowing his eyes. "And you call me cryptic."

"Come on, you two. Taxi's here. Steph, you're in the middle." Sara wave us over.

Hades held his hand out for me to walk in front of him.

"Why do I always get the middle?" I grumbled.

Sara and Hades stood beside each other.

She motioned between the two of them. "You see how tall we both are, right?"

"Point made," I mumbled.

We all slid into the back seat. I pressed my knees together and kept my elbows at my sides.

"You can lean on me, you know? I promise I won't break," Hades whispered.

No. But I might. Something told me Sara wouldn't appreciate us making out in the seat right next to her.

"Sidari Beach, please," Sara told the driver.

Hades' eyes narrowed. "Interesting beach choice, Sara. Any particular reason?" He leaned past me to look at her.

"The Canal d'amour, of course," she responded with a grin.

Hades smirked. "I had a feeling. You know those legends precisely that, right?"

"Wouldn't be so sure," our driver piped in, smiling at us in the rearview mirror.

"What's the legend?" I asked, trying to ignore the feel of Hades' leg brushing against mine.

"When a couple swims the canal, they're destined an eternity together," the driver said, raising his eyebrows.

"And for singles, if you hop in when the canal is in the shade, you'll always be lucky in love," Sara added with a smile.

Hades rolled his eyes. "Like I said, only a legend."

"Bit of a pessimist, are you?" The driver asked.

"I'm someone who knows."

I eyed Hades sidelong.

"Have an in with Aphrodite? If so, please give her my number," the driver said, bursting into a fit of husky laughter.

My body tensed. Hades nudged the side of my thigh with his knuckle. I looked over at him, and he winked.

It didn't take long to arrive at the beach, and the driver dropped us off near the canal entrance. He told us it was a decent walk to reach it, but worth it. We made our way over a bridge leading to a dusty road framed with foliage. The sun beamed down on us, the blue of the sky matching the Ionian Sea water, not a cloud to be seen.

"You have to be sweltering in all that black. How do you do it?" Sara asked as we made our way down the path.

"I'm hot-natured," Hades replied, staying near me while Sara led the pack.

It was so strange hearing his answers now and knowing there were subtle truths to it all.

"Hades and I are entering that dance contest," I blurted.

"Really?" She whipped around to face us, walking backward. "You can dance like that, Hades?"

"Admittedly, I've never seen the movie, but I can—pick things up rather quickly. I wanted Stephanie to have the chance to do it."

"Huh. That's nice of you," she said with a smile before turning back around.

At the end of the path, the famous canal came into view. A rock formation withered away by erosion and time, a slit down the center creating the canal itself. There were several tourists scattered across the rocks. Some were at the very top, others climbed down and sat on the rocks. It was a quaint, quiet cove with gentle lapping waves at the opening.

"Legend or not. This is gorgeous," I said, staring at one of Mother Nature's masterpieces.

"Yes, it is." Hades' gaze pierced the side of my face.

I looked at him and gulped.

Sara grabbed each of our hands. "Come on, that water is calling my name."

"I certainly don't hear the same calling," Hades said, allowing Sara to lead him to the edge of the rocks.

Sara wasted no time, whipping off her shirt and shorts, down to her bikini. "You can either jump off from here." She leaned over the edge, staring down at the water. "Or there's a rope over there. Pretty sure you know what I'm doing." She gave a wicked grin, ran forward, and leaped off the rock.

I gasped, running to the edge just in time to see her splash into the water. "She's fearless. I'll give her that."

"I take it you'd rather use the rope?" Hades asked.

"You're coming with me, right?"

Hades leaned over the edge, sneering at the water. "Would you...*like* me to?"

"I certainly don't want to climb down there by myself." I bit my lip to keep from smiling.

He cleared his throat and dragged a hand over his beard. "Alright."

Was it wrong I felt some kind of deep-rooted satisfaction in watching the god of the Underworld squirm?

"I'm getting pretty lonely down here," Sara shouted.

We made our way to the rope. I paused with my thumbs in the tops of my shorts, feeling Hades' presence behind me. Taking a deep breath, I whisked the shorts and shirt off before I could talk myself out of it. I turned to face him in my bikini. As his eyes roamed my body, he gave a subtle lick of his lip. I didn't feel compelled to cross my arms over my chest. It was… liberating.

"So, are you going to hop in there fully clothed?"

"Well, since someone didn't tell me I'd need swim attire, guess I'm improvising'." He slipped off the short-sleeved shirt.

My heart thudded.

He squinted, watching me watching him as he slid his hands under his tank top and pulled it over his head. I sucked my bottom lip and let it snap back out. Hades, shirtless, standing on a rock in the middle of Greece. And he most certainly had the 'V.' Muscular, tanned, and carved like a fleshy marble sculpture.

He didn't take his eyes off me as he slid down his pants, standing now in only a pair of black silk boxers. As he walked past me, he held his hand up, and a quick surge of smoke wafted through my hair, tossing it over my shoulder.

I gasped.

His eyes brightened before he swung his leg over the edge.

"I'll go first."

I waited until he was at the bottom before starting my descent. My coordination wasn't the best and trying to find rocks to rest my feet on was more difficult than I'd imagined.

"How much further do I have?" I asked.

"You're almost there. Put your right foot directly beneath you, darlin'."

I moved my right foot but to the right and down instead of directly below as instructed. My foot slipped, and I let go in a bout of panic. Hades caught me, and I lay draped in his arms.

"Have I told you before you're clumsy?" He focused on my mouth.

I nodded, not saying a word, and ignoring the goosebumps sprouting all over my skin from his touch.

"The water feels amazing," Sara said, beckoning us with her hands.

Hades set me down, and I smoothed out a skirt I wasn't wearing.

Once in the water, I let out a contented sigh. "It's the perfect temperature."

"Little cold for my taste." Hades grimaced as he moved into the water inch by inch.

Sara looked between us with a warm smile before focusing on Hades, who hadn't taken his eyes off me since we were at the top of the rock.

"You two should take a little dip through the canal. I've already done it." Sara swirled her arms through the water.

"A dip together? What about the legend?" I risked a glance at Hades.

Hades appeared at my side, his hand slipping over my hip underwater. "Darlin' I promise you won't want to inexplicably marry me after some swim in 'magical' water."

"And if I do?" I turned to face him, slipping my hand over his.

He squatted further into the water, wincing when it reached his chest. His lips pressed to my ear, the brush of his beard against my cheek tickling my skin. "Let's test it then. Swim with me, Stephanie."

Sara swam backward, canting her head and back and forth as she continued to watch Hades. I knew exactly what she was doing, profiling him. When she told me she wanted another chance to talk to him, I knew what she *really* meant.

"Alright. But what if that supposed dark heart of yours melts in my hand afterward?" I grinned.

"Not even Aphrodite herself could force this black heart into love. If it's meant to melt…it will."

My grin faded and I bit down on my bottom lip, staring up at him. As we swam side by side, the heat from his body coiled around me despite the frigid temperature of the water.

"Does Poseidon control the water here?" A question to distract myself from the varying knots my stomach formed.

"He hasn't been in Greece for some time. I have no idea where he is now. I've been otherwise occupied, remember?"

"Right. I keep forgetting, sorry. Though I'm not sure how I could forget, given what I've seen."

What I've felt. What I continue to feel.

"You don't need to apologize. It's a whole new world for you."

And there were undoubtedly a hundred thousand things to see.

We reached the end of the canal, where the rocks narrowed into a gap not big enough to squeeze through.

"We swam the canal together. Should I propose now?" He gazed at me through the wet strands of his hair. His lip curled slightly.

Queen of the Underworld.

I couldn't be certain if I'd say no.

We stared at each other for a beat, swishing our arms through the clear blue water. His head cocked to the side when he noticed I didn't smile, nor answer his question. He moved closer, lifting his hand from the water to pinch my chin within his grasp. Water beads rolled off his skin, trickling over my chest.

"So, did you set the date?" Sara asked, suddenly appearing beside us.

I widened my eyes and splashed her. She shrieked, paddling away with one hand while covering her head with the other.

We spent the rest of the day swimming through the canal, letting ourselves dry off on the rocks and diving back in when we got too hot. Several times, Hades remained on the rocks, just watching me. He wasn't kidding when he said he despised the water, but the water did *not* despise him. It left little to the imagination, clinging the boxers to his legs. And they could write poems on the way it made his abdominal muscles sparkle.

The sun started to set, and Hades insisted we stay for dessert. We found a small café, and Hades ordered something called Sykomaïtha.

"You'll both love it. It's a fig-based cake. Corfu staple,"

Hades said.

I sat next to him with Sara across from us. She had one elbow propped up and her chin resting in her hand.

"Are you Greek by descent?" Sara asked Hades.

"Yes."

"How'd you end up with a southern accent?"

Hades leaned back and rested one arm on the back of his chair. He pursed his lips, making the dimple in his cheek more prominent. "Greek descent, American born. Georgia, to be exact."

"Uh-huh. And what is it you do in Georgia?"

I dropped my face in my hands. She was interrogating him. It was more terrifying than watching her interview charged murderers.

"I don't live in Georgia anymore. I mostly work from home."

Her eyebrows shot up. "Doing?"

"Odds and ends. I take the jobs as they come. Sometimes with either of my brothers."

"Two brothers? Where do you fall in the order?"

"Oldest."

She shifted in her seat. "And your middle brother's name?"

"Simon." He narrowed his eyes.

It was like watching a tennis match.

"Dogs or cats?"

"Dogs. Definitely dogs."

She grinned from ear-to-ear. "Okay, I like him, Steph."

"Oh, come on, Sammy isn't that bad," I quipped.

Hades cocked an eyebrow.

"Her pet cat," Sara said. "And you're right, as far as cats go, he isn't *that* bad, but give me a day of playing fetch and excited jumping when I come home any day of the week."

The waiter arrived with our order just in the nick of time.

"Oh, look! Food's here," I yelped, grabbing my fork.

The waiter placed a plate lined with large green fig leaves, and a glazed brown patty between us.

"This is supposed to be delicious?" Sara quirked of a brow and poked one patty with her fork.

I dug in. "What happened to your sense of adventure?"

I glanced at Hades from the corner of my eye. He beamed at me, showing that dimple again. He watched me as I took the first bite. It was sweet, nutty, and a tad spicy—overlapping flavors I wasn't expecting.

"Oh, wow. This is different."

Sara dug in next and ran her pinky under her lower lip, scraping away the crumbs. "No kidding. It looked like a cow patty. This is delicious."

Hades reached past me for his portion. "Told you."

We spent the next hour finishing our savory fig cake and talking. Hades did his quick smoke trick several more times, mostly because I think he didn't want me to forget who he was regardless of how normal the conversation seemed. He could touch me without touching me. And…I liked it. Thankfully, Sara steered away from more questions about Hades and focused more on telling embarrassing stories about me. Ironically, those stories were far less stressful than worrying about how Hades would answer questions like: What were your parents like growing up? What's your favorite pastime?

Or, who's your favorite sports team?

The cab ride back to the resort was different. Sara seemed more relaxed and didn't look at Hades like he would flip his lid at any given moment. We stood in the lobby after the cab dropped us off. Nighttime had rolled in painting the sky with glowing stars like paint spatters. Except for the hanging sconces, the only other light source came from the moon.

Sara yawned as she walked away. "I'll meet you back at the room, Steph."

"Have dinner with me tomorrow," Hades said, slipping his hands into his pockets.

"Dinner?" I sheepishly smiled.

"It'll give us a chance to talk alone. I'm sure you have a lot of questions I couldn't answer around your friend."

"About that. You've never tried to hide who you are around me, but you did with Sara. I mean, Simon? Who even is that?"

"Poseidon. It's the mortal name he goes by. And I played the part with Sara because I can tell it's important to you."

"I don't know. It's also kind of exhilarating hearing you talk about it so candidly." I smiled and kicked an imaginary pebble.

"Stephanie Costas has a courageous side. I'll remember that."

"I'd like to have dinner with you. As long as your offer includes a glass of wine, I'm in."

"I'll make it an entire bottle if it helps you."

The spark in his gaze made me forget for a brief moment what he was. Maybe it truly was possible to see past it.

"I should get going. I'm sure Sara's lurking around the

corner spying on us anyway."

He nodded. "Good night."

"Night."

I may not have felt the urge to marry him after swimming through the Canal d'amour, but one thing was certain…I felt *something*.

TEN

I FELT A RESPONSIBILITY now to keep his secret. If I were to tell anyone I knew the god of the Underworld, they wouldn't believe me anyway. It killed me inside, not telling Sara. We told each other *everything*. Sometimes a little too much. As much crazy crap as she'd seen, I knew this would be something beyond her out-of-the-box thinking.

The only other dress I had with me aside from the one I bought for the ball was reserved for the dancing contest. Sara let me borrow one of her little black dresses. She laughed, stating Hades and I would match, guaranteed.

Hades insisted we meet at the Greek restaurant at the resort. Odd, there was only one considering we were *in* Greece. I asked for the farthest table away from everyone else so we wouldn't need to have an entire conversation in whispers. The restaurant bustled with dozens of conversations. Forks clanked on plates, laughter, and Byzantine ambient music played over the speakers, while fake candles on every table provided dim lighting.

It was hard not to notice when Hades walked in. He wore black dress pants and a long-sleeved button-down shirt with the sleeves rolled up to his elbows. He squinted like Clint Eastwood when he first entered, peering at the maître d' through strands of hair. Women turned to stare at him as he passed, whether they had company or not.

Had they been doing that at the bar and I didn't notice?

My heart raced the closer he got, and I fidgeted with my necklace.

He slid into the booth seat across from me, eyes unabashedly roaming over my attire. "I applaud your color choice."

"It was Sara's idea. She thought it was funny. We look like we're getting ready to go to a funeral."

"The night *is* young."

I stared at him.

"That was a joke."

"Do you have any idea how frustrating it is when I don't know if you're being serious or not?"

He canted his head from side to side. "Probably about as frustrating as it was convincing you I'm the god of the Underworld."

I wanted to retort, but the waiter appeared, displaying a wine menu to Hades. They both conversed in Greek, occasionally pointing at the menu before the waiter left. Women from various tables gazed at Hades like he was the world's yummiest chocolate bar.

"Do you have seduction powers or something?"

He sputtered his water. "Seduction powers?"

"You had every woman in here drooling as you passed."

"Mm, yes. More than likely it's the presence of a god and what it exudes. We give off this…tone if you will? They all react differently to it."

Was what I felt for Hades—thinking I felt for Hades—real, or was it this bizarre power?

"Wait, do I react differently?" I frowned.

He interlaced his fingers on the table. "It's one of the reasons you intrigue me. It doesn't seem to affect you at all."

"How would you know?"

"Trust me. I'd know." He gazed at me, the flicker of the fake flame glinting in his eyes.

"Sara hasn't tried to jump your bones or anything. What about her?"

"It's there, but she suppresses it. I've only seen a handful of mortals able to do it. Must be her profiling abilities. But you…no, you are—" He squinted. "Different."

A lump formed in my throat. "If you have that effect on women, then why did Perseph—" I pinched my eyes shut, shaking my head. "I'm sorry. I didn't mean to—"

He leaned back in his seat, draping his arms over the back. "No, no. It's a fair question. Will you allow me to tell you what happened? What *truly* happened?"

"Of course."

"No interruptions?"

I propped my elbow on the table, holding up my pinkie finger. "Pinkie swears."

He looked at my hand before wrapping his pinkie around mine. His touch sent a chill down my arm, and I slid my hand away, shoving it into my lap.

"As you can imagine, ruling the Underworld is a lonely existence. I ruled that throne for thousands of years in solitude. My brothers both had queens—"

Brothers. Hades. Zeus. Zane was Zeus.

My eyes bulged from my skull. "Wait a minute—"

"Hey," he said, raising a brow. "You promised." He held up his pinky finger.

I made the gesture of zipping my mouth shut and sat back.

"As I was saying, my brothers had their queens, several of them. And neither of my brothers appreciated the companionship. I never imagined any woman would ever want to live in the Underworld, let alone agree to be with someone like me." The corners of his jaw popped; his eyes focused on the table.

The waiter arrived, resting our wine glasses with blood-red liquid in front of us. I wrapped my fingers around the stem of the glass as Hades continued.

"When I saw her picking flowers in the field through my portal to the aboveground, my heart stopped. She was the most beautiful thing I'd ever seen. So sweet. So innocent." He brought the wine glass to his lips, taking a long swig, and rolling the stem between his fingers afterward. "Loneliness and desperation drove my actions. I had to have her. So, I went to Zeus, asked for his blessing, and he agreed. Even assisted me with luring her to the Underworld."

"I sat in my chariot, my heart racing, watching her grow closer and closer to the flower. There was a moment I even thought of backing out, but the idea of having someone to share my eternal life with was too great of an opportunity to let pass."

As he told his story, I imagined him painting pictures of the event in his brain and the pain it must cause to conjure the memories.

"Hades, you don't have to—" I started, but clipped my words when his scowl pierced me.

"I want to finish, so you know the truth."

I nodded, cupping my glass with both hands, and taking a long sip.

"Once she was in the Underworld, I made it very clear if she were to eat anything—anything at all—she'd be stuck. I only wished for the chance to allow her time to know me, to find out if she could see a future with me. Looking back, I know the methods Zeus and I took to get her down there, had already damaged any chance of her truly loving me." His eyes glazed over, and he downed the rest of his wine.

"After she ate the seeds and I knew she was there forever, I did everything in my power to make her happy. I made her Queen and let her rule by my side as an equal. No other god has done such an act because they're all too obsessed with their power to share it." His hands balled into fists. "She asked for a realm where all the good-hearted people could live out their eternal lives. I created the Elysian Fields—for *her*. Everything I did was for Persephone."

I was beside myself. To hear this firsthand was surreal. Hades' intentions may have been selfish, but it was clear Persephone became his whole world.

"How did she escape?" My voice cracked.

"Theseus. He'd always wanted her for himself. And he got

close to it once, but I trapped him. Heracles rescued him. I assume, given what I know now, that during the six months Persephone went to the surface, she spent her time with him. And they hatched a plan. She left her shade in the Underworld so her physical form could be with him."

"Shade?"

"You may know of it more as a—soul."

I frowned. "She left her soul behind?"

He smirked, running a hand over his face. "She was with me for over a thousand years and yet was so repulsed by me, she was willing to leave it if it meant being rid of me."

I reached for Hades' hand. He quirked a brow, but obliged, resting his hand on the table.

"Trickery and abduction aren't really taken in the best light. I understand why you did but—"

His hand stiffened beneath mine. "It was a long time ago. You don't need to tell me it was wrong."

"*But*," I continued. "What you did for her when you knew she couldn't leave was entirely selfless. And Zeus eventually let her go to the surface."

"Because I talked him into it. She'd been weeping for days, missing her mother and friends. I had to practically grovel at his feet before he agreed to the deal."

"He really is an asshole."

"You have no idea." His eyes fell to my finger, idly stroking one of his knuckles.

I hadn't noticed I was doing it and slid my hand across the table, back to my lap. "You're not at all what I imagined you to be. You walk around with this permanent scowl and act so stand-offish, but there's this whole other side to you. Why don't you show that part of you more often?"

"It's tiring trying to convince people I'm not who they think I am. It's easier to just—give in."

His eyes cast downward, and I studied his expression. He'd spent so long wearing this façade, it was hard to see himself as anything but darkness and gloom.

"Have you ever tried to—I don't know, smile? Does wonders for the spirit." I grinned.

The left side of his face grimaced, his lip twitching like he was sneering.

"What are you doing with your face?"

He blew out a breath like the act took a great deal of effort. "Smiling, I thought."

"Know what? I'm making it my personal mission to put a real smile on your face."

His eyes darted to mine. "I appreciate your candor, but you're going to be very disappointed. They don't come as often as they used to. When you haven't smiled as long as I have, you lose the knack."

"We'll see." I took a sip of my wine, peering at him over the rim.

The waiter showed up, and I fumbled with my menu.

Hades waved his hand. "I got it. Don't worry." After exchanging more conversation in Greek, the waiter took our menus and left.

"I *was* looking at that. What if you ordered something I don't like? What if I'm allergic to it? What if—"

"Are you?"

I snapped my mouth shut. "Am I what?

"Allergic to anything?" His eyes brightened.

"Yes." I folded my arms. "Pollen."

His dimple deepened, the left side of his lips quirking ever so slightly. "I promise there isn't any pollen in what I picked for you." He leaned forward, resting his elbows on the table. "Do you trust me?"

A tiny smile played at the corner of my mouth. "Hypothetically."

He pressed his back to the seat, draping an arm over it. "Good."

What was this man doing to me?

I played with my necklace.

He picked up his wine glass, holding it out to me. I clanked mine against his.

"Yamas," he said. After taking a sip, he lowered the glass to the table, keeping his fingers wrapped around the stem. "Tell me about yourself."

"Me?" I chuckled. "My life is pretty boring compared to yours."

"I've also been around for thousands of years. That's hardly a fair comparison."

"You think the unfair comparison is how long you've been around? Not the whole—god thing? With powers?"

He raised his eyebrows as he tapped his finger.

"Fine. I already told you about my mom. My dad retired after the fire incident and moved to a cabin by himself in Alaska when I moved out. He didn't take what happened to Mom very well and preferred to be away from everyone.

Including me, his only kid." My grip tightened on the glass. "He died out there. Alone."

Hades' brows pinched together. "Stephanie—"

I shook my head at him. "I finished at the top of my class. I love knowing I help put bad guys behind bars even if it's only from the digital perspective. And I love Disney movies, comic books, and girly romance books." I shrugged, finishing the remainder of my wine.

"And *Dirty Dancing*." He tipped his glass.

I smiled, curling my feet underneath my seat. "And *Dirty Dancing*. And eighties music. I can't get enough of it."

"Hades music?"

I blinked.

"Another joke."

I grinned. "The god of the Underworld makes jokes. That's the second one tonight."

"You have to have more questions rumbling around in that head of yours. Ask away." He took a sip of his wine, keeping my gaze.

I tapped a finger against my lips. What did you ask a Greek god? "If you're Hades…and Zane is your brother…that means he's—" I raised my brow, rotating my head in a circle, begging him to finish my sentence for me.

He arched a brow, cocking his head to the side. "Judging from that strange look on your face, I'd guess you know exactly who he is, sweetheart."

"But he—I mean, *why* is the King of the flipping Gods practicing law as a criminal defense lawyer?"

"We've already established he can be a dick. Every decade

or so, he'll come to Earth disguised as someone different. He thought it'd be amusing to help criminals avoid sentencing. I also think it may be a jab against me."

"You? Why?"

"I think we both know the likelihood of a criminal changing their ways once they've gotten away with it. They normally end up doing something worse. When they arrive in the Underworld, it makes their punishment more extreme. Contrary to how the media and stories have depicted me, I don't particularly *enjoy* torturing people. It's simply a part of the job." He took a sip from his glass.

My throat constricted. I tucked a finger underneath my necklace, working it back and forth over the chain.

He leaned forward. "Am I scaring you?"

"No."

His gaze dropped to my fingers trailing over my collarbone as I played with the chain.

"I've barely wrapped my head around the idea of you being real, let alone Zeus. Have I met any other gods I don't know about?"

"Not while I've been with you. I just resurfaced, so I couldn't tell you where most of the others are."

I tightened my grip on the chain. "This is so crazy."

"It's no less crazy for me. I've never been around mortals this long. Somehow, I find it—comforting. Being amongst life. Vibrance."

For the first time, the turquoise colors mixed with gray rather than fighting its way through.

"You *are* life, Hades." I slid my hand over his, not feeling

131

the need to recoil.

His gaze dropped to my knuckles and he traced a finger between them—up and down like each one was a hill to be conquered. "I'm simply the keeper of it once its departed Earth, Stephanie."

"And there you go again selling yourself short."

He slipped his hand into mine and lifted his eyes. "You're one to talk." The words rumbled from his chest like a masculine purr—the male form of a Siren's call.

My heartbeat thumped harshly against my chest. I thought it'd snap a rib. The waiter arrived with our food, and my brain wanted to jolt back to reality but I kept Hades' gaze. His thumb brushed the inside of my palm and the pastel colors brightened around him.

The waiter cleared his throat as he finished setting a bowl with overlapping sliced tomatoes and melted cheese in front of each of us. The smell snapped me from whatever trance I'd put myself in, my eyes finally tearing away from his long enough to scope our meal.

"What is this? Looks amazing." I slid my napkin over my lap and held the fork up, ready to dig in.

"Moussaka. Minced lamb. Potato. One of my favorites."

After dipping the fork into the cheesy deliciousness, I shoveled it in. I moaned from the flavors exploding in my mouth—cheese, onion, and, cinnamon. "And here I thought you ate worms and eyeballs."

He stopped his fork halfway to his mouth, frowning. "I *am* trying to eat here."

I'd stuffed another hunk in my mouth and shoved it into

one cheek as I flashed a smile at him.

"Is it strange I enjoy watching you eat?" He watched me, absently holding his fork.

"If you were anyone else, I'd say maybe. But I can't imagine you don't see many mortals eating in the Underworld. Or that you'd want to, considering they'd be damning themselves to eternity there."

"Intuitive, as always."

"Par for the course in my profession."

His eyes flashed. "Mine too."

"Why were you, in particular, charged with the Underworld? Did you draw the short straw or something?"

"No. He'd never say it, but Zeus knew I was the only one capable of handling such a task. Poseidon is far too adventurous, and Zeus too frivolous. Neither of them would've lasted a week down there, let alone eons." He shook his head, glaring into his glass.

"You're the most stable." My heart fluttered.

"If you want to put it that way, then yes. I've accepted what I need to do. It means I can't be on the surface for a great amount of time, otherwise, there'd be thousands of souls with no direction."

I scraped my fork against the bottom of my plate, eating every bit of sauce I could. Would it be bad manners to lick it? Probably. "That is extremely mature of you."

"Is that a compliment?"

"Oh, it is. Trust me. Especially with the way some men are these days." I winced. "Not that you're—a man. I mean you're—"

"I know what you meant. Thank you."

I bit down on my lip. "Could we maybe take a walk on the beach?"

His face brightened. "Of course. Let me pay our bill."

I grinned, scooting out of the booth. "I'll meet you outside."

As I made my way down the wooden ramp leading to the shoreline, the moon glowed bright, casting a white hue over anything it touched. The stars, as clear as day, twinkled with intensity. With all the lights and smog around Chicago, you'd have to drive hours before seeing a sky like that. His hand touched the back of my arm, and I tensed.

"Didn't mean to startle you," Hades said.

I turned to face him. "You didn't startle me. I just didn't hear you. Did you float over here on smoke or something?" Grinning, I stepped closer to him.

"I could, but figured it might turn too many heads."

I slid off my flats, letting the sand seep between my toes.

"I'm thankful you asked for a romantic walk along the beach under the moon. But I can't help but feel you have an ulterior motive," he said, his eyes squinting.

I simpered, curling my hair over my ears. "I wondered if you could—do the smoke trick again? Now that I know. That I...believe."

The skin at the corners of his eyes crinkled as he scoped the deserted beach. The tips of his shoes brushed my toes as he moved in front of me. The black smoke built up at our feet, swirling like a pinwheel around us. It traveled over my chest, then flowed over my neck and cheeks. The eerie calm put me at ease, and I closed my eyes.

"Where is this coming from?" I asked through a sigh.

It flowed through my hair, shifting some of it to fall over my shoulder.

"The Underworld. More specifically, the river Styx. It's the current that helps the souls travel to their destination."

My eyes flew open. "I have dead people caressing me right now?"

A corner of his mouth quirked. "No. Just smoke."

"Was that a hint of a sliver of a smile I saw?" I nibbled on my lip.

"You wish."

The smoke hovered over my chest. I looked down and shot him a glare. "Are you copping a feel with your smoke monster?"

He pressed a hand to his chest. "I think I'm offended." A wicked glint formed in his eyes.

"I like this side of you."

"The side which unabashedly sneaks a feel of you without using my hands?" His brow raised.

I laughed and swatted his arm, leaving my hand on his bicep. "The playful side. Makes you seem so—human."

"It's a side of me I thought was lost." He stared at my hand on his arm before shifting his gaze to my face. "I may have been wrong."

The smoke faded away, but my hand remained glued to his arm. My lashes fluttered as we stared at each other in silence.

"I should probably get back to the room," I said. "I appreciate you telling me the real story behind Persephone. Put a lot of things in perspective."

"I'm glad."

"Will you meet me in the pool tomorrow?"

He cocked his head to one side. "The pool?"

"We need to practice the lift."

"You remember the part about me being a god, right? Strength being a given?"

"Please?"

"As you wish." He bowed his head.

Princess Bride. How did he keep doing that? Did he even know he was?

"I'll be seeing you" I said, turning away.

"What kind of gentleman would I be if I didn't escort you to your room?"

I turned on my heel, biting back a smile. "Your southern charm?"

"You don't seem to mind the accent I chose for my mortal form, darlin'." He shook his head.

"Why did you choose that accent? This…look? Do you all get to choose how you appear at any given time?"

We walked on the tiled pathway to my room. He sunk his hands in his pants pockets.

"We can appear as anyone or anything we choose. The American southern accent for whatever reason has always been comforting to me. And anyone who has an issue with it, well—" He locked our gazes. "I'll see them in Tartarus."

I grinned. "And your appearance?"

"Random."

We walked the rest of the way in silence and arrived at my door. I curled my hair over my ears and rummaged through my clutch for the key.

"You seem nervous," his voice rumbled.

I found the key and held it up in the air like a piece of gold. "Nervous, why would I be nervous?"

He pressed his hand against the doorframe near my head, leaning forward. His eyes searched my face as if judging my reaction to his proximity. His gaze dropped to my lips.

The King of the Underworld was about to kiss me.

His mouth hovered over mine before moving to my cheek, giving it a peck. "Goodnight, Stephanie."

"Good—" I stood frozen like a statue, still feeling the brush of his beard on my skin.

He backed away, giving me a mischievous curl of his lip.

"Night," I finished.

I'd seemingly brought out a new side to Hades. A deeply buried side. And he liked it.

ELEVEN

![decorative Greek key border]

"HOW MANY MORE TIMES are you going to look for him?" Sara asked, fishing for her straw with her mouth.

My eyes fixed on her after peering over my shoulder for the twentieth time since we'd sat down at the swim-up bar. "What are you talking about?"

She rolled her eyes. "You've barely said a word and keep looking around. Is he supposed to meet you here or something?"

Her gaze moved over my shoulder, fingertips tracing over the dip between her breasts.

Behind me, Hades took labored steps into the pool, clad in a pair of black boardshorts. I kept my fist under my chin to keep my jaw from dropping. He winced when the water hit his stomach, making his muscles clench. In turn, it caused something of my own to clench. It wasn't an exaggeration of how close he resembled a Greek statue, right down to the individually carved abdominal muscles. I'd already seen him shirtless, but somehow, he managed to look even sexier today. He waded over to our stools; his hands balled into fists beneath the water.

"Well, hello again, Hades." Sara took the opportunity to scan him.

He nodded. "Sara."

I gripped my stool to keep from falling off it.

"Darlin'," he said to me, with a mischievous glint in his eyes.

"Hi," I squeaked.

He put his hands on each side of the bar top, caging me in. "Did I ever tell you how much I hate the water?"

"Yes." I gulped.

"And yet you've managed to coax me into it for the second time since we've met."

I chewed on my lip, and my gaze dropped to his chest. "A sick, sick ploy to continuously get your shirt off."

"How naughty." His lips brushed my ear, and he whispered, "Careful. I may need to punish you in Tartarus."

Goosebumps littered my skin, and I tried not to squeak again.

"Umm, should I leave you two alone?" Sara asked.

He stepped back, and I threw a glare at Sara.

Hades leaned on the bar beside me and jutted his chin at the bartender. "Whiskey. Neat."

"Well, look who decided to join the crowd," Rupert said.

"Oh, boy," Sara mumbled, pulling on the brim of her floppy hat.

Hades cocked an eyebrow. "Something I should know?"

"Rupert's been a bit of a pill lately. He insists on drinking like a fish and doesn't like it when Michelle tells him he shouldn't," I whispered.

He narrowed his eyes, staring at Rupert over the rim of his glass.

"I thought they were going to bloody well carve your name into that stool at the other bar," Rupert said to Hades, chuckling.

Michelle batted his shoulder. "Be nice."

"Well, I'm surprised they haven't etched your name into every bottle across the resort," Hades retorted, casually sipping his drink.

Rupert slipped his sunglasses onto his head with a glare. "What did you just say?"

Michelle grabbed Rupert's shoulder. "He's just a bit antsy about the dance contest is all." She patted him.

"Oh? Did you two enter?" I asked, scooting back on my stool. I would've fallen off if it weren't for Hades' hand pressing against my lower back, steadying me.

"We did. It's a shame it's for Valentine's Day, being couples only and all. You love that movie, don't you?" Michelle asked.

Hades' arm slipped around my waist, his hand resting on the top of my thigh. If I'd been capable of melting, I might have. "She is here with someone as luck would have it. Just established last night. Isn't that right, darlin'?"

I leaned into him as if it was something I'd done a dozen times already. "That's right."

Sara gave me a look over the top of her sunglasses. I wanted to kick her in the shin.

"How bloody convenient," Rupert muttered, leaning on the bar near Hades.

I tugged on Hades' arm. "Can I talk to you for a second?

Once we were out of earshot from everyone else, I grabbed his arm. "Are you sure you're okay with this?"

He eyed me sidelong. "Okay with what exactly?"

"Acting like we're *together*."

He took a long deep breath through his nostrils and curled his hand over my hip. "I may not be as familiar with female customs as I'd like to be, but correct me if I'm wrong when I say you're attracted to me."

My stomach caved in on itself. "You would be correct."

He pulled me to him, his abs brushing my elbow. "I'm attracted to you as well."

I lifted my chin to peer up at him, my jaw chattering.

"Given this would be an opportunity to touch you more without abandon...I most certainly am okay with it." He circled my cheek with his thumb.

My brain no longer communicated with my mouth.

"Would you be more comfortable entering the contest with someone else?" He asked.

No, I really wouldn't. I wanted it to be him more than anything.

I shook my head.

"Good." He took my hand and led me back to the bar, slipping his arm around my waist. Hades cocked his head to the side until Rupert looked at him. Neither man said a word, but Rupert's eyes widened, and his bottom lip quivered.

"You're looking a little pale there, Rupe," Hades said, still staring him down.

I lifted my sunglasses. Rupert was more than pale. Talk about downright terrified.

Rupert reached behind him for Michelle, grasping at nothing but air the first several tries before latching onto her arm. "Let's uh—let's go to the other side of the bar, eh?"

"What? Why?" She asked as he pulled her away.

I spied the red tendrils flowing through the darkness around Hades like paint in water. "What did you do to him?"

He finished his drink. "Nothing he didn't deserve."

"Hades…"

He planted a quick kiss at the corner of my brow and moved to the open space of the pool. "You ready to try this lift?"

It happened so quickly, so naturally, I was at a loss for words. I traced my finger over the spot he kissed, staring down at my legs.

"Hey, space cadet. Hades is calling for you," Sara said, nudging me with her elbow.

I tossed her a glare and hopped off my stool. She forced her grin so wide it made her look like a crazed clown. Hades stood in the middle of the pool, his arms stiff at his sides.

"You should probably make this look somewhat difficult for yourself," I said.

His brow furrowed. "By doing what?"

"I don't know. Drop me a few times?"

"You want me to drop you? On purpose?"

"It's a pool. That's why the creators used a lake in the movie. So, no one would get hurt."

He dragged a hand through his hair, slicking it back with water. "Whatever you say, darlin'. Am I just lifting you over my head and holding you there?"

"Right. You haven't seen the movie. Yes. Lift me over your head by my hips. That's it."

"I can handle that."

My heart raced with excitement as I moved to stand in front of him. "Ready?"

He lifted his hands out of the water, making come hither gestures. I took a step forward. He used both hands, gripped my hips, and hoisted me up over his head. I sported my best superman pose, ready to balance, and he let go. I belly-flopped into the water with a loud *clap*. The gasps and laughter from people sitting at the bar were so audible I could hear them underwater. Mortified couldn't begin to describe it.

I sputtered water and parted my wet hair away from my face. "Why did you do that?"

"You told me to drop you."

"Yes. Yes, I did. But that doesn't mean to simply…let go." I flicked my wrist, spraying water.

"So, you want me to drop you, but *not* by letting go of you?" One of his eyes squinted.

"No. Well, yes—in a manner of speaking?"

He continued to one eye squint.

"You know what? Forget it. Just lift me."

He didn't give me time to prepare myself. His hands gripped my hips, and he lifted me over his head. His arms weren't even shaking. I was so giddy, I forgot to strike the pose, but didn't care. He let go, while simultaneously turning my body.

I fell into his arms with a gasp. Biting my lip, I curled an arm around the back of his neck.

"Was that about right?" He asked, tantalizing me with his gaze.

I nodded.

He let go of my legs, and I quieted a whimper, already missing the feeling of being cradled in his arms for the second time. Michelle abandoned Rupert on the other side of the bar. She stared at Hades, biting the plastic straw in her drink. Rupert hid as far away as possible.

"Tell me, Hades, what do you do for work?" Michelle asked, turning her body to face him.

He leaned on the bar. "Odds and ends. I work from home now, but before that, I was mostly the carrier and divider of souls."

I choked on my drink, stepping between him and Michelle. "He's a—funeral director. So, in a way, he assists in carrying their uh—souls to the afterlife."

Hades beamed at me.

"Interesting. How does someone direct funerals remotely?" Sara cocked an eyebrow.

Amidst the lying, I'd forgotten Hades' lie from yesterday.

"Uhhh—well," I started while twirling my hair.

"The bodies aren't part of my jurisdiction. For the final… arrangements is where I come in," Hades said with the coolness of a cucumber. "But recently, I've had more of a hand with the bodies themselves due to a coworker up and…quitting."

Sara narrowed her eyes.

Guy entered the conversation. "Did I hear you're a funeral

director? Must be a pretty grim job, eh?" He asked, claiming a stool.

"Grim doesn't begin to scratch the surface," Hades responded.

Sara tapped her fingernail against her cup. "You failed to mention the funeral director part yesterday. Must get pretty lonely. Hanging out with dead bodies all day who don't uphold their side of the conversation?"

"If anything, it's usually begging and pleading, so I tune them out," Hades said, sipping from his glass.

Everyone froze.

I cleared my throat louder than necessary. "He's kidding. This guy is a regular jokester, aren't you Had?"

His eyes gleamed. "I'm a comedian."

"Well, you two have something in common, Sara. Only you see fresh dead bodies." When everyone remained frozen on their stools, I quickly followed up with, "She's a detective."

Guy grinned. "You are? You haven't said anything. That's pretty cool."

Sara's lips pursed. I could feel her glare, even though her sunglasses masked it. Michelle scooted closer to Hades.

"I have to admit I've never seen a funeral director who looks," she paused, motioning with her hand over his physique. "Like you."

"Oh? What should I look like?" He asked, leaning on the bar with one elbow. He reached his other arm out and guided me to his hip.

Michelle laughed, draping a hand over her mouth. "The polar opposite, I suppose."

"Shelly, let's get some bloody food. I'm starving," Rupert said from afar. He didn't look in Hades' direction, beckoning Michelle with an outstretched hand.

She sighed and slid off her stool. "Until next time." She flashed a smile at Hades.

A strange pit formed in my stomach. "Would you mind toning down the godly tone?"

He moved his hand to my hip, curling one finger over it at a time. "Your eyes are taking on the color of emeralds, my dear."

My cheeks flushed. "You can't tell people you divide souls for a living."

He released his grip and pressed his back against the bar. "Whatever happened to my candidness being exhilarating?"

"Are you screwing with me?"

"Yes." He stared down at me, the dimple in his cheek deepening. "I haven't had this much fun in—ever."

I gave a lopsided grin and folded my arms. "If you've never seen *Dirty Dancing*, how did you know the corner quote?"

"Swayze mentioned it."

He's must've said "lazy." Most certainly, he didn't say, Swayze. "Did you say, Swayze?"

His eyes shifted. "Yes. Patrick Swayze."

"I know—" I grabbed his arm. "I know who Patrick Swayze is, but how is that possible considering he's d—" How I'd forgotten who I was talking to was a mystery, but the idea of him chatting it up with Swayze in the Underworld chilled me to the bone.

"Dead? Yes. We briefly talked when I escorted him to the Fields."

I gripped his shoulders, shaking him. "How can you talk about this so nonchalantly?"

"Stephanie, I talk to thousands of people every day. He was just another kind soul."

My eyes blinked so rapidly it blurred my vision. "Well, tell me everything. You can't tell a girl you spoke with Patrick Swayze and not elaborate."

"Hey, you two are being incredibly anti-social," Sara said, pulling on my arm.

I ground my teeth together. If she only knew she interrupted the story of a lifetime.

He dropped his lips to my ear. "I'll relay the entire conversation to you later. In private."

The word "private" made my stomach tighten. I rolled my shoulders and turned my attention on Guy. "Is Keith still sick?"

"He said he'd come down if he could manage to stand up without feeling like hurling," he said, chuckling. "Poor bastard."

"Speak of the devil," Sara said.

Keith entered the pool, with skin a full shade lighter than when I'd last seen him. He gave us an awkward wave. "Hey. Surprised to see me alive?"

"Yes," Hades clipped.

I elbowed Hades in the ribs, making him grunt.

Keith squinted at Hades. "What the hell are you doing in the pool? Shouldn't you be crying into your whiskey glass or something?"

"I decided the view in here is decidedly much better." Hades looked at me, and my neck warmed.

Keith looked between us. "Seems I missed a lot."

"Good to see you out and about, man," Guy said, patting his back.

"Do you want water or something?" Sara asked.

"Are you kidding? Now more than ever, I need a damn beer," Keith said with a snicker.

"He's back!" Guy threw his fists in the air.

Hades glared off in the distance. I followed his gaze, seeing an older man sitting at a table, staring back at him.

"Do you know that guy?" I asked.

Hades didn't budge. If anything, his eyes narrowed more. "No."

"Then why are you looking at him like that?"

The older man stood from the table and with his arms pinned to his sides walked to the pool's edge. Without hesitation, he hopped in, fully clothed. He didn't blink, and his body stayed stiff save for his feet moving him. I'd seen some bizarre things in my time, but this took the cake.

"Can you tell me what it's like?" The man asked Hades.

Hades' face softened, and he canted his head to the side. "The greenest grass you've ever seen. Never a cloud in the sky. Any food your heart desires."

An orange hue curled around Hades like the sky hugged him. The sight brought tears to my eyes. Compassion from the God of the Underworld.

The man smiled as a tear streaked down his face. "Will I see Louise again?"

Hades gave a single nod. "Yes."

The man broke into a sob, patting Hades' hand.

"Don't be afraid, Markos. You're a good man who's lived a

good life. You deserve to live your eternal life in happiness," Hades said.

He continued to sob as he nodded at Hades.

He turned away and walked back the way he came, but this time he didn't walk stiff as a board.

"Care to fill me in?" I asked.

Hades rubbed a hand over his chin. "He's dying."

"Dying?"

The man hoisted himself from the pool.

"How can you tell?"

Hades arched a brow.

"Right. I keep forgetting."

He scratched his beard. "I've never been approached by them on the surface."

"Them?"

"Those close to death. It's not my job to send them to the Underworld."

"Then whose is it?"

The corners of his jaw tightened. "Thanatos."

TWELVE

SARA BEGGED ME TO go snorkeling despite my known fear of underwater life. Specifically, the kind with pointy, sharp teeth. Hades said he'd put in a good word with his brother and promised I wouldn't get eaten by a shark, so I eventually agreed to go. Far too caught up in his brooding, Hades had no desire to come, so it was the perfect opportunity for some girl time.

"At least you didn't try and get me to go scuba diving," I mumbled, twirling the snorkel mask around my finger by its strap.

"I knew I didn't stand a chance with that one," Sara said with a snicker.

"Beautiful day for a swim, ain't it?" Rupert asked.

I put a hand over my eyes to block the sun. Rupert and Michelle walked up, snorkel masks in their hands.

Sara rolled her eyes. "Great."

"Rupert saw you two walk past with your masks and thought

it sounded fun. I'm just glad to do something other than drinking like a fish at the bar, frankly," Michelle said, giggling.

"How convenient," I responded with Rupert's words from yesterday, narrowing my eyes.

Several other people arrived in spurts. The resort host was the last to arrive, standing at the front of the group.

"A few ground rules before we embark. First, we are to stay as a group. There are things in the water that could harm you, and if you stray from the group, it's harder for us to help you. Second, if you see a shark, we'll use the universal symbol," he put a hand over his head like a fin, "to let everyone know there's been one spotted. At this time of day, I've only ever seen one while doing these snorkeling excursions, and I've been doing this for years. Don't worry."

I made a 'pfft' sound, haughtily crossing my arms over my chest.

"The most important rule is everyone has fun and enjoys peering down into the mysteries of the sea. Make sure the mask is tight and secure over your eyes, so no water seeps in and keep that tube above the surface. Unless you have a set of gills, human lungs aren't a big fan of water."

He smiled, and a couple of people chuckled at his corny joke.

"If any should get in, simply blow out." He winked and slipped the mask over his face. "Let's go!" He shoved the tube into his mouth and hopped off the dock.

I barely had my flippers on when everyone jumped in. Sara and Michelle hopped off the dock. I was about to follow when Rupert's hand gripped my arm.

I squinted behind my mask. "What are you doing?"

"What does Hades *really* do for a living? We both know he's not a bloody funeral director," he said, his grip tightening on my bicep.

"I have no idea what you're getting at."

His nostrils flared. The skin under his right eye twitched. "Bloody level with me here. Is he in the mafia? Some kind of organized crime unit?"

"You're hurting me," I growled.

His chest heaved, and he let go, running the back of his hand under his nose. "I'll figure it out." He slipped the mask over his head, the flippers making flapping sounds as he walked past me and jumped in.

I rubbed my arm, staring down at him in the water as he swam to catch Michelle. After jumping in and swimming so fast it made my arms and legs burn from the strain, I clung to Sara's side. Sharks were nothing compared to the dark, killer instinct that reflected in Rupert's eyes. I'd seen that look far too many times through my career.

Sara yanked the tube from her mouth. "What's wrong with you?"

I swam in circles. "Rupert." It sounded more like roo-purr from the tube still in place.

"What'd he do?"

I plucked the tube from my mouth, sputtering saltwater. "He asked me the strangest questions about Hades, had this crazed look in his eye, and gripped my arm so tight it'll probably leave a bruise."

"He did what?" She'd raised her voice, the familiar flames

igniting in her gaze when she was about to release the inner tigress.

I grabbed her shoulders, my head dipping underwater several times due to my frantic brain forgetting to tread water. "Don't say anything. Not right now. Let me talk to Hades first."

"What's he going to do that I can't?"

Oh, if she only knew. "There's no reason to potentially ruin our vacation with things getting blown out of proportion."

She stared at me. The corners of her jaw popped. "Fine. But don't get caught alone with Rupert. I knew he was going to be trouble the moment I laid eyes on him."

"Trust me. He's the last person I want to be alone with."

The rest of the excursion went off without a hitch. We saw fish of all shapes and colors and a couple of sea turtles. Even a dolphin stopped by to swim through our group. I wondered how much of the experience was due to Hades putting in his supposed word with his brother. Was Poseidon possibly one of the people in our group? Or was he a person at all? Maybe he *was* the dolphin. It all made my head ache.

Sara helped me out of the water, glaring daggers at Rupert from across the way. "Come on, Steph. Let's get a head start, so he doesn't have an excuse."

Rupert pulled himself onto the deck, wincing and holding his side. When Michelle reached out to help him, he slapped her hands away. I picked up my pace.

"Aside from creepy Rupert, that was pretty fun," I said, smiling at Sara.

"Good. Figured we needed to see a little more of this gorgeous island, you know?"

"I can't believe I never thought about coming here. Not that I inherited much of the Greek part of my genes." I referenced my body with a chuckle.

"Face it, Steph, you've been slacking on going anywhere or doing anything other than working."

The word "slacking" gave me pause, and I grabbed Sara's arm. "Slack. File slack. Oh my—Sara, I never thought about checking the file slack."

Her eyes shifted. "What the hell are you talking about?"

"The hard drive. There could be residual data from anything deleted in the *file slack*." I grinned and jumped up and down.

"Great. You'll have a lead when we get back. See? Vacation worked."

"Oh, no. I can't wait until we get back. Are you crazy?"

She pointed a finger in my face. "Stephanie. You promised. The case has waited all these years; it can wait a little longer for us to get back."

I pouted. "Please?"

She raised a brow.

With a groan, I kicked an imaginary pebble on the ground. "Fine. I'll wait until we get back."

"Good. Let's get back to our room. I say today, we order room service and enjoy that veranda we've been neglecting. There's even a TV out there." She draped an arm over my shoulders with a wide grin.

"Is this your way of avoiding Rupert?"

She tapped my nose. "That too."

I popped out my contacts and slipped my black-rimmed glasses on, given her intent on barricading us inside for the rest of the day. If only my eyes could sigh in relief. I changed into a pair of lounge shorts and a spaghetti strap tank top, devoid of a bra. The beach view from the veranda and the wind whipping through the trees sent a wave of calm over me.

We'd been channel surfing for the past hour, nothing jumping out at us. Trays littered with dirtied plates and glasses rested on the table in front of us. There was a knock at the door. Considering we'd ordered another round of drinks, and I was in a drowsy stupor, I didn't think to look through the peephole before opening the door.

"Am I interrupting something?" Hades asked, pressing his forearm against the doorframe above my head.

I froze. "What are you doing here?"

"I haven't seen you all day. Figured I'd stop by to see if you wanted to practice this dance," his eyes dropped to my chest.

The A/C mixed with the sight of him casually standing there in the hallway had my nipples at full salute. I slapped an arm over my chest with a nervous bout of chuckles. "Practice? Right now?"

"All we've done is the lift. The contest is tomorrow night. You need to teach me the rest of it."

"Oh, of course." I adjusted my glasses. "What was I thinking?"

"Have you always worn those?" He tapped my glasses with a twinkle in his eye.

I gave a sheepish smile and slid them off. "During the day I usually wear contacts."

"Don't take them off on my account, darlin'. I like them." He lifted my hand toward my face, urging me to put them back on.

Sara brushed past me. "Feel free to practice in our room. I was going to hang out by the pool anyway." She smiled at me, despite my unspoken pleas for her not to leave me braless.

After she left, I stepped aside to let him in. When I shut the door, the clicking noise it made sounded more ominous than usual. I contemplated bringing up the Rupert situation right out the gate. Chances were, he'd whisk off to give Rupert a piece of his mind, and we'd get no practice.

"Let me change first," I said, power walking past him.

"If you insist," he said, wickedness lacing his tone.

I ducked into the bathroom and changed into a bra, shirt and, shorts. When I walked back into the room, he sat on the armrest of the couch, watching *Dirty Dancing*. My heart raced at the mere sight of it.

"What are you doing?" I asked, marching over to him like he'd done something wrong.

He arched a brow and turned the volume up. "This is the movie, correct? I figured it'd be easier if I just watched it."

"Are you like Neo and kung fu? You spend five minutes watching something, and inexplicably know it?"

He folded his arms and furrowed his brow. "I'm a fast learner."

Of course, he was. The all too familiar music blared from the TV speakers as Swayze walked on stage, beckoning Jennifer Grey with his finger. I couldn't watch him, watching my favorite movie of all time. Why was this making me so nervous? I bit my thumbnail and started to pace the room's length, occasionally glancing over at the TV and gauging his expression. As always, the man's face was stone-cold the *entire* time even when Swayze did his slow-motion leap off the stage.

Once the scene finished, he turned the TV off and stood up, crossing the room with three powerful strides.

"Before we get into this, you owe me." I held my hands in front of me like their presence would stop him.

"Owe you?"

"Relay your conversation with Swayze."

He squinted. "Alright. He arrived in the Underworld, and it took me only a moment to know he led his best life. I asked him what he felt he gave most to society."

I clasped my hands under my chin. "And what'd he say?"

"He said, entertainment, but mostly acting, and forever giving the world the line, 'Nobody puts Baby in a corner.'"

"He seriously said that?"

He held up a finger, signaling for me to be quiet. "He quickly followed up with that last bit being a joke, and I didn't need to ask any more questions. I was more than prepared to guide him to the Fields."

I didn't say anything for a beat, staring at him wide-eyed before motioning with my hand to continue.

"That was it." He blinked.

"What do you mean, that was it? I'd hardly consider that a conversation."

"I'm not sure what you think it's like in the Underworld, but normally the last thing most of the newly departed feel like doing is chatting."

To say my curiosity piqued at seeing the Underworld would've been a gross understatement. I imagined it would be breath-taking or downright terrifying. Probably both. "Fair enough. Well, thank you. I'm glad to know his sense of humor continued despite his untimely demise."

His eyes morphed into that sexy, narrowed thing he often did. He didn't say a word, closed the space between us, and slid his arms around my waist. I tensed. He took my right hand into his left and, without warning, dipped me. I backpedaled away, pushing my glasses further up my nose.

"We don't need to practice that whole beginning part. Maybe we should concentrate on the trickier coordinated pieces."

He retook my hand, leading me to him until he was behind me. "Dancing is like a symphony." He lifted my arm to curl it over the back of his neck. "One melody flows into the other with intricate moving parts. If you were to rearrange them or only play one part, it ruins the entire composition." He dragged his fingertips down the underside of my arm.

I tried to suppress a shiver. It didn't work.

I crossed an arm over my stomach, slipping my hand into his. He gripped my hip with his other hand but failed to perform one of the smallest of gestures. In the movie, Swayze kissed her on the nose before going into the first move. It was subtle but adorable. Oh, well. He spun me, and we delved into the dance I've known since I was a kid. He didn't miss a beat even with the absence of music, but I could hear the instruments and lyrics in my head. I started to mouth the lyrics.

We performed every step without error until he spun me several times in a row. I forgot to spot something in the room to focus on and got dizzy. My feet tripped over each other, and he gripped my hand to keep me from falling.

I stared up at him. "How are you *so* normal?"

"And how are you so *not* normal?" He lifted my arms above my head, moving his hands to my ribcage, and I swayed from side to side.

"You rule a kingdom of ash and bone, and yet here you are rehearsing dance moves with a mortal woman who can read your aura. Why?"

We shimmied together; our elbows parallel to one another. "So many questions."

I glared up at him, my lips curling into a sly grin. As he spun us in circles, I clasped my arms around his neck.

"Rehearsing dance moves as if I *wasn't* the god of the Underworld is exactly what I need." He pulled away from me, our fingers interlaced until he slid his hand away. "I get to pretend I don't have the responsibilities." He walked backward. "Pretend as if I'm simply a mortal man spending time with a mortal woman."

He motioned with his hand, beckoning me. I bit my lip and ran forward. He wrapped his hands around my hips and hoisted me above his head. This time I didn't forget to pose. The room fell silent. The only sound was my steady breathing while suspended in the air. He lowered me, letting our bodies slide against each other until the tips of my toes touched the floor. I stared up at him, my gaze dropping to the thin shape of his lips. I couldn't be sure if it were the dancing or the intensity in his stare, but with shaky hands, I touched my lips to his. He tensed before reciprocating, sliding his lips against mine. He tasted like charcoal.

I gasped and pulled away. "I'm sorry."

"For what?" He licked his lips.

I forgot who he was. What he was. He seemed *so* human. "I shouldn't have done that."

"Kiss me, you mean?"

"I mean—we can't."

He glared. "Why? Because I'm a god or specifically because I'm the King of Ash and Bone?"

His words felt like lemon juice in a papercut. "That's not what I meant, I—"

"It is. I knew this was too good to be true. Who put you up to this?" He snarled. "Zeus?"

My sinuses stung. "What? No. I—" I couldn't get the words out. A tear rolled down my cheek.

"I'll do the contest with you because I already promised, but rest assured, once it's over, you never have to see me again." The skin above his nose creased, and his jaw tightened.

When he turned for the door, I took a step forward. "Hades."

His forearm tensed, holding the door open, and he tossed a scowl over his shoulder. "What?"

"Rupert's acting strange. I'm worried that—"

His grip tightened on the door, and he interrupted me to say, "I'll take care of it."

"Okay—" The door slammed. "Bye."

I flopped onto the couch and sobbed.

THIRTEEN

IF THERE WAS ONE thing I knew about myself, it was the inability to leave work at work. I snuck out of our hotel room first thing in the morning in my PJs and went to the computer lab. That and I could hardly sleep given the way things ended with Hades. The disappointed look on his face haunted me. A face I'd put there.

Sara had a knack for making me feel guilty, and if she caught me, it'd be like I stole her last Cinnamon Bun Oreo. I secured myself in the corner of the lab, making sure to keep my head low. The light from the monitor glinted in my glasses.

The file slack. I can't believe I didn't think to check it before. Or I'd gotten so burnt out with the case it slipped my mind. Wouldn't be the first time it happened nor the last. Examiners were human beings as much as we'd like to think of ourselves as robots. Essentially, files are never entirely deleted. Instead, their data is moved around the hard drive as it makes space for other files. It could get tricky when less and less of the file was available, or if it became so fragmented, piecing it all together from varying points on the drive. For anyone trying to hide something, deleting a lot of data was usually a first step in covering their digital tracks.

Making sure to keep my head level with the monitor, I started processing. The sound of the door opening made my head dip lower.

"You've got to be kidding me," Sara said, standing at the end of the row with her arms crossed.

I chuckled, sitting straight up. "Fancy seeing you here."

"Stephanie Rose Costas. You. Promised."

"Sara, I know, but we only have two more days here, and I didn't want to waste them wracking my brain over this working or not."

She stomped over, glaring down at the screen. "You know this is confidential evidence. Sifting through it on a public domain could get you in some deep shit."

I drummed my fingers against the desk. "Not if I'm logged into a virtual private network."

"Stephanie." She loomed over me. "You would've had to set that up *at* work."

"Look at you, knowing how VPNs work."

"Which means you knowingly set it up before we left. You had every intention of logging in before our plane left the tarmac, didn't you?"

I blinked. "I may have a serious problem."

"I know you're passionate about your job and want to help people, but you need to start putting yourself first, Steph." She stood up with a sigh.

I traced a fingertip over my lip, remembering the kiss with Hades. The scowl that creased into his brow when I'd stupidly said it shouldn't have happened.

"Did you at least find something?"

I jolted in my chair. "Hm, what?"

"The process is finished." The word "complete" flashed on the screen.

"Right."

After scrolling through the broken data, it wasn't looking good. I sighed, leaning back in my chair with a humph.

"From the way this data is patterned, it's as if he knew the possibility and added meaningless files to override the data continuously," I said.

"Is that why I keep seeing the filename: catmeme.jpg repeatedly?"

"Exactly. And I already checked. That file is an actual cat meme. Son-of-a-bitch." This was a whole new level of frustration. There was always a shred of evidence. *Something*. I pressed my face into my palms and started crying.

"Don't be so hard on yourself. It's not as if the physical side of things was any better. He knew what he was doing. He didn't get messy, as so many other serial killers do. Committing suicide was probably the smartest thing he could've done."

It wasn't about the case. The crying turned into full-on sobbing.

"Steph, my God. What's the matter?" Sara said, taking a seat next to me and rubbing my back.

"Hades."

"Did he do something? Say something?"

I sniffled. "No. It was me. *Me.*"

"Sweetie, you're going to have to give me a little more here."

"I kissed him."

She stopped rubbing and dipped her face into mine. "Was it bad?"

"No." I started sobbing again. "It was perfect. Beyond perfect."

"Stephanie." She turned my chin to look at her. "Are you going to tell me or what?"

"It was a great kiss that shouldn't have happened."

"Why?"

"Because we can't be together, and it'd just hurt more in the end."

"Why can't you be together?"

I rubbed the back of my hand across each cheek, wiping away tears. "Do you remember the movie *Labyrinth*?"

She narrowed her eyes. "I remember David Bowie's codpiece and her name being Sarah mostly, but yes."

"Sarah is pulled into the Goblin King's spell. Like it starts as a wicked ploy on Jareth's part at first, but then Sarah really does start feeling something for him." I pinched my eyes shut, remembering Hades call me "real." "He'd been known for wicked deeds and ill intents but went through everything to lure her into the labyrinth. Seduce her, to make her his."

All Hades wanted was to feel normal for a short time while he was on the surface. With one action and few words, I ripped that way from him.

"You're starting to lose me here, Steph."

I sighed. "Do you think under different circumstances, Sarah would've become the Goblin Queen?"

I looked at Sara pleadingly, as if I needed to hear her say it. To tell me what I was feeling was alright.

"What if he hadn't kidnapped Toby, but rather approached her in the normal sense?"

Or knew what he'd done in the past was wrong and vowed never to do it again…

"But then…" I pursed my lips. "She wouldn't have been able to be with him anyway. He was a being from another realm."

An immortal god with a kingdom to rule.

Sara cleared her throat and wrapped her hands around mine. "I'm not sure why you're using analogies to get to your point, but I'll humor you. She could've been with him if she agreed to become immortal. But you're right. He didn't deserve her after all the shit he pulled. I don't care how much he claimed to love her."

Become immortal. My heart sunk to my feet.

"You need to talk to him, Steph. Clearly, you both like each other, and he seems pretty understanding, so talk to him."

I wanted nothing more than to tell her everything. Get her opinion on everything. But I couldn't.

"Come on." She grabbed my shoulder, pulling me back. "Shut all of this down. We have a contest to primp you for."

"Primp?" I asked.

"We still haven't used our free spa passes, remember?"

Who could think of relaxing at a time like this?

"Go change. I'll meet you there," she said, shoving me toward the door and slipping our passes into my pocket.

I stood outside of the spa, chewing my thumbnail. When she said to meet her here, I didn't realize she meant in twenty minutes, which is how long I'd been standing here. I was sure of it.

"I'm going to take a wild guess and say this isn't a whiskey tasting, is it?" Hades said from behind me.

I spun around to face him, and my heart raced. "Hades?"

He dipped his chin down. "Hey, darlin'."

"Sara, she must've—" Tears threatened my eyes, but I held them back.

"She did." He smirked. "Rather clever, I have to say."

I stepped forward. "About yesterday, I'm sorry. I didn't mean to hurt you."

He held up a hand. "You don't have to explain."

"No, I do. I said that we *can't* because I didn't know if we *could*."

His face fell blank.

It was better than that scowl of his.

"So, you *don't* regret kissing me?" His brow raised.

Gulping, I shook my head. We stood in awkward silence, staring at each other.

I glanced behind me at the spa. "I probably know the answer, but have you ever been to one of these before?"

He smirked. "No."

"Me either. I can give these passes to another couple," I said with a shrug.

He walked up to me and slipped his hand into mine. "Or we can experience it for the first time together. I can power through it if you can."

My throat constricted, and I tightened my grip on his hand, letting him lead me into the spa.

The attendant, a young man, greeted us with a warm smile. "Kalimera."

Hades bowed his head.

"Eísai mazí?" the attendant asked, cocking an eyebrow at Hades.

"Naí," Hades replied with a nod, pressing a hand against my lower back. "Passes, sweetheart?"

"Oh, right." I dug into my pocket and held them out.

The attendant motioned with his hand for us to follow him.

As he led us to the back, I leaned toward Hades. "What did he ask?"

"If we had passes." His lips thinned.

I narrowed my eyes. "Are you screwing with me again?"

He gazed down at me with brightened eyes but said nothing.

"This is what I get for letting that Greek Rosetta Stone collect dust."

The back area of the spa had several doors leading to changing rooms.

The attendant pointed to the left. "Gynaíkes."

"Women," Hades translated.

I locked eyes with him as I slipped into the changing room. We gazed at each other until the door closed, breaking our trance. Several white robes hung from silk-lined hangers, and there were cubbies to store personal items. I removed my shorts and shirt, standing in only my bikini.

I had a choice. Keep the bikini on or not. A simple choice, but it made my mind reel. A week ago, the version of me that arrived in Greece wouldn't have stewed on it for long. She'd have kept the swimsuit on. The one-piece.

I pulled on the strings and let the suit fall to the ground. The robe caressed my bare skin when I slipped it over my naked form. It was soft and fluffy terry cloth. When I returned to the hallway, Hades walked out of his room at the same time. I clenched the neckline of my robe and stared at his bare chest peeking out.

His eyes roamed down my body. When he reached my feet, he cleared his throat and rubbed the back of his head. "You ready?"

I nodded. In truth, I wasn't even sure what I should be ready for. Were we getting massages? Facials? I bit back a laugh at the thought of Hades with a clay-based mask on his face.

The attendant held his hand out toward another room. Two tables situated side by side with face pillows and white sheets draped over them. He rattled something off in Greek with a wide grin and left. I shuffled into the room, playing with the ties of my robe. Hades walked in behind me, shutting the door with a light click.

"He said they'd be with us in a moment and to get comfortable under the sheets," Hades said.

Under the sheets.

My stomach clenched.

I moved to one table, undoing the ties of the robe. Glancing over my shoulder, I caught him staring. He shot his gaze skyward, rubbing the back of his head again.

"I can turn around," he said.

I should've been lady-like and asked him to, but surprisingly I *wanted* him to watch. Instead, I let him make up his own mind, kept my back to him, and slipped the robe over my shoulders. As bold as I felt, I couldn't bring myself to take a peek at him. But the sound of a husky breath letting out of him as I crawled under the sheet told me he hadn't bothered turning around.

I shoved my face into the pillow and turned my head when I heard his robe coming off. My cheeks warmed when his perfectly rounded and muscular butt stared at me. He slipped under the sheet, and I turned my face away with a grin.

"I saw that," he mumbled.

We spent the next hour being massaged by Georgios and Alexandra. Hades asked for Georgios, claiming he'd have the stronger hands to handle his extremely tight muscles. A small part of me hoped he asked because he knew Alexandra had a good possibility of trying to take the massage to a whole other level once the godly tone kicked in. Involuntary groans escaped my throat when she'd worked my lower and upper back. Sitting at a computer desk all day had been taking its toll. They rubbed large chunks of salt against our skin, wiped it off with hot towels, and instructed us in Greek before leaving us to slip on our robes.

Hades lay on his back, staring at the ceiling with heavy eyes. "I never thought in a million years I'd do something like this. Have to say, I've been missing out." His dimple made an appearance as he looked over at me with a smirk.

I laughed. "Me too. Sara will never let me hear the end of it." Sitting up, I wrapped the sheet around me.

He leaned on one elbow and watched me.

"Did they say what's next?" I asked.

He gave a subtle nibble on his lower lip. "Soaking in the mineral bath."

"Guess I better get my bikini back on, huh?"

He nodded.

We slipped back into our robes without any attempts to disguise our ogling of each other.

After slipping into my bikini, I followed the attendant to the bath where Hades already was. Scented candles surrounded a colossal square-shaped tub that could have fit a dozen people. Vanilla, lilac, and cinnamon permeated the air. Steam floated over the water, and there sitting at one end was the god of the Underworld himself. One knee poked out of the water, propped on the bench seat. He swirled his finger, watching the ripples with squinted eyes.

My feet made light flapping noises as I walked toward the edge of the tub. He lifted his chin and pierced me with his gaze. I kept eye contact as I dipped a foot in the water.

"Warm enough for you?" He asked.

I sat on the bench seat across from him and closed my eyes with a contented sigh. "It's perfect."

"I took the liberty of making it a tad more…inviting."

My eyes fluttered open. He had that wicked glint in his eye and continued to circle his finger in the water.

"What's the Underworld like?" I asked with a voice barely above a whisper.

He stopped twirling his hand. "What do you wish to know?"

I pushed from my seat and waded through the water until I was on his side. Shimmying across the bench, I scooted until I felt his thigh brushing mine. "Everything."

He glanced down at our legs touching before waving his hand in front of us. The black smoke fog swirled over the water. "The river Styx," he started, and the smog morphed into a projection of a river. Bodies poked from the water as a boat sailed past them.

"Who are those people?"

"Souls on their way to judgment."

I looked at him. "To you?"

"To me, yes." He wiggled his fingers, and the fog morphed into a tall throne with spires. "The river leads to my throne room. It's where I spend most of my time." Cave-like walls and a high stone ceiling surrounded the throne. The boat pushed into the sand of the river's shoreline. "The sand is black. My throne is black. Everything about the Underworld, Stephanie is dark and dreary."

I slipped a hand over his knee. At first, he tensed but then relaxed against my touch. "Tell me more, Hades."

He stared at me before waving his hand again. A dog with three heads snapped its jaws at a faceless figure. "My guard dog, Cerberus. It doesn't happen often, but when a soul escapes or wanders away from Tartarus, Cerberus is duty-bound to bring them back."

"Tartarus. Is it all fire and brimstone like I imagined it to be?"

He pursed his lips. "I'd rather not get into details about Tartarus. If you've ever pictured what hell would be like, then it's truly all you need to know."

I made absent circles with my fingertip over his knee. "And the Elysian Fields?"

"My powers couldn't show the true brightness and colors of the Fields. It's paradise."

My belly warmed. "Sounds amazing. Are people happy when they see it? Does it help them not be so afraid?"

He turned to face me, draping one arm on the edge of the tub. "It does. So curious, you'd think to ask such a question."

"Have you thought about it? Taking on another Queen?" It left my lips before I had a chance to think about his reaction.

His jaw tightened, and he looked away. "I have. But I'd never feel right asking. Since last time, it'd have to be a choice. An eternity in the Underworld isn't exactly an easy sell."

He forgot it was a package deal, a package that included *him*.

"Anything else your smoke monster can do?" I gave a coy grin.

His tongue grazed his lip, and he whispered into my ear, "Shut your eyes."

I kept my grip on his leg and closed my eyes. A touch like a rose petal caressed my arm. It lit every nerve on one side of my body on fire, liquid fire coursing through my veins. The sensation traveled up my neck, and I moaned. My hand clenched his knee, and he slipped a hand over mine, clenching it back. It skirted over the back of my head, dipping over my shoulder to my breasts. I gasped, and my lip trembled. The sensation dripped to my core, tantalizing me, and tightening. My head flew back. I grabbed for him for fear I was falling.

"What is it you find so attractive about me, Stephanie?"

The fog continued to flow over me as his kissed my shoulder, grazing his teeth against my skin.

"Is it the power? The godliness? The fact I oversee a kingdom?"

He trailed two fingers up my inner thigh underneath the water and I had to grip the edge of the bench to keep from slipping off.

"I'd be lying if I said none of those things appeal to me," I said through a shaky bout of breaths.

His tongue trailed up my neck, giving it one quick peck. "But?"

I opened my eyes to gleam at him, making sure he heard every word I said by pushing a hand on his chest and willing his gaze to mine. "All those things pale in comparison to the fact you possess it all and yet humility and kindness blossom in you."

His eyes turned feral, amorous, as he wrapped his arm around me and pulled me against him. The fog wrapped around us, curling over our limbs and breezing through our hair. I stared up at his ravenous gaze. His nostrils flared. He dipped his chin, kissing me with the same fiery intensity I'd felt across my skin. The fog swirled around us, and I fought back a groan. The door creaked open and Hades' arm shot out, using the fog to slam it shut.

I slipped onto his lap, straddling him, grinding against him as I worshipped him with every lap of my tongue. Showed him I didn't care who or what he was with every graze of my lips. He curled one hand into my hair while the other found my butt, grabbing it with a deep purr vibrating in the back of his throat.

He peeled away with a snarl, gripping my hips. "I want nothing more than to have you, but at any moment they're going to get past that door and I couldn't promise how I'd react with being interrupted." His fingers dug deeper into my waist. "Especially given what I had planned."

My body shuddered at the thought.

The door burst open and the attendant's eyes widened at the sight of me still straddled on Hades' lap. The old me would've been embarrassed but this version of me, the version who opened herself to the Underworld itself, wouldn't have cared to even get caught.

The attendant cleared his throat, averted his gaze, and spoke in Greek.

"He said our time is up." Hades slipped a finger into the top of my bikini bottom, dragging it over the crease of my butt.

Ironically, our time really was up. Hades would have to return to the Underworld, leaving me with nothing but memories of his molten touch.

"I still don't regret kissing you," I said for me as much as I said it for him.

He traced his knuckles down my cheek. "I only regret I can't stay."

"We still have tonight." I forced a smile.

As Hades walked me back to my room, the older woman from the resort I'd seen him talk to days before ran up to him. She looked pain-stricken, grasping his hands within her gnarled ones.

"Fovámai," she kept saying over and over.

Hades glanced at me before wrapping an arm around the woman's shoulders and leading her to a bench. Her hands trembled, and tears streaked down her face. A butterfly appeared in his hand, and he held it out to her. It was beautiful in shades of purple, delicately flapping its wings, allowing the woman to hold it. The woman smiled. Smoke swirled in patterns around her body, emanating from the butterfly. She didn't seem to notice, staring down at the insect, grinning, until she slumped over motionless.

I walked over. "Is she..."

His face hardened. "Yes. Her time had come to an end."

I gasped, tears threatening. "I thought you said you guided the souls once they're in the Underworld, not here."

"I did say that, and it still holds. Something's not right. I *have* to go back soon."

I stared at the woman in horror. It was a natural process of life, but being so close to it sent a chill down my spine. The only sense of comfort was seeing her serene face when he'd calmed her.

"Stephanie," Hades said, gently touching my elbow.

I jumped and peered down at the man who had shared such intimacy only moments ago. It felt bizarrely normal despite conversations of the Underworld and animated fog. I should've been scared of him after witnessing what I just had, but couldn't bring myself to be.

"Yes?" I asked through a cracked voice.

"Can you please go get someone? Tell them what happened

to her."

"What about you?"

His brow creased. "What about me?"

"What if they…" I lowered my voice. "What if they think you killed her?"

"They won't. Trust me."

He kept my gaze and waited for his words to sink in.

I gave a firm nod and turned away. His hand caught mine.

"I'll see you tonight," he said.

Tonight. The dance.

I sat on the couch in my pink chiffon dress and nude-colored flats, waiting for Hades. Sara had been rather proud of herself when I got back to our room. When she asked how it went, I left out all of the steamy details. He wasn't going to be around forever. It was just as unfair to her to make it seem otherwise. She helped me with my hair and hurried off to claim her front-row seat in the atrium. Thoughts of the older woman consumed me. It was a grim realization of who he was.

A light knock sounded at the door. I stared at the peephole before opening it to reveal Hades leaning against the frame with his hands in his pockets. He wore a black silk collared short-sleeve shirt with several buttons undone and black pants.

I sucked on my lower lip. "You're going all out. Same outfit and everything."

"Figured you would appreciate it." His eyes dropped to my dress.

My body hummed. "Oh, I do. Very much."

"You look beautiful."

"Thank you." Heat flushed over my cheeks. "Is everything alright? With the woman, I mean?"

"Yes, but you shouldn't have to think about that right now. Tonight is for you." He reached for my hand and curled it around his arm, escorting us to the atrium.

"What happens to all the souls when you're not in the Underworld?"

"They remain in the river Styx until I'm there to guide them in the right direction."

My grip tightened on his bicep. "That's awful. It's like a sort of limbo?"

"Time works differently down there. They don't know how long they've been there. But, it's also why I can never be on the surface for a prolonged time. They might not know, but I do." He squeezed my hand.

"That's quite the burden you have on your shoulders."

He shrugged. "You get used to it. I was never meant to lead a normal life. No waking up, brushing my teeth, and brewing a pot of coffee."

"You'd take your coffee black, I assume?"

"Naturally. And I'd guess you have a little coffee with your sugar?"

I laughed. "And two creams."

His eyes twinkled, peering down at me. My breath hitched. The murmurs from the inside crowd muffled through the atrium doors once we reached them.

"Ready to win this thing?" he asked, pulling the door open

for me.

"I have full confidence in you. I just hope I don't trip and fall flat on my face." Nerves prickled my skin.

"You know I wouldn't let that happen, darlin'." He pressed his hand against my lower back, steering me toward the table with sign-in sheets.

The woman looked up at us unenthused. Her gaze landed on Hades, and she smiled wide. "You look amazing."

Hades was a juicy steak, and I was a window.

My hands trembled as I picked up the pen. Hades touched his fingertips to my arm, gently taking the pen from my grasp.

He nodded at the woman. "Thank you."

After he signed our names in that gorgeous scroll of his, he led me past signs reading "Contestants This Way." We went backstage where a man stood, holding square pieces of paper with numbers on them. He handed us a number six and pointed to a far corner.

"Are you okay? We got this. Not sure why you're so nervous," he said, massaging my shoulders.

My eyes closed, remembering the feel of the fog pooling over my chest.

"I'm fine. I've only wanted to do this pretty much my entire life. I have the perfect partner, the perfect scenery. Hardly seems real."

"Perfect partner?" His breath breezed against my ear.

I tensed and turned to face him. *(I've Had) The Time of My Life* blasted through the speakers as the first couple took the stage. "Guess we should watch our competition?" I moved to the wings.

Several couples went before us, most of them messing up one move or the other, and *none* of them were able to complete the ending lift. Rupert and Michelle were next. I secretly hoped Rupert broke a leg.

Okay, not really. But still.

Hades stepped behind me, gripping each of my hips. I watched them go through the routine flawlessly, and my heart raced.

"They won't be able to do the lift," Hades whispered.

"How can you be so sure?"

"Trust me."

Rupert trotted to one end of the stage, motioning for Michelle. He planted his hands around her hips and hoisted her straight into the air. She remained suspended until Rupert winced, clutched his stomach, and she landed flat on her butt. She was lucky she didn't land on her head.

Several resort workers ran on stage, helping Michelle to her feet. One bent over to help Rupert, but he slapped their hand away. Michelle cried as they led her off stage, Rupert following behind, still clutching his side. Hades' expression turned predatory as Rupert passed us. When he spotted Hades, that same look of pure terror engulfed Rupert.

Hades' expression softened. "We're up darlin'." He took my hand and led us to the dancefloor, but I couldn't help look over my shoulder at Rupert.

Why was he so scared of Hades if he didn't know who he was? And what was he hiding? Or was Hades the one hiding something?

The song started, and as we practiced, he wrapped a hand

around my back, dipping me. Sara gave an enthusiastic "woo" from the front row. I turned my back to him, curling my arm around his neck, and right before he gripped my hip to spin me, he kissed the tip of my nose. It threw me so off guard I almost didn't move my feet with the turn.

As we went through the cha-cha moves, spins, and dips, we made eye contact whenever we faced one another. I got lost in his gaze several times, staring at amber-colored eyes. Did his true form have the same color? He wrapped a hand around my waist, lifting me, and spinning several times. It was the first of two times I'd be entirely at his mercy during the dance.

When we neared the end, ready to perform the final move, he squeezed my hand, backing up to the edge of the stage. Was he going to—? His eyes flashed before turning as he leaped off stage. I stared dumbstruck, pressing a hand to my chest. Sara sat between Keith and Guy, and she elbowed them both, motioning toward me. Begrudgingly, they both got up to help me down from the stage. I thought I was about to cry.

I ran at Hades, his hands wrapped around my waist, and with no effort in the slightest, I was up in the air, doing the best Baby pose I could. The crowd went wild, but I was far too preoccupied with Hades lowering me back down. I gulped, staring at him as I slid to the ground. He searched my face, looking about as confused as I felt. At some point between the feel of my chiffon skirt floating like a cloud around me and the longing in Hades' eyes every time we drew close, a realization crept over me like a flame on a lit match. Whether we won the contest or not, I couldn't be sure because my mind caught on the fact that I'd fallen for the god of the Underworld.

FOURTEEN

WE STOOD STILL STARING at each other while everyone else around us cheered. Hades brushed a strand of hair from my face. The subtle touch of his fingertips grazing my cheek made me shudder.

"Oh, my God! That. Was. Amazing. I felt like I was watching the movie all over again." Sara grabbed my shoulders.

I gulped and slipped away from him.

"You two, okay?" Sara asked with a crinkled brow.

Hades' eyes glinted. "Never better."

"Well, come accept your award." She grabbed our hands and dragged us toward the stage.

"They haven't announced the winners yet," I mumbled.

She cocked an eyebrow. "Oh, please. You guys were smoking. And the only couple who did the lift."

A resort worker walked out on stage with a microphone and envelope. "I'm sure I know whose names are in this envelope, but may I announce the winners?

The crowd cheered, pointing at Hades and me. I turned to face him, shoving my forehead into his shoulder. My inner introvert screamed. Being the center of attention made me want to crawl in a hole. Hades' body tensed.

"And the winners are…" He opened the envelope, paused, and smiled. "Stephanie and Ha—des. Hades? Did I read that right?"

Heat sprung up the back of my neck as Hades led me to the stage. The resort worker handed us an envelope. "Tomorrow evening, we're having a special guest. And you two have been given VIP access."

"A band?" I peeked into the envelope. Inside were two badges, and once I read the name Apollo's Suns, I almost lost it. "Apollo's Suns?"

Hades rolled his eyes.

"That's right! Not only will you watch the entire concert from the wings, but you'll also get the opportunity to meet the band itself."

"I'm overjoyed," Hades said monotone.

I slapped him on the shoulder with the envelope. "They're one of my favorite bands."

"Of course, they are."

As we walked off stage, I grabbed his arm, turning him to face me. "Can you stay through tomorrow?"

He licked his lips, holding his head low. "Does the concert mean that much to you?"

"I hoped to watch it with you, but I also can't be so selfish as to keep you from wandering souls." It alarmed me how normal that sounded.

"I doubt one more day will hurt. I'll stay for the concert and then I have to go back." His jaw tightened. "In the meantime, I have a few things I must do. I'll meet you back here tomorrow night."

I frowned. "You're not sticking around?"

"I'll see you tomorrow." He curled his hand around the back of my neck and kissed my forehead.

He turned away and walked off before I had another chance to protest.

It was our last day in paradise, and I was depressed for more reasons than one. Admittedly, the thought of never seeing Hades again was at the top of the list. I sat on the stool of the swim-up bar next to Sara, who was with Guy. Sara leaned into Guy, and they couldn't stop smiling at each other. The ice had melted long ago in my hurricane drink, diluting the color to pale orange. I stared into my glass, stirring its contents.

"We're going to have to go on vacation more often," Sara said.

I took a sip. It tasted so watered down it made my nose scrunch. "Why?"

"Look how depressed you are."

Not over what she thought. "Yeah. More brain breaks couldn't hurt honestly."

"That's what I'm talking about." She shook my shoulders.

"Too bad you girls aren't sticking around for one more

day," Guy said, tossing his hair from his face.

"Why's that?" Sara asked.

He grinned and moved his face closer to hers. "Because *we're* here one more day."

I bit down on my straw with such force it cracked. "I think the concert is a perfect end to our vacation."

"Oh man, Apollo's Suns? Their singer is steaming," Sara said, fanning herself. "And you finally get to meet him, Steph."

Guy smirked, taking a long guzzle of his drink. "If you like the blonde pretty boy look."

"Methinks someone is jealous," I said, elbowing Sara.

She elbowed me back. "Methinks you're right."

"I can hear you. You know that, right?" Guy asked.

Sara grabbed a cocktail napkin. "Can I borrow a pen?" She asked the bartender. After scribbling a series of numbers, she slid the napkin to Guy. "Tell you what, Canuck. You ever want a tour of Chicago, you let me know."

Guy's eyes sparkled. "Chicago isn't too far away."

"Not at all," she responded, popping the cherry from her drink into her mouth.

Seeing them so happy made me nauseous. I'd grown feelings for Hades, and here he was about to crawl back underground to play soul keeper. "I'm going to get a refill."

"Why don't you get it from this bar?" Sara asked, but I didn't look back.

I slurped down the rest of my drink and waded through the pool. Once I reached the bar Hades frequented, I plopped my empty glass down and pointed at it. "Another hurricane, please."

Michelle emerged from a corner of the walkway. I crouched

my head down, as if I were a turtle with a shell, hoping Rupert didn't follow her. Much to my dismay, he did. I tensed, moving to the opposite side of the bar. Michelle's face looked pain-stricken, and she wrapped Rupert's arm around her shoulders. Most of the color had drained from his face, and he clutched his side like he had a stab wound.

They passed by the bar, Michelle dropping him several times as she dragged him along. I ran over to them. "Michelle, do you need help? What's going on?"

She shook her head frantically. Rupert groaned. "He has a stomach bug or something. I'm taking him to the infirmary. I'm fine. Thank you."

Stomach bug? I had my fair share and didn't remember looking that bad. I stepped away, feeling guilty for not being able to help.

"Why the frown?" Keith appeared beside me.

Rupert's business was his business.

"Last day," I said.

"Ah. Yeah, that's always a bit of a downer." He patted his hips, looking around.

We stood there for a few awkward moments.

"Everything good with, uh, Hades?" He scratched the back of his head.

"Hm?" Between Hades and the enigma that was Rupert, my mind couldn't concentrate on anything else. "Yeah. He had some business stuff to take care of, but he'll be at the concert tonight."

"Cool." He nodded. "Well, it was good talking to you."

"You too."

He brushed past me, and I slapped a hand over my face. Tonight couldn't get here fast enough.

I waited outside of the atrium, bouncing around on my heels. Hades was running late. It was like first date jitters. Only this wasn't a date and not the first time I'd hung around Hades. I wanted to make the most of it. The final night together. I wrung my hands before clasping them around the lanyard on my neck. Maybe he had to go back and didn't have time to tell me?

"Think I wouldn't show up, darlin'?"

My breath caught in my throat. The smell of ash and burning firewood hit my nose, and I turned to face him. "I would've understood if you had to go back unexpectedly."

"And that's precisely why I made it a point to show." He dipped his chin, those sexy strands of hair falling over his cheeks.

With a stiff arm, I shoved another lanyard at him. "Here you go."

"Ah, yes. How fortunate we're VIPs." He plucked the badge from my hand and slipped it over his neck with a grimace.

"What do you have against Apollo's Suns?"

He led us toward the entrance. "Their singer is my egocentric nephew."

Hades walked forward, but my feet froze to the ground. He opened the door, waiting for me, and did a double-take when he saw I was several feet away.

"The front man of Apollo's Suns is the *actual* Apollo?"

"As I said—egocentric."

I shuffled forward, but my arms remained stiff. "I've been a fan of them so long. I'm not sure how I'm going to look him in the face."

He slipped his arm around my waist. "You look me in the face without issue. Just try not to get blinded by his sunshine smile." Sarcasm laced his words like venom.

A resort worker spotted our badges and motioned for us to follow him. Without knowing, I gripped onto Hades' shirt, my heart racing as we got closer and closer to the stage.

"You have no reason to be nervous. He has half the power I do. Maybe even less."

I narrowed my eyes. "Did you ever stop to think I'm nervous about meeting a rock star, not the fact he's a Greek god?"

He frowned. "Sorry."

Now I was double nervous. I often heard rock stars referred to as "gods" in their own right, but never in the literal sense. It was ingenious. His cover—was essentially himself. Ingenious or extremely arrogant. The resort worker led us to the wings. We were so close you'd be able to see the sweat rolling down their faces.

"Here we are. The show should be starting in a few minutes. You'll be able to meet the band after the first act. Enjoy!"

Hades folded his arms over his chest, a scowl distorting his features. The lights dimmed, and I clapped. The band entered the stage from the opposite side, the drummer taking his position first, followed by the bassist and guitarist. The crowd roared, waiting for that pivotal moment when Apollo made his grand entrance. A burst of flames ignited in the middle of the stage. Ace or rather, Apollo stood with his iconic silver and ivory guitar with glowing orange suns down the neck.

"Oh, brother," Hades mumbled.

I stopped clapping. "That wasn't pyrotechnics, was it?"

"No. It wasn't."

Apollo stepped to the mic stand, throwing the rock symbol into the air. "How are we tonight, Corfu?"

He wore skintight metallic gold pants and a leather vest with no shirt underneath. His bleach blonde hair hung to the nape of his neck, draping over his perfectly sun-kissed skin. Every time he ran his fingers through his hair, it only made him more attractive as it fell in a perfect frame around his chiseled facial features. He had the brightest blue eyes I'd ever seen, a broad jawline, and just as Hades described—an electric smile.

The drummer began their first song. Apollo strummed his hand over the strings of his guitar, sun rays blazing from it toward the audience. I'd seen the effects before, but it was crazy to know they weren't parlor tricks. Every time he did something, Hades' eyes would fall shut and he'd shake his head. Considering he was stuck underground every waking day of his life, it must've been annoying to watch another god flaunt their powers so openly.

The songs I knew had a different meaning now. The lyrics centered around Apollo's life. Lyrics I previously thought were a complete myth. I curled my hands around the strings of my lanyard. Apollo moved to the front of the stage, swinging the guitar on its strap behind him. He grabbed the mic stand and leaned forward, reaching out to various women screaming and clawing over each other to get to him.

I elbowed Hades. "Aura?"

"Aura and an ego the size of Olympus," he mumbled.

"We can't help who our family is."

"Very, very true, darlin'."

Apollo worked the crowd, especially the ladies, occasionally hopping down to roam the aisles. Fire, sunbursts, and blinding flashes of light went off throughout the performance. When they played the final song of the first act, he turned in our direction, and my heart quickened.

Oh, my God. He was coming over. My inner fangirl went into overdrive. This was my chance to redeem myself from the airport.

He dragged a hand through his hair, grinning wide when he spotted Hades. The guitar slung over his shoulder, and he rested one of his hands on the neck of it. "Uncle. Long time no see."

"You're hilarious," Hades replied, narrowing his eyes.

Apollo bit his lip, letting his steely blue gaze drop to me. "You look familiar."

I snorted, feeling my cheeks warm. "Stephanie. Steph." Keeping one hand on my lanyard, I stuck the other one out to him.

He snapped his fingers. "The airport. You were that shy little mouse who couldn't bring herself to talk to me." He gave a snarky grin and shook my hand.

Why in the world did he have to remember? The heat from my face traveled down the back of my neck. Hades stepped between us, breaking Apollo's hold on my hand.

"So, this is what you do with your time? Pretend to be a rock star? Exhibit your powers openly?" Hades slipped an arm around my waist.

Apollo looked at me with a cocked eyebrow.

"She knows," Hades said.

"She knows? Well then, that changes things entirely, doesn't it?" He grinned at me. "And I'm not pretending to be a rock star. I am one. Are you able to subscribe to Spotify in the Underworld?"

Hades sighed. "Considering none of us are ever in the same place by coincidence—why are you here?"

He pointed at Hades and spoke to me. "This is why my dad gave him the Underworld. He's a smart cookie."

His dad. Zeus. Uncle Hades. Underworld. Apollo. I'd warped into the Twilight Zone.

"My visit comes with bad news, I'm afraid," Apollo started, draping both hands over his guitar.

Hades rolled his shoulders. "I'm listening."

"Thanatos has abandoned his duties."

"What?" It came out more like a growl.

Apollo held up his hands. "I've no idea how or why. But something tells me you've noticed."

Hades dragged a hand over his face.

"What does that mean?" I asked.

"It means, my dear Stephanie, Hades here is in charge of souls both on the surface and below." Apollo pointed at the ground with a smirk.

His smile annoyed me. "This doesn't sound like a funny situation."

"Maybe not for my uncle. He'll be a very busy man." He slapped his shoulder.

Hades growled again, balling his hands into fists. "I'm

powerful, but even I can't be in two places at once."

"Sounds like you need to have a little talk with Thanatos." Apollo shrugged.

It unnerved me he didn't offer to help, and on top of that, he acted like this was all no big deal.

Apollo rubbed his chin. "I'm curious. How did you go about telling her about, you know?"

Hades cocked an eyebrow. "I showed her."

"You just—" Apollo's eyes widened. "You took her to the Underworld?"

My body stiffened.

"No, you idiot. I showed her power. The fog from Styx."

"And that was it? Just like that, she was cool with it?"

"More or less."

Apollo frowned.

"Is there a particular reason you're asking?" Hades said.

"No. Nope. Just curious," Apollo replied, looking away.

The lights faded on the stage before brightening again.

Apollo raised a single finger. "That's my cue. It was a pleasure meeting you, Stephanie. And Uncle, charming as always." He flashed a smile before returning to his waiting audience.

Hades paced like a caged lion. "I'm sorry. I wish nothing more than to spend time with you, but I've got to take care of this."

"I understand." Tears built up in my eyes, but I fought them back. "Will I ever see you again?"

He frowned. The deepest frown I'd seen on him yet. "I've never lied to you, and I won't start now. I don't know."

There was no stopping them. Several tears rolled down my

cheeks.

His face fell, and he cupped his hands around my face, wiping the tears away with his thumbs. "This may sound strange to you, but mortal tears over me is one of the most beautiful things I've ever seen."

I gulped, staring up at him, wishing with every fiber I could go with him. Before, the thought of the Underworld terrified me, but facing the harsh reality of never seeing him again terrified me more. He dipped his head and kissed me. A kiss so tender no one would have ever believed it came from a man who tortured the evil in Tartarus. And then he vanished. The faint smell of fire hung in the air, the taste of ash on my lips.

FIFTEEN

⛩⛩⛩⛩⛩⛩⛩⛩⛩⛩⛩⛩⛩⛩

FOR THE REST OF the concert, I felt numb. Gone were the excited jitters. I didn't even bother sticking around for the encore, yanking off my lanyard, and tossing it in the closest garbage can. I texted Sara to tell her I was going back to the room and not to worry about me as I didn't feel right. In reality, I wanted to be alone, go for a walk, and try to forget Hades.

After half an hour of wandering the resort grounds, it was proving impossible. How did he know I couldn't go to the Underworld with him? He didn't even try. Maybe he toyed with me like all the other gods. My insides twisted. The night grew chilly, and I rubbed my arms as I passed by a series of rooms.

Clank.

I stopped.

Following the direction of the sound, I heard it again. It sounded like chains rattling against each other. I pressed my ear to a door, hearing a man's pained moans. Either someone was into some severe kink, or they were in trouble. This was one of those moments I should've stepped away, but my conscience wouldn't allow it. I pushed my ear harder, and the door creaked open.

My heart raced as I pushed my fingertips against it. The room was pitch black save for a sliver of moonlight sneaking through the curtains. Against my better judgment, I stepped inside, a chill running down my spine. I held my breath, taking cautious steps forward.

"Don't come any closer," a voice said from the darkness. The clanking sound happened again, followed by him grunting.

The voice sounded like several voices speaking at once. One was no louder than a whisper, and the other two were in different pitches. But the tone was deep and husky.

"Who's there?" I stopped, squinting into the darkness.

"It's me, darlin'. Don't come any closer, please."

The southern accent was too recognizable.

"Hades?" Ignoring his plea, I continued forward. "Why? You sound like you're—are you chained up?" My heart thudded so quickly I thought it'd burst through my ribcage.

"Stephanie, please. I don't want you to see me like this." He spoke low and gravelly.

I rounded the corner and gasped. The moonlight spilled over Hades, illuminating his half-naked body. He was barefoot and shirtless, wearing only his black pants, chained shackles around his wrists.

"Oh my God," I stammered, running to him and dropping to my knees.

He lifted his head when my hands clamped around the

chains, and I gasped again. His hair was white, flowing down to his stomach. It floated around him as if in water. He had no facial hair, and his irises were a vibrant white. His skin looked inhuman in a pearl-like sheen, and ears that came to a point like an elf.

I cupped his face with my hands, a tear rolling down my cheek. "Is this the real you?"

"Yes." Those white eyes gleamed up at me, his brow crinkling, and with the staggering whispers of his real voice.

I thinned my lips, staring down at the true him. Should I have been afraid? Aghast from his appearance? Because I wasn't. In a warped way, I preferred this side of him. "Why are you chained up? Who did this to you?" I pulled on the chains, eyeing the connection to the shackles.

"You're not afraid of me?" He dipped his head to look at my face, his hair floating behind him.

"I haven't been afraid of you since the day we met. Why would this change anything?"

His nostrils flared as he stared at me. His lips parted several times, but in the end, he pursed them together, saying nothing. I opened the drawers of a nearby desk. What did I expect to find? It's not as if hotels stored toolboxes in each room.

"You won't be able to remove the chains. They're cursed."

I slammed the last drawer shut, fishing through my hair for a bobby pin. I squatted on the floor next to him. "Like hell, I can't."

The chains clattered together as Hades' arms tensed, hands balling into fists. The faint sound of a revolver's hammer pulling back filled my ears, followed by cold metal pressing into my head's side.

"Step away, love. No sense in you getting tangled up in all this," Rupert's voice said in a hushed tone.

Hades growled, trying to stand up, only to be brought back to his knees. "When you arrive in the Underworld, I will *not* be merciful. Mark my words, mortal."

My hands trembled as I held them up and rose to my feet. Rupert pressed the gun harder against my skin, and I pinched my eyes shut.

"As long as I keep you chained, no one has to die. And I've got far too many things left to do with my life."

I grunted. "What the hell are you talking about?"

"Oh, come now, love. What kind of a Greek myth trivia winner are you? The story of King Sisyphus and the god of death?"

It wasn't easy drumming up Greek myths with a loaded gun to your head.

"He tricked Thanatos and chained him with the same chains the gods were going to use to punish him. Without the god of death roaming free, no mortal could die or go to the Underworld." He chuckled.

And with Thanatos relinquishing his duties...

"Rupert, can't we talk about this?" I asked, gulping.

He pushed on the barrel. "Sorry, love. There's nothing left to talk about. I knew as soon as Hades showed me his true face, I was dying. Bloody bleeding ulcers. I didn't expect this to work, honestly. But a little voice in my head told me otherwise."

Think. Think. In the story, Ares freed Thanatos. But Ares was a god, capable of bypassing the curse.

"Did you stop to think what happens when you don't get away with this?" I asked, trying to keep my voice from shaking.

He poked my head with the gun. "The only thing keeping me from getting away with this right now—is you." He pressed his lips to my ear. "Don't worry. You won't die completely. Remember?"

I never thought I feared death until now. The thought of my life being ripped away by someone else felt unfair. The same way my mother's life was torn away by a stranger. Was it fate to be killed? Shouldn't we all die of natural causes?

The faint sound of the revolver clicking filled my ears.

"No," Hades roared. He let out a ferocious yell, wings sprouting from his back. The arches of the wings glowed with fiery embers, morphing into smoke and ash. Remnants of singed feathers floated around him. "These chains may make me weak, but it doesn't mean I can't hurt you."

Rupert shoved me in front of him, his free arm crossing over my chest. His body trembled, and he pushed the barrel into my head with such force it made me wince. "You come any closer, and I *will* pull this trigger."

Hades' chest heaved, the ash from his wings suspended in the air, floating around him. He wrapped his hands around the chain, pulling it taut. He snarled, revealing teeth shaped like a wolf—sharp and deadly. His hand splayed, and the black fog swirled up my leg before passing over Rupert. It curled around his neck. Hades closed his hand into a fist, and his eyes glowed with a white intensity.

The pressure of the gun against my head fell away. Rupert gurgled and gagged behind me. I launched my elbow into the side I'd seen him clutching. He let out a strangled cry of pain and pulled the trigger. A stinging pain blasted over my shoulder, my blood spraying me in the face.

"No," Hades roared.

I yelped but caught the revolver when Rupert dropped it.

The fog loosened its grip from him, floating back to Hades. I winced as I lifted the gun, aiming it at Rupert.

Rupert laughed as he rubbed his neck. "It's no use, love. As long as Hades is in those chains, I can't die. And none of us can break them. Not even me."

"How did you even *get* magical chains?" I said through gritted teeth.

Rupert snickered like a hyena. "They fell into my hands in the right place at the right time."

"You have a gun pointed at your head. Do you really think now is the time for riddles?"

"I'm already dead, darling. Makes no difference to me."

Darling wasn't his word to call me. I growled under my breath and pulled back the hammer, holding the hilt with both hands.

"Stephanie." Hades' shades of voices passed over me like liquid silk.

I gazed over my shoulder at the beautiful image of him standing in his true form. Embers, smoke, and singed feathers floated around him.

"Killing him will do nothing but damper the light inside you. He's not worth it." The chains rattled as he tensed his arms.

"Now I see why it was so easy to get you into those chains, mate. Threaten to kill your dearly beloved, and bring the god of the Underworld to his knees. Literally. It's embarrassing." Rupert shook his head.

I was dearly beloved. My chest tightened, and I released the hammer, lowering the weapon but not letting go.

Hades growled, vibrating the paintings hanging on the walls. "Keep. Talking. I dare you."

The chains. Break them.

A distant whisper fluttered over my ear. Using only my eyes, I looked around. No one and nothing else were in the room. Where did it come from?

The chains.

I ran over to Hades, clamping my hands around the chain. He looked down at me with a quirked brow.

"What in Tartarus are you doing, Stephanie?"

"Something crazy." I kept his gaze as I yanked the chain with ease.

Blue sparks flew as each link broke. It turned into dust and fell to the ground in a pile.

I blew out a breath, staring at my palms. There was no rationalizing this one.

"What? How? They're cursed. It's not possible," Rupert stammered, backing away toward the window.

Hades' wings flapped once, and he stood toe-to-toe with Rupert. Hades puffed his chest and clenched and unclenched his fists. Rupert's entire body shook as he looked up at his fate.

"You have no idea the torturous eternity you've condemned yourself to," Hades said, his wings starting to wrap around Rupert. "And your time expired hours ago."

I looked away, shoving my face into my palms.

A hand touched my shoulder, sending me writhing back on my heels.

"It's only me," Hades cooed.

I blinked up at him, in awe at the sight of his hair floating around him and the brightness of burning embers at the arch of his wings. "Where's Rupert?"

"The Underworld. I'll deal with him soon enough." The staggered whispers of his voice were deep. Masculine. Commanding.

"What are you going to do with him?"

"You don't want to know, Stephanie." His gaze turned sinister.

I gulped. "Do people try that with Thanatos often? Try to bargain with him for their lives?"

"Everyone wants to go to an afterlife in paradise, but no one wants to die." He said, shaking his head.

Rupert most certainly wasn't going to the Fields.

I stood up, groaning from the pain shooting down my arm.

He turned my shoulder. "The bullet only grazed you."

I stared up at the menacing, yet angelic form of the real Hades. If he would've appeared in front of me this way only weeks ago, I may have passed out…again. His appearance was intimidating, but he still had an ethereal quality to him, a gentleness that gripped my very soul.

"I can help you with this, I need to—" he started, but was cut off by a gust of wind.

A figure loomed in the corner, blocking the moonlight from illuminating the room. Hades turned around and moved me to stand behind him, his wings wrapping around me like a cocoon. His nails were black, thick, and pointed.

"Thanatos. You've made quite the mess," Hades said.

I leaned around him, attempting to see into the darkness. Thanatos himself was the night. His tattered black cloak draped to the ground, and he floated forward on a bed of fog. All he was missing was a scythe, and he'd be the grim reaper himself.

"I will not go back. Too long have I been feared when it is you who guides my hand. I am nothing but a pawn." A hand slipped from his sleeve, pointing at Hades. I half expected it to be skeletal, but it was a pale, human hand.

"I may be your King, Thanatos, but Zeus is king over us all. He gave you your reign. You uphold it."

"We, who are *all* descendants of Titans, reduced to following an arrogant man with a lust for power. You are almost as bad as he is, Hades." It was pure macabre the way he stood motionless, fog wafting around him.

Hades wrapped his wings around me tighter, pieces of ash fluttering against my eyelashes. "We both have our roles. I've never marveled in the cards I've been dealt, but we do what we must because it's our responsibility."

"Says the man with near the power of Zeus." Thanatos snarled.

"Says the man who can never remain on the surface. I'm not going to discuss whose existence is more pitiful over the others. You are a god. Act like one." The embers on the top of his wings glowed brighter.

The sound of a sword blade sliding against stone reverberated in my chest. "I will not go back. Even if it means killing you in the process, my lord." A pair of black as midnight wings sprouted from his back—as beautiful as they were intimidating.

Hades' wings shifted, spreading wide, but his hand still held me behind him. "Don't be foolish. You know you can't win."

"Has anyone ever tried?"

Thanatos launched forward. The ground beneath me disappeared, replaced by a hole glowing orange and billowing smoke. I started to fall, but Hades wrapped one arm around me, suspending us in the air with his wings.

The world dipped into slow-motion as we succumbed to the beckoning crack in the earth. And right before it sealed, the hotel room door swung open, revealing a wide-eyed Sara, staring at the scene like the world's most grueling murder spree. Thanatos' hooded head whipped over his shoulder, catching Sara's gaze before darkness enveloped us.

Dark water flowed below. The surrounding torches reflected flames on the surface, illuminating the whaling ghosts who swam within it. I remained in Hades' embrace, his wings the only thing keeping us from plummeting.

The animated fog Hades used to show me the Underworld in the spa paled compared to its real appearance.

Thanatos raised a large sword above his head, its blade the length of his body. He propelled forward with one might flap of his wings. Hades growled, diving us toward the water. I pinched my eyes shut, and my back collided with wood.

I expected to feel cold and wet in the river, but instead, I was nestled within a boat, floating on its own toward a cave entrance. Thanatos and Hades fought in the air. Thanatos swung his sword while Hades used his smoke power as a guiding force against him.

A pair of ghostly hands gripped onto the edge of the boat, a gangly head following. The only hair it had was a few strands sprouting from the top of its head, darkened cavities in its skull where eyes used to be. When it wailed, holes formed in its cheek, showing teeth. I gasped, scooting to the other side of the boat. Would it have been disrespectful to stomp its hands away with my feet? As it pulled itself out of the water, I didn't care and stomped my feet at it until it fell away, re-joining the other lost souls.

The river Styx. I *was* in the Underworld. Panic tugged at my insides, but there wasn't time for it. I needed to focus.

As the cave entrance grew closer and closer, panic tugged at my spine. According to Hades' explanation, the river was about to end in his throne room. Above me, Thanatos reached for Hades' wings, but only managed to grab bits of feather and embers.

"Your burning wings shouldn't be an advantage," Thanatos snarled.

Hades grabbed him, plunging them into the water. The souls crawled over Thanatos as Hades flapped back into the air. The souls cried in agony, but Thanatos shrugged them away, floating back up.

Darkness flooded over the boat as it made its way through the tunnel. I gripped onto the edge of the vessel. Just ahead, an enormous throne stood, made of burnt bone. Pillars surrounded the throne with a moat of fire. Sconces hung from the ceilings by chains, blue flames flickering within them.

The boat stopped when it beached itself on a sanded shoreline—black sand. I hoisted myself onto the bank, gripping my arm. I backed away from the water, watching as the souls climbed into the abandoned boat, crying when they found no one inside. All these poor people stuck in limbo with no direction on where to spend their eternal lives.

I walked toward the throne, a chill traveling down my back, trying to imagine what Hades looked like seated on it. All imposing and merciless when he needed to be. Hades came crashing through the cave entrance, his arm clipping the edge of a stone pillar. Rocks flew into the surrounding walls and plunged into the water. I pressed my back against the side of his throne.

"We could do this until the end of time, Hades. Why can you not simply let me be?" Thanatos roared. The sound of his sword slicing echoed through the cavern.

"I need someone on the surface. I can't do both," Hades snarled. "And you call Zeus selfish."

"Very well. You leave me no choice but to persuade you."

Thanatos appeared in front of me. Red fog eked over my hands, working its way up to my face. When I looked up, the hood of his cloak draped over his head, disguising his face in a hollow shadow.

Hades made a shrill whistle. A canine growl followed by several snapping jaws sounded. Three pairs of glowing red eyes emerged from a darkened corner of the throne room. A massive creature with three heads loomed over Thanatos, drool dripping down its jaws. Cerberus.

SIXTEEN

𐂷𐂷𐂷𐂷𐂷𐂷𐂷𐂷𐂷𐂷𐂷𐂷𐂷𐂷

HADES POINTED AT HIS guard dog. "Watch her."

Cerberus slid in front of me, his claws scraping across the stone floor. In the fog scape Hades showed me, Cerberus was as big as my forearm. In reality, he was as tall as a skyscraper. There was something oddly comforting about having such a large creature defending you. It didn't keep my knees from shaking at the sight of him, however.

"You think your pet can stop me?" Thanatos asked, the fog under his feet carrying him backward.

Hades glared, still suspended in the air. His flapping wings sounded like a flickering flame. "His bite is far worse than my bark. Do you want to continue with this charade?"

"Like all the other gods, here you are underestimating me," Thanatos growled. He slammed the blade of his sword into a nearby pillar, sending rocks into one of Cerberus' heads.

The other two heads snapped at Thanatos, but Cerberus

kept his ground in front of me as his master ordered. The head the rocks pummeled blinked one of its eyes, and snarled, claws digging into the ground.

Hades flew down like Superman and collided into Thanatos' chest. The impact sent both gods in a violent tumble of fog and smoke.

Cerberus' feet twitched. Hades threw punch after punch at Thanatos' face before being tossed away, slamming into the side of his throne. Cerberus slid forward but stopped again.

Thanatos raised his sword above his head with both hands, bringing it down over Hades' shoulder. Hades disappeared in a flash of swirling smoke. The sword clashed against the throne, sending sparks flying but doing no damage. Hades reappeared behind Thanatos, throwing his arm around his neck in a choke hold.

"Where is this *coming* from, Than?" Hades growled, his grip tightening around Thanatos' hood.

Thanatos twirled the sword, making the point face Hades, and thrust it behind him. With a snarl, Hades dodged out of the way and relinquished his hold on the god of death, shoving him away.

Thanatos no longer floated as he paced back and forth across the sand, leaving no footprints behind. "Hades. The everlasting poster boy for the Underworld."

"You can't be serious. This is all about some bitterness toward the way mortals view us?"

The tension in Cerberus' legs eased as the two gods spoke rather than fight.

Thanatos pointed at Hades with the sword. "I guide their

souls to their eternal resting and yet the mighty King of the Underworld oversees *all*. They already all think it, I simply made it so." His ebony wings flared.

Hades' jaw tightened. "I cannot help how mortals perceive us any more than Homer described us in his words. It's up to them how they view it all. How they view *us*."

Focusing on their conversation helped ignore the hunger pains twisting in my gut. I winced as my stomach rumbled.

"You abducted Persephone and yet somehow were depicted as a romantic." A chilled laugh resonated from the shadows of the hood. "I wonder if they would think the same of Death itself."

The expression on Hades' face softened as if a realization washed over him like a water bead trickling down his cheek. "Zeus. He talked to you, didn't he?"

The King of the Gods name said out loud somehow made the agony in my abdomen hurt that much more.

"It doesn't matter. He was *right*," Thanatos roared as he flew up and came crashing down over Hades.

Hades threw his arms forward, forming a shield of fog.

Cerberus' claws sprung out and his stance widened.

I delicately touched the fur on the canine's leg. The nearest head lowered, eyeing my fingers. It sniffed me and let out a huff, sending my hair flying backward. I suppose I should've been glad there wasn't snot to accompany it. "I think it makes more sense for you to help him defeat Thanatos rather than be stuck in this corner by me, wouldn't you say?"

His head shook before he snorted and nudged me with his forehead. I stumbled, my heart racing. Cerberus charged forward, capturing Thanatos, wings and all, in one of his massive jaws, tossing him back and forth like a rag doll.

Thanatos cackled. "Does this ignorant canine think it can snap me like a twig?"

"He's distracting you," Hades boomed, his eyes bursting with white, wings glowing a furious orange. "Don't make me do it, Than. Blood or not you're my *brother*. We're both tied to this eternal life of death and woes. Talk to me."

Thanatos laughed again, only this time it sounded pained— genuine. "We've been partners in this game for eons. Not once have we had a heart-to-heart. What would be the difference now?"

I cocked my head to the side, staring at Thanatos, casting my eyes over his shoulders, his head. For the first time, I saw no colors. No pure darkness. No light. Pure. Nothing.

"You'd be surprised how healing a simple conversation can be." I gulped, interlacing my fingers behind my back to keep my hands from shaking.

Thanatos snapped the hood in my direction before slowly craning it back to Hades, Cerberus holding him firm within his mouth. "Ah. Is this the reason you suddenly have the desire for a little chit chat? Your pet?"

A low snarl vibrated in the back of Hades' throat, making Cerberus join in an intimidating chorus with his own growl.

"Come on, Hades. You have the courage of your convictions. *Do it*." Thanatos roared his last words.

Hades' lip twitched and he threw his hands forward, arms shaking, as a blue swirl eked from Thanatos' chest.

My stomach growled. The kind of hunger pains that make you feel nauseated. How could I be thinking about food at a time like this? It was so excruciating it made me grip my stomach in agony.

Cerberus rested Thanatos on the shoreline as Thanatos stared at his hands, shaking his head. His wings disappeared like quicksand. "Does she really mean all that much to you, Hades for you to remove my essence? My power? Strand me here or face becoming mist in the wind were I to try and go to the surface?"

Hades floated down with clenched fists. "I'll give it back to you as soon as you *talk* to me. As you said, we've been upholding these jobs for eons and not once have you pulled something like this."

Thanatos made a tsking sound before dropping in a slump on the wet black sand, holding his head low. "Bargaining with me to reveal my out of character motives. Maybe you really are as cruel as they say, brother."

A pain formed in my chest hearing Hades be called cruel. It had been almost distracting enough until my stomach twisted harder.

"What choice did you give me? You show up on the surface in your godly form. You stop ushering souls to the underworld." He sat on the sand next to him, narrowing his eyes. "And then you threatened Stephanie's life."

The words pulled me from my food frenzy daze and I walked over to them, eager to help in any way I could. I sunk toward the ground, not caring about the wet sand that'd soak into my dress upon sitting on it. Hades flicked his wrist and a black stool appeared in time to catch me before I reached the ground.

Thanatos threw off his hood, to reveal as human of a face as Hades had. His hair fell in long wavy tendrils black and sleek like raven wings with skin so pale it was almost iridescent. His light eyes glared at the river ahead of us, the skin above his thin sleek nose wrinkling in dismay. He was tragically handsome and the polar opposite of how I envisioned Death.

"You've always thought because I'm able to walk on the surface that I'm no lonelier than you are, Hades."

A lump formed in my throat and I shifted my glance to the god of the Underworld. Hades' face tightened and he stayed quiet, letting Thanatos speak his thoughts before responding. The teal colors around him rippled with the urge to help the defeated god next to him.

"I believe it far worse to be amongst them—to feel them, to experience their life and laughter. And having to avoid showing myself. *Truly* showing myself or risk scarring them for the rest of their mortality."

I leaned forward, resting my arms on my knees. "Have you ever tried without the hood? You don't look any different than the rest of us without it." A meager smile tugged at my lips.

"You can only see him this way because we're in the Underworld, sweetheart." Hades met my gaze.

Thanatos smirked and drew an abstract skull into the sand. "He's right. Up there, all they see is how they envision death. I couldn't say what they all imagine, but can only assume it's the head of a skeleton, a half-rotting corpse, face-less."

I folded my hands in my lap. "You've both been dealt pretty harsh deals but shouldn't you be confiding in Hades versus blaming him? I mean—I know misery loves company and all but…" Without thinking, I gave his shoulder a reassuring squeeze.

Thanatos tensed under my touch and his already thin lips thinned even more as he stared at my hand. I went to move it but he slipped a hand over mine, his skin as cold as ice, making me gasp.

"You *really* do not fear us. Do you?" Thanatos' eyes searched my face like a newborn enamored by the sky.

The pain twisted in my stomach, swallowing any shock I had from Thanatos' touch and I shook my head.

His hand dropped and he turned his attention back to Hades. "I understand now and I envy you."

"Never in the thousands of years of my existence have I met a woman like her. But she exists, Thanatos. Which means there must be more like her." Hades caught my gaze over Thanatos' head—his eyes softening as he took me in.

My chest hummed and I could feel my *own* aura bursting with pastel pinks and reds.

"Have we spoken lately of how infuriating Zeus can be?" Thanatos raised a thick dark brow with a hint of a grin at the corner of his mouth.

Hades punched his shoulder. "It's been at least a decade."

"I'm a fool." Thanatos sighed. "He caught me at a more vulnerable moment and I somehow let his words overshadow my purpose."

"It won't be the first nor the last time." Hades held out his hand. "Are we good, Than?"

Thanatos slowly nodded and shook his brother's hand. "Yes. You return my essence and I'll return to my duties."

I sniffed the air. The smell was impossible to ignore. A small table, decorated with a scarlet ornate table cloth, sat in the corner. And resting on top, displayed on a silver platter, was a pile of Cinnamon Bun Oreos. My stomach growled like Godzilla.

Hades bowed his head and turned his palm up. Blue tendrils misted and swirled from his skin as Thanatos' essence flowed back into him, billowing in a cascade from Hades' arms. Feathers from the majestic black wings poked from his shoulder blades within the robes until they fanned out to their full span.

Thanatos turned his gaze on me. "Your friend with the obsidian eyes. What is her name?"

I cocked my head to one side. "Sara."

"Sara," he repeated, casting his eyes downward. "Princess." A small smile tugged at his lips.

I'd have probably made more out of his reaction to my best friend's name if it weren't for the food calling to me—luring me in like a prized bass. I eyed the delectable plate of Oreos, biting my lip, and moving toward them.

Thanatos slipped on the hood. "You shouldn't expect my insubordination again, my lord."

"Don't make promises you can't keep old friend."

The sound of scattered whispers echoed off the cave walls as Thanatos disappeared.

I reached out for the plate of Oreos. Just one tiny nibble. So hungry. So very, very hungry. The textured surface of the delicious cookie brushed my fingertip, and I picked it up. My mouth salivated as I brought it to my lips.

A hand grasped my wrist, stopping me.

"Stephanie, no," Hades said, glowering down at me.

I blinked, staring down at the Oreo inches from my lips, and dropped it. "I don't—I don't know what came over me. I would've been—"

"Stuck here." He frowned.

I gazed down at his hand wrapped around my wrist. "But you didn't let me."

"I told you before I would never let that happen again. She deserved a choice."

My heart thrummed. I let pieces of his floating hair slide through my fingers.

He peered down at me, caressing his cheek against my hand, and closing his eyes.

"I really must get you back to the surface. The Underworld is no place for a mortal. It's already starting to affect you," he said, his chin dropping.

"Am I really never going to see you again?"

The tips of his pointed ears drooped. "It's better that way."

My sinuses stung, and I bit the inside of my mouth to keep from crying.

"There is one last thing I wish to do for you, however, if you are willing."

My throat clenched. "What is it?"

"Your suicide murderer. Remember when I told you I could allow you to interrogate him here in Tartarus? The offer is still on the table."

My eyes widened. Interview a dead serial killer? This took the idea of *Interview With The Vampire* and put it on an entirely different playing field. "It'd—it'd give the information I need to convict him."

He gripped my shoulders. "I must warn you—he is a slime of a human being."

"I wouldn't expect much less. Will you help me?"

"Help you?" He quirked a brow.

I traced a fingertip over the tip of his ear. "It's called 'Good Cop, Bad Cop'."

"I assume I'm to play the role of Bad Cop?"

"Please? As you can imagine, I've never been any good at it."

He dipped his head. "Very well."

He gave one extravagant flourish with his arm, kicking up swirls of smoke. An irradiating heat slapped me in the face. We stood in the middle of a charcoaled entrance where lava flowed through the cracks. Hundreds of screams, wails, and crying poured into my ears. It was so deafening, I had to clap my hands over my ears. Hades touched my shoulder, and the world silenced.

"I apologize. It's been a long time since I've escorted a mortal in the Underworld," he said, his tone hushed and soothing.

"Are we—" I slipped my hands from my head. "Are we in Tartarus?"

"Yes. It's the only area he can roam. We have to conduct the interrogation here. Did you still want to continue?" He delicately turned me to face him.

My teeth chattered, despite the increasing temperature. "I don't have a choice. I can help so many families knowing this information. I'll have to get over the fact that probably three feet away someone is getting tortured."

"I promise you won't see or hear any of it."

I nodded, staring up at his stoic expression, a serene glimmer in his gaze. "Let's get this over with."

He bowed his head before passing his hand over his face and body. As his hand progressed, he transformed into his mortal guise. The "Sawyer" guise.

"They get a false sense of security when I appear human."

Well, this was going to be interesting.

In another whoosh of smoke, we were in a room surrounded with sleek black walls. Low lighting pointed at a man with a ball and chain attached to each of his limbs. My heart raced. Earnest Fueller. Across from me at arms-length was the man I'd made eye contact with years ago in the interrogation room. A man I knew was guilty with every fiber of my being. Here he was in the deadly flesh. He looked the same: Balding, average size build, scruff over his chin, broad nose, and bushy caterpillar eyebrows. And just as his aura was all those years ago as he sat on the witness stand and lied through his teeth—pure blackness. Not one microscopic shrivel of color to suggest anything but his cold heart had given up and there was no turning back.

"To what do I owe the pleasure of my torture break?" He grunted, the chains rattling together.

Hades remained in the shadows, leaning on the wall with his arms folded. "We need to ask you a few questions."

It was one thing to be behind the safety of a two-way mirror when looking at a person you hoped to convict. This was another matter entirely. "I only need to ask you a few questions about the murders, and then you're free to go."

He snorted, spitting on the ground. "Yeah, because I'm in a hurry."

Hades pushed off the wall. He stood in front of him and leaned forward until their noses almost brushed. "The longer this takes, the more excruciating your torture becomes. Permanently."

Earnest gulped.

So far, so good. I expected Hades to start ripping off fingernails already. "How many victims were there?" We knew of seven, but I wanted to be sure.

"Seven. My lucky number," he said with a smirk.

The tip of Hades' finger glowed orange, and he poked Earnest's shoulder with a sizzle. Earnest yelped.

I grabbed Hades by the elbow and pulled him over. "What are you doing?"

His brow furrowed. "He's a smart ass."

"But he's still giving information. The idea is to be the 'bad' in 'bad cop' when he refuses."

He narrowed his eyes. "Fine."

"Your first three victims were inconclusive due to no physical evidence, but witnesses were saying they saw someone who matched your description. Was it you? Alleyways? Rainy nights?"

"Yes," he clipped, glaring at Hades from across the room.

My nerves dissipated, and I took a step closer. "After the fourth victim, you were pulled in for a field line up. Why was the witness not able to identify you?"

"They needed glasses?"

Hades swiped his hand in the air, and Earnest arched from his chair, gurgling and shaking. I widened my eyes at Hades, and he dropped his hand with a shrug.

"Earnest, you're dead and have already been judged. What good does it do you to lie?" I asked, trying to keep my tone sympathetic.

He groaned. "It was dark, and I always wore a baseball cap."

And that explained why there were rarely any witnesses who could confirm his face.

"Your fifth victim. I found evidence on your phone, which clearly showed you setting up a time to meet with an unknown number an hour before they were found dead. Was that the victim?"

"Yeah. But they didn't show up. I even *let* the cops into my apartment to do their little search. Did they find anything?" He chuckled. "Who the hell are you anyway? Snooping on my phone?"

Hades stormed in front of me, the arches of his wings peeking from his back. Earnest leaned back, shaking. He tried to lift his hands to his face, but the chains prevented it.

"*She* is asking the questions. You've just escalated your punishment." The wings slipped away, and he stepped aside.

Earnest whimpered.

He was right. They didn't find anything in his apartment, not a single piece of evidence. Irritation boiled in my core all over again.

"The sixth victim. I found your name in police logs, which I later found out officers forgot to document. They stated they found you loitering near Lincoln Park. You had a hammer on you. They said you stated you were going to help a friend repair a leaky roof. Another rainy day. Tell me the true story." My body tensed.

"People can't repair roofs on rainy days?"

Hades didn't bat an eyelash and launched forward, morphing into his Underworld form with a flash of fire and ash. He raised his arms above his head and roared in Earnest's face. "Answer the questions you insolent toad!"

He was going to make this guy pee his pants and go mute before I had a chance to finish. I yanked on Hades' arm. He whipped his head over his shoulder, chest heaving as he looked down at me.

"A word?" I asked, motioning with my finger.

The wings folded behind his back, and he followed me to the corner.

"You've been torturing him for how many years now? I think all you need to do is glare or pretend you're going to swat him to get him to cooperate."

"You said," he pointed at me. "I was bad cop."

"Yes. Bad cop. Not terrifying cop. He has to be able to speak."

Hades blinked. "I think you underestimate my level of intimidation."

"I'm almost done. Can you keep it to a bare minimum? Please?"

The corners of his jaw popped. "As you wish." He stepped aside, displaying his hand toward a fidgeting Earnest.

I cleared my throat and flattened my dress. After clasping my hands in front of me to assure Earnest I intended to do nothing with them, I lowered my voice to barely above a whisper. "Earnest?"

His bottom lip trembled, and he stared at me wide-eyed.

"A few more questions and we're done. Good?"

He nodded, not blinking.

"The last victim is where things got especially confusing. The cops found the victim with a hammer near the body. They went to your house from prior suspicions. Your arm was bandaged up."

Earnest shifted in his seat, digging his heels into the ground as if he were trying to back away.

"The suspect's blood more than likely got washed away from the rain, but that particular victim fought back more than the others, didn't he?"

"He damn near broke my arm," he mumbled.

Confirmation. My heartbeat quickened.

"Did you use a hammer?" I asked, biting down on my lip.

"Yes."

"The hammer inexplicably disappeared from the evidence locker. Did you have something to do with that?"

"I had someone on the inside."

My throat constricted. "Who?"

"Never got his real name. Called himself Bulldog. But he was a cop. I can tell you that much."

And another can of worms opened. I'd file that one for later.

"Where's the hammer now?"

He smirked. "Oh, you have no shot at finding it. Threw it into Lake Michigan."

Tears stung at my sinuses. Here I was interviewing a dead murderer, and even getting all the answers out of him led nowhere.

"Give me *something*, Earnest. There has to be something, anything that could tie you to these murders. To prove it." I lurched forward, pointing a finger in his face. "You owe the families that much."

"You know, when I was a kid, my mom used to take me to Lincoln Park Zoo every Sunday. We'd walk on the path, and I'd point at every damn animal I saw. It was a time just for us," Earnest said, gaze dropping to his feet.

I leaned back, thrown off guard. The darkness of his aura sputtered with fractals of white.

"My mom died when I was eight."

And now we had something in common.

"A burglar. She'd been taking a nap on the couch. I was downstairs playing video games. I heard a gunshot, ran upstairs, and caught sight of the guy running out of the house with our VCR. Mom's blood stained the area rug in the living room." His face contorted into pure fury, his wrists pulling at his chains. "She died over a fucking VCR."

I gulped, thinking back to the night I found out about the fire. It was unsettling, realizing our pasts were so similar. Who wanted to share a similar backstory with a serial killer?

"I'm sure they noticed all the men I killed had a similar look. I found people who reminded me of him, and beat their skulls in with a hammer because it made me feel better. But then I'd get angry soon after and have to do it again."

Hades pressed his hand into the small of my back.

Earnest studied my face and smirked. "You'll want to go to Lincoln Park. There's a huge willow tree that droops due east. At its base, buried several feet down—you'll find what you need." His shoulders hunched forward. "Do you know why I committed suicide?"

"To avoid paying for your crimes?" Hades mumbled.

Earnest stared at the floor, tears welling in his eyes. "Because I knew I was going to hell, but I wanted to be damn sure about it." His aura turned coal black.

Dizziness washed over me, and I staggered backward, grasping my head.

Hades caught me.

"Thank—" I started to say to Earnest, but he disappeared in a puff of smoke.

"We need to get you back to the surface, Stephanie."

Hades kept me standing upright and turned me to face him. I fought back the tears as he traced his fingertips over the side of my forehead.

"Both of our mothers died tragically. He wound up a serial killer. What if I have that inside of me?"

"You're not him," Hades said. He pulled me flush with his chest, wrapping his arms around me and stroking the back of my head. "People respond to tragedy in different ways. You went a different path. You sought the passion in humanity versus giving up on it altogether. One of the many reasons you're a remarkable human being."

I shoved my face into his shoulder, memorizing the scent of burning wood. "High praise from a god."

He peeled back, peering down at me. "High praise from *me*."

My eyelids grew heavy. "I've never felt this tired." Exhaustion was more like it. So much so, I started to sway.

"You need to go. Solve the case. Give those families a gift only you can bestow." He kissed my lips with such delicacy; it felt like a passing breeze. His hand grazed my shoulder, making it tingle. "I'll always be watching over you." He winced.

His words disappeared like a whisper caught by the wind. Before I could say anything else, I was back in my hotel room.

SEVENTEEN

𝄢𝄢𝄢𝄢𝄢𝄢𝄢𝄢𝄢𝄢𝄢𝄢𝄢𝄢

THE NEXT DAY WAS a blur. Sara was unusually quiet when I'd shuffled my way into the room. She'd been staring at the wall, unblinking. I tried to talk to her about what she saw. What we both saw but she'd held up a hand, silencing me. I remembered shoving clothes into my suitcase and saying final farewells to Keith and Guy because Sara insisted. The next thing I knew, I was sitting on the plane. I had no recollection of the cab ride, going through security, claiming my boarding pass, none of it. My time with Hades engraved itself into my brain. Him. The Underworld. I'd never forget any of it.

"Stephanie," Sara beckoned.

I snapped to attention, sucking air through my nostrils. She'd walked me up to my apartment after our cab ride from the airport, but I'd been standing in the middle of my living room, purse still resting on my shoulder. I trailed a hand over my arm, the bullet graze wound no longer there.

"I need you to level with me. Did I see you and two men with wings plunge into a hole yesterday?" Sara clutched the lapels of her jacket, not meeting my gaze.

I curled my arm with hers. She let me. "Yes."

Her throat gurgled and her arm pressed against my hand, pinning it to her side. "It's not possible," she whispered.

"I didn't think so either, Sara. But it is. Hades is Hades. And the other one..." I turned her to face me, shaking her arm when her gaze didn't meet mine. "Thanatos."

Tears filled her eyes, making them glisten. After a harsh swallow she forced them back, not letting one escape to roll down her cheek. "Greek gods are myths. Maybe we were drugged, I know this one that gives you halluc—"

I delicately pressed a hand over her mouth and shook my head. "No, Sara. Those hours I was gone? I was in the Underworld. Those two fought. Cerberus, yes, the three-headed dog, showed up. I almost *ate* the food."

"You would've been—" Her bottom lip quivered.

A warm smile tugged at my lips as I opened myself to her aura for the first time in years. Luscious greens floated from her shoulders like vapor. Fresh thoughts plagued her mind. It meant she believed me.

"But I'm not. Hades stopped me."

She pinched her eyes shut, slapped a hand over her forehead, and turned away. "This is absolutely crazy, Stephanie. Do you understand that?"

I blew out a harsh breath, making my bangs flap. "Me more than anyone, yes. I've been coming to grips with this for days now."

She whirled back around. "Are you and Hades—I mean… you two have gotten close."

"Nothing gets past you, detective." I tried to smile but could only manage half of one. My eyes fell to my feet, remembering how they looked against the contrast of the Styx's black sand. "I'm going to miss him," I whispered.

In two quick strides, she crossed the room and wrapped her arms around me in one of her trademark hugs. It was enough to make me melt, and I rested my head on her shoulder with a disgruntled sigh.

"He didn't say anything about meeting up with you again?"

"He can't." I slipped away, sniffling and rubbing the back of my hand over my nose.

"Why?" A scowl pulled at her face.

"It's complicated, and I really don't want to get into it. Please. We should really get some rest. Did you want to stay here tonight?"

She narrowed her eyes, studying me. The human lie detector at work. "No, I'll be fine. Surprisingly, I've seen much worse on the job than two Greek gods pulling my best friend into a hole leading to the Underworld." She clutched her tongue against her cheek. "I'll see you at work tomorrow. I'll make sure to get extra shots of espresso in our coffees. We're gonna need it." She nudged my shoulder and slipped out the door.

I spent the next ten minutes standing in the middle of my living room, unable to function like a normal human being. All things Hades aside, there was still the matter of Earnest Fueller. The reason, "it came to me in a dream," wasn't going to cut it. I'd have no choice but to get Sara involved and beg her to say the tip came from an anonymous call. She was a sworn-in officer. Her word meant gold compared to mine. Being able to look Mrs. Conroy in the face, and tell her with absolute certainty who killed her husband would hopefully ease the pain I felt. After popping a couple of Tums in my mouth, I readied myself for a restless night's sleep.

Sunrays beamed on my face, stirring me awake. With a yawn, I sat up…in the middle of a meadow. A flower meadow. A white nightgown replaced my usual sleeping attire of shorts and an Apollo's Suns tank top. My hair was down and wavy, and despite no glasses or contacts, I could see with the clarity of an elf.

"Hello, Stephanie," a female voice said, her voice sweet and buttery.

My feet glided over the blades of grass, their touch cushioning my feet like clouds. A young woman in a pale pink dress with waves of golden hair down to her knees, flowers braided within it, bent to the flowers in the middle of the meadow. She plucked a tiny white one and added it to the growing bouquet in her grasp.

As I moved closer, the lighting turned everything into a tranquil haze, making my mind mushy and relaxed. "Hello. Where am I?"

A honey-warm smile pulled over her lips as her blue eyes lifted to look at me. "Greece."

My heart raced as my brain pieced it together. "You're… Persephone."

The sight of her aura made my heart burst—radiant pinks, yellows, oranges, purples and blues. The woman wore a rainbow halo of exuberance.

"Yes. I thought it would be unsettling to appear to you in the flesh. So I chose this instead. I hope that's alright?" She moved toward me with the elegant stride of a swan and held the flowers out to me.

Considering it was a dream, I hoped my allergies were safe here and took them with a grin. "Absolutely. I can only assume what you wish to talk to me about?" A lump as coarse as charcoal formed in my throat.

"Hades. Yes." Her smile didn't fade. "I wish to tell you my side of the story in hopes it will ease your mind about him."

A nervous twitch coiled in my chest. "My mind?"

"You want to be with him but don't understand how it's possible or if you're truly capable of accepting the responsibility that goes along with it."

I raised a single brow. And I thought Sara was intuitive.

Her eyes panned to a blue bird landing on a tree branch above us. "There was a time I hated him. And there were times I loved him. But it took far too long to realize that he was all I knew."

This should've felt stranger. Standing in a dreamscape with Persephone. A goddess. The same goddess who was hurled into the Underworld. But I *wanted* to hear her—wrap myself around every word and seal it off in a secret chest buried in my brain.

"I know Hades would've moved mountains for me. And that's the part of me that kept me from completely losing my mind. He isn't cruel like the modern media try to portray. He is a man with a job thrust upon him, a dedicated man that will uphold that job to the best of his ability and he was lonely. So, so, lonely. I don't blame him and I forgave him a long time ago."

I wrapped my arms around myself, picturing the expression melting over Hades' face when Thanatos had me in his grasp.

"The Underworld changed me. Made me someone I never wanted to be and that's no one else's fault but my own because I let it happen." She held her hand out and the blue bird flew to her finger. "I know I hurt him by leaving but at the end of the day, he'll see that it was better for both of us. To bring us *both* true happiness." Using her knuckle, she caressed the bird's crest.

"Theseus?" I whispered.

Her sky-blue eyes met mine. "Yes. Even as a mortal you're capable of so much, Stephanie."

"I'm just a digital forensics examiner from the suburbs of Chicago." I shrugged and gave a half-smile.

"You were given a gift." She lifted her hand and the bird flew off. "You're able to see beings for what they truly are. What they are or are not capable of." She squeezed my shoulder. "You were meant for more than a life on Earth and I think deep down you *know* that."

"I have to ask…are you talking to me more for Hades' benefit or mine?"

A full smile spread over her lips. "Both of you. Hades doesn't think he deserves happiness after me. And you question whether you could have it with him. Keep it in your thoughts, Stephanie."

Words escaped me as I stared at the brightness glowing through every strand of her bright blonde hair.

She leaned forward and kissed my temple.

I jolted awake, slapping a hand over my chest at a loss of breath. I'd have convinced myself that it was only a dream— my subconscious playing games with me until a tiny white flower petal rested on the bed next to me and the faint scent of pollen permeated the air.

Running the petal between two fingers, Persephone's words fluttered through my mind like a slide show and I sneezed.

"Can you tell me what we're doing roaming tree after tree in Lincoln Park, please?" Sara asked, rubbing her arms over her leather jacket.

I squinted behind my glasses as I turned several times. "Which way is East again? Never." I turned. "Eat."

"Soggy Waffles? You still use that third-grade trick to figure out your directions?" Sara raised a brow.

"It's as solid of a method as any." I frowned, facing what I thought was east, but seeing no trace of a willow tree.

She grabbed my shoulders. "Or, you can use the sun." She turned me to the right, and there in the corner beckoning me like a rainbow sprinkle cupcake was the tree.

I ran over and dropped to the ground, not caring about grass stains on my knees.

"Sara, come help me," I yelled over my shoulder.

The ground was harder than I thought, and I broke a nail the moment I tried to dig.

Sara crouched down. "What are you doing, Steph?"

"This might sound crazy, but—" I adjusted my glasses. "I spoke with Earnest."

"Earnest. The dead killer?"

I nodded.

"Do I even want to ask how?"

I one-eye squinted. "Hades took me Tartarus to interrogate him."

Sara stared at me for a solid ten seconds before her head slowly began to nod. "Does this get easier?"

"To believe myths are real?"

"Sure."

"Yes."

After sighing, she looked around the park, which was conveniently far less crowded than it usually was. "If you knew you were going to dig a hole, why didn't you bring a shovel, you silly goose?"

"Wouldn't it look a bit suspicious walking through Lincoln Park with a shovel?"

She shrugged. "If anyone asked, I'd have said we were planting a tree."

"It annoys me at times how much sense you tend to make at every turn."

"We'll improvise. Here." She handed me a flattened rock.

We both went to work, slamming our rocks in the ground and breaking off bits of hardened dirt little by little. Every few thwacks, Sara would lift her head, making sure no one was watching us. A corner of a bag sprung out. The once clear plastic had turned cloudy from the years spent underground. I reached forward, and Sara slapped my hand. She dug into her pocket and handed me a rubber glove.

"Do you always have rubber gloves on you?" I slipped it on with a snap.

"Of course, I do."

I held the bag up, and it unrolled. Inside was a stained hammer. "That son-of-a-bitch lied," I whispered.

Sara leaned around the bag, staring at me. "Does that surprise you?"

"It shouldn't. It really shouldn't. I can count on one hand the number of people I've seen with nothing but darkness clouding them. It's hard to believe some human beings aren't capable of being saved."

Earnest lied even after Hades upped his torture sentence. Being one of the world's most putrid worms was ingrained into his very soul.

She narrowed her eyes but then cocked her head to the side, examining the bag. She removed another glove, slipped it on, and yanked the bag out of my hand. "This is one of our evidence bags. How did he get it out of the locker?"

"He mentioned a cop helping him." I bit my lip, eyeing her sidelong.

She handed it back to me, glaring at the ground. "Now I need to figure out who."

"That was years ago. They might not even work there anymore. If they were smart, they would've quit after the trial." I rolled the bag back up and filled the hole.

She dusted off her hands. "If they were smart, they wouldn't have ever knowingly assisted a serial killer. Which leads me to believe they still work for us."

"Sara, I know you've done a ton of favors for me lately, but I need to ask for one more."

Sara gently took the bag from my hands. "I received an anonymous tip on where to find evidence proving Fueller's guilt."

There were times I questioned whether I deserved such a profound friendship. Sisterhood.

"I know it's lying, but—" My brow creased.

She shook her head and interrupted me with, "Come on, let's get it back to the station before someone sees us."

When Sara announced the anonymous call to the department, most of the troopers hadn't believed her. Until they took a look at the evidence bag and realized it was an older version they no longer used. They questioned several times why someone was only coming forward now with the information. Slick Sara shrugged and told them fear could make people do all sorts of things. A trial was set for a month later to close the case for good.

Sara was on the stand to testify her finding the hammer and presenting the DNA lab results. I curled my hands in my lap after swallowing a Tums, waiting for the judge to start his questioning.

"For the record, Detective Hickman can you state your

involvement in the Fueller case?" The judge asked, his squared reading glasses resting on the tip of his nose as he shuffled papers.

The witness stand. A necessary evil in my profession. I'd always hated it, but Sara was a natural with it.

"I was the lead detective," Sara answered.

"How did you come across the murder weapon as evidence in the Fueller case?" He tapped a pen against his gavel.

"I received an anonymous phone call. The voice was distorted, but they were explicitly clear of the location under the willow tree in Lincoln Park." Her eyes surveyed the few people in the courtroom—me, Mrs. Conroy, a few of the troopers from the department, and several others.

"They stated they'd seen Fueller bury it there, but feared connections to Fueller might have come after them or their family."

The judge nodded slowly, scribbling something down on a piece of paper in front of him.

The room was silent as the grave. Images of Earnest's snarky face as he told me the hammer was at the bottom of Lake Michigan poked at me. I held my breath.

The judge rubbed his hands together. Mrs. Conroy was in the first row, tears rolling down her cheeks. She clasped her hands together in silent prayer.

"Given the evidence presented to me today and Earnest Fueller's DNA found on said evidence, I find the defendant guilty. If he were alive, I'd have sentenced him to two life sentences in prison. I'm sure wherever he is, he's receiving a far worse punishment. Case closed." The sound of wood hitting against wood vibrated in my nears as he brought the gavel down.

If the judge only knew how right he was.

I pinched my eyes shut, relief washing over me. Mrs. Conroy leaped from her seat, bawling her eyes out. Once Sara stepped down from the stand, she ran over to her and hugged her so tightly it made Sara blow out a breath.

"Thank you so much, Sara. You have no idea how amazing it is to feel this sense of closure," Mrs. Conroy said through several sniffles.

"Thank the anonymous tipper." Sara gave me a knowing smile over Mrs. Conroy's shoulder.

Mrs. Conroy wiped the tears from her cheeks and turned around to see me. She wailed again and wrapped her arms around me.

"Thank you so much for your help, Miss Costas." She squeezed my shoulders and ran out of the courtroom.

If only I could thank Hades. He was the only reason any of this was possible. I sighed, slipping my hands into the pockets of my dress.

"We just won a cold case. Why do you look like someone pissed in your Cheerios?" Sara asked.

"No reason. I mean now, what am I going to obsess over, right?" I grinned.

She draped an arm over my shoulders. "We're celebrating at your place tonight. I'll bring champagne. Got some more news too."

"Oh?"

She nodded with a huge smile. "I'll tell you tonight."

Later that night, I curled up on the couch with Sammy, stroking his fur. When a knock sounded on the door, I was relieved to have a distraction from my thoughts.

Thoughts about you know who.

I whipped open the door. "Thank God, you're here." She held two giant bottles of champagne, and I snatched one.

"Wow. Miss me that much, huh?" She smirked and closed the door behind her with a bump of her hip.

"Always," I said, resting two flute glasses on the countertop.

Sammy jumped up, curling himself around the champagne bottle. Sara hissed at him. He gave her a disapproving stare before walking off with a flick of his tail. She took out her cell phone, scanning her thumb over the screen. I held the bottle away from me, turned my head, held my breath, and pulled on the cork. *Pop*. Fizzy alcohol sprouted from the bottle, and I squealed, holding it over the sink.

"So, are you going to tell me what else we're celebrating tonight?" I asked, pouring us two glasses.

She grabbed one and rested her phone on the counter. "I found our sneaky cop accomplice."

"Seriously? Who was it?"

"Leonardo Michaels." She shook her head.

I blinked. Leo, the creep-o. "Why doesn't that surprise me?"

"Because he's a sleazeball who's going to get what he deserves. You should've seen his face when we arrested him. I thought he was going to bawl."

"Wait. Why Leo? I know he's a perv but that doesn't explain why he'd knowingly assist a criminal. Especially a murderer."

"Valid question. I looked into all connections to Fueller and cross-referenced them with past *and* current employees. It turns out, Fueller and Leo lived in the same neighborhood as kids. Fueller served a year in juvie for a grand theft auto conviction."

"Was Leo involved too?"

"Yup. Charged, but Fueller confessed to doing it himself, and Leo tried to stop him, which is the only reason he was there."

I narrowed my eyes. "But we both know he lied for Fueller."

"Exactly. So, when Fueller approached him about the hammer, I think Leo felt he owed him. And when I asked why he didn't quit and leave town, know what he said?"

I raised my brow.

"He thought it'd have looked too obvious." Sara smirked. "I'll tell you this much, if it weren't for me being an officer of the law, I'd have kneed him straight in the balls."

"Should've let me tag along, then." I pointed to myself. "Civilian."

Sara laughed and held up her glass for a toast.

"To the Fueller case," I said.

"And here's to hopeful promotions for both of us." She tapped her phone and *Push It* played.

Without bothering to set our glasses down, we danced in my kitchen. As the night wore on, we drank both bottles, danced to our song a total of thirteen times, and I didn't think about three-headed dogs, floating smoke, or the King of Ash and Bone. It wasn't until I went to bed with a fuzzy head from copious amounts of alcohol that my mind betrayed me. I had feelings for Hades, feelings I never had the chance to voice to him. The way he looked at me, he had to feel something for me too. Lust? Admiration? Mrs. Conroy wasn't the only one who needed closure.

EIGHTEEN

I WANTED TO SEE Hades in the Underworld. We deserved a proper goodbye. I refused to let things end the way they had. Hades said the only way to the Underworld was either by him or death. Thanatos himself was death. It was worth a shot. I found an empty area in Lincoln Park far enough from prying eyes.

After taking a deep breath, I clenched my fists at my sides. "Thanatos?"

The wind rustled through the trees. Fall had come and gone, and the once vibrant leaves colored orange and yellow were turning brown and snapping away from the branches. I wasn't sure how one communicated with a Greek god, not to mention one who only showed up when it was time to meet your demise.

"Thanatos, please. I need your help," I implored, turning circles, my feet brushing against the grass.

In a burst of smoky red fog, he appeared, his head held low. The hood of the cloak draped over his eyes. "I do not normally appear simply because someone calls out my name."

My hands wrung together behind my back. "I should feel so lucky then."

"Can I help you with something, Stephanie?"

"I need you to take me to the Underworld."

The hood of the cloak lifted. "That's a tall order. Why did you not ask its King?"

"He has my best interests at heart. He wouldn't want to bring me back."

He cocked his faceless head to the side. "You want to say goodbye."

Tears welled in my eyes. "Yes. Our last meeting was—cut short."

"Tell me one thing." He slipped the hood from his head, revealing the same face I'd seen in the Underworld. "What do you see?"

A gooey smile pulled over my lips. I cupped his cheek, not taken aback by the feel of cold death on his skin this time. "You, Thanatos. I see you."

His lips parted. "Not a skeleton?"

"Not a skeleton, or half-decaying head, no. I see the eerily handsome face of Death."

"So, it *is* possible." His eyes darted back and forth as his gaze dropped to his feet.

"It is. And now you realize why I need to see him again. Even if it's the last time." I choked back tears.

The red fog swirled under his feet. "You realize no *living* mortal can remain there? Only immortals? Gods?"

Only immortals. Was it possible for a mortal to become immortal?

"Yes. And I know Hades won't let me stay long enough for it to hurt me."

"Then I'm pleased to escort you." He flung his robe around me in a foggy flourish, and we stood on the banks of the river Styx.

An empty boat waited and Thanatos held out his hand. After positioning my hair over my ears, I climbed in. He waved his hand, and the boat floated downstream.

"Are you not ferrying me?" I remembered the countless lost souls attempting to climb on board. The thought made my skin crawl.

"This is between you and Hades. I must return to my duties." He disappeared in a puff of smoke.

I opened my mouth and snapped it shut before shuffling to the center of the boat. The water was dark, bleak, and not overrun with souls like before. Occasionally, one would appear on the surface like a gray mirage. It hadn't taken Hades long to catch up with his job. I wrapped my arms around myself, going over the first words I intended to say to him.

It would depend on his reaction. If everything went the way it did in my deepest fantasy, he'd greet me with the one thing I never got to see on him—a genuine smile. Then he'd wrap his arms around me in a warm embrace, make us float using his ember wings, and we'd make love on his throne. I scrunched my nose. Maybe not the throne. The river flowed right past it. There'd be too many witnesses.

As the boat grew closer and closer to the throne room, my heart rate skyrocketed. What if it was a bad idea? He could chastise me for foolishly coming back and send me right back to the surface. I dragged a hand over my face with a groan. The boat turned the corner, the familiar pillars of Hades' throne room blazing into view.

My breath hitched. There Hades was in his true form, seated in a slump on his throne. One leg was draped over an armrest, his long white hair partially falling over his face. A crown of floating flames circled his head, and he had a scowl that could've made Cerberus whimper away. I wrung my hands together as the boat drifted to the bank. Hades' head lifted, and the frown melted away, replaced by surprise.

He stood and squinted. "Stephanie?"

"The one and only." I stepped out of the boat, the black sand shifting beneath my shoes. "Well, not the only Stephanie in existence but the only—" I cut myself short when I noticed the scowl was back on his face.

"What are you doing here?" He snarled, still standing in front of his throne. His face softened, and his eyes bulged. "No. You're not—" He stormed forward and grabbed one of my shoulders. He stared at me, shaking his head. "Your soul is still intact. How did you get down here?"

I looked up at him, taking a moment to stare at how ethereal he looked. His fiery crown flickered, his hair floating around him like a wispy frame. "Thanatos."

"How?" He dropped his hand.

I shifted my eyes. "I…asked."

"And he brought you here?" His brow furrowed.

"Uncharacteristic of him."

"You know, I didn't expect you to run up to me and whisk me off my feet at the sight of me or anything, but I thought you'd at least be happy?"

"I'm elated to see you." His tone took on a whole new form of gruffness.

"Really? Because normally frowns, growls, and standing there like a statue suggests quite the opposite." I slid an inch forward.

His hands relaxed at his sides. "I'm still trying to make sense of a mortal woman purposely making her way into the Underworld."

"It doesn't take much thought, Hades." I continued with cautious steps until we stood toe-to-toe.

He cocked a brow.

"You." I raised to the balls of my feet, craning my neck back. "I came for you." I planted my lips against his. My eyelashes fluttered, waiting for him to reciprocate.

His arms slid around my waist, and he kissed me. It started tender but soon turned ravenous. Deep. Like the weeks we spent apart compared to living without a part of your soul. The taste of fire and ash exploded in my mouth. I missed it. I missed him. He pulled away, staggering backward. I stood there, blinking and tracing a finger over my lonely lips.

"This isn't fair to you." His words were pain-stricken. He growled and cast a hand through the flames of his crown, making it disappear.

"Fair for me? Don't I get to have a say?" My chest heaved.

"You can't stay here. What kind of man would I be if I

were to bed you, only to send you back to the surface straight after?" His rigid stance overtook him again.

I sighed. "I knew full well before I decided to see you that I couldn't stay here. But I wanted that one final chance to be with you." I interlaced our fingers. "I've never felt this way about anyone."

He lifted our hands and ran his thumb over my knuckle. "Neither have I."

He cocked his head to the side, running one of his hands through my hair. He pulled me to him, wrapping his arms around me. I pressed my ear to his chest and closed my eyes. When I opened them, we stood in the middle of a vast room.

There were Victorian gothic-styled bookshelves, a round table with half-melted black candles, dressers, and lounge chairs in each corner. Darkened ionic columns bordered the bookshelves, leading into ornate designs carved in mahogany, traveling to the ceiling. A large, unlit fireplace framed by Corinthian columns settled against the back wall. The mantle had spires like medieval castles.

It was a room fit for a king.

He walked past me and threw his hand toward the fireplace. It roared to life in a blaze of blue, morphing into orange and white flickers. "Did you find the evidence you needed for your case?" He continued to stalk around me, like a wildcat on the hunt.

In the center was a bed that could fit my entire apartment with black sheets, black marble headboard with meander scrollwork, and an equally as dark frame. Cranberry-colored and black silk pillows rested at the head. A cranberry curtain draped on the wall above it.

A lump formed in my throat. "Yes."

He wriggled his fingers at the table with lit candles. The lighted intensity dimmed until the room felt eerie yet inviting. "Was he found guilty?"

"Yes." Every breath escaping my nostrils and pulling into my lungs made me acutely aware of what was about to happen.

He crossed the room, his glowing white eyes brightening from the darkness. "And, are you absolutely certain you wish to lay with me, knowing what I am and that I'm incapable of giving you what a mortal man could?" His long white hair floated around him, and he peered down at me, patiently waiting for my answer.

A relationship. The god of the Underworld being someone's boyfriend? It sounded absurd. Was I crazy for doing this? Probably. But I didn't care. My heart punched against my ribcage. "Yes."

He morphed into the Sawyer look-a-like I met at the resort and dipped his mouth to mine.

I pushed a hand against his chest. "No."

He leaned back, raising an eyebrow. His lips thinned.

"I want the *real* you." My heart raced so fiercely it felt like a caged bird yearning to free itself.

A tiny smile tugged at his lips. "As long as I've been alive and yet I can still somehow be surprised." He nodded and transformed into the god of the Underworld.

My eyes fell on the points of his ears sticking out from his hair. I traced a finger over one. He closed his eyes before sliding his lips over mine. He cradled the back of my head, kissing with such fervor it bent me backward. His other hand curled around my lower back, supporting me. I reached my hands into the folds of his robes, but only managed to get lost in the never-ending fabric. He took my hands into his and leaned back.

The robe began to disintegrate into embers, floating away like flying pieces of burning paper. He stood naked and motionless. His mortal guise looked like a Greek statue, but somehow his godly form was even more muscular, hard, and toned. The fire-lit room created the perfect shadows over his muscles. Each stood out as if carved from marble.

I clutched my shirt, bunching it at my neck. We'd been naked in front of each other at the spa, but this was different. So very different. I was about to give myself to him completely. It was the epitome of vulnerable.

"If only I had the power to read your mind." He took a tentative step forward, the muscles in his legs flexing.

Suppressing a whimper, I turned my back to him.

His hand cupped my elbow, and the other shifted the hair from my neck. He lowered his nose to my nape, his breath prickling my skin. "Stephanie, we don't have to do this."

He'd seen the back of me already, and the newfound confidence within me returned with one touch from him. I slid my hands underneath my shirt and peeled it away. Once I stood in my bra and pants, I turned to face him. He clasped the back of my neck and kissed me so deeply I felt weightless. I had to open one eye to be sure we weren't floating on smoke again. He pulled away only to trail his lips across my chin and peck his way to my neck. His tongue lapped against my skin as he kissed it, finishing with a light nip.

We locked gazes as I undid the clasp of my bra. His knuckles grazed my shoulders as he slipped one strap down, followed by the other. It fell to the floor, and my chest swelled, watching his lips curl into a grin.

He pulled me against him, dragging his knuckles down the side of my face. "You are, without a doubt, the most beautiful mortal I've ever seen." He trailed his fingers across my pants, making them crumble into embers.

I nibbled my lip. "I'm going to need those."

"Later," he whispered.

He backed me to the bed until I felt my calves hit up against the coolness of the frame. It was so high off the ground I'd have to take a running leap to get on it. He curled a hand around each of my hips and hoisted me up. The soft comforter soothed against my skin once he laid me down. I rested my head on one of the many cranberry throw pillows, and he stared down at me, letting my hair fall through his fingertips.

"Pomegranate. Definitely your color," he said, his eyes ablaze.

His lips pressed against the valley between my breasts, and I gasped. The fog floated over my hair, traveling across my chest and hovering over my stomach. He took one breast into his mouth and circled his tongue around my nipple. The tingling sensation from the fog mixed with his mouth was damn near enough to drive me insane.

My back arched as he pulled his mouth away, grazing my breast with his wolf-like teeth. His nose dragged over my ribs, making his way further down my body. As he traced the tip of his tongue over my abdomen, I forgot entirely about who and what he was. It wasn't until his fingertips brushed the insides of my knees, coaxing them apart, I became lost in his glowing white eyes.

I'd been with other men before. Seen the carnal look in their eyes, knowing what they were about to receive. His gaze was different. Predatory, yet anticipatory. Like eyeing baked goods behind the glass, wishing you could devour each one. I opened myself to him, and he lowered his hips. The white hair floated as he peered down at me. I traced my hands over his shoulder blades, expecting to feel slits where his wings sprouted. It'd be surreal to see them in a moment like this.

A masculine purr vibrated from his throat. "You want to see my wings again, don't you?"

"I thought you couldn't read minds." I played a wicked grin, one to rival his own.

"I don't have to." He lowered himself further. His hardness pressed against me, and it made every muscle in my lower half clench. "You've played with their sheath repeatedly."

My hands ran absent circles over his shoulder blades in an unspoken plea to see them come out to play.

"I rather like you've such a fascination with them," he said.

The wings peeled out from his back, their span nearly the entire width of the bed until he folded them back. Smoke tendrils wafted through the air. Sparkling orange embers fell, and ash trickled over my skin before disappearing.

"Will it burn me if I touch them?" I lingered my fingers over the glowing orange feathers.

"Only if I wanted it to."

I smoothed my hand over the fiery arch on his left wing. He groaned, his length pushing harder against me. They felt like any other feather I'd touched. But these were composed mostly of fire and smoke. His lips crashed against mine, conquering me with a kiss. He pushed at my entrance, and I gasped when he thrust himself forward. He situated his forearms on each side of my head and began slow rhythmic motions. Smoke tendrils swirled around my arms, cascading over my breasts like silk. His nose brushed against my chin as he kissed my neck. The smoke intensified, playing through my hair and over my cheeks.

"Eímai dikós sou," he whispered into my hair.

The words flowed from his tongue like a rolling tide. I had no clue what he said, but the way he said it sounded like a carnal declaration. His hand dragged down my ribs and curled under my backside. While supporting himself on his other arm, his thrusts quickened. The smoke traveled over my hips and caressed my inner thighs. Between his practiced motions within me and the feel of warm silk against my skin, it was enough to send me straight over the edge.

My back arched, head pressing into the pillows. I gripped the sheets as every muscle within me tightened, and I quaked and quivered. When my eyes managed to flutter open, Hades gazed down at me. A smirk creased the corner of his lips. He sat up straight, resting on his haunches. His fingers curled around the back of my knees, and he gave one quick tug. My back slid forward until our hips met.

The smoke spiraled around him. His wings stretched wide, and he paused, peering into my very being. The fireplace crackled and popped. Seeing him surrounded by animated smoke was like being transfixed by a painting.

"Would you be offended if I said you were beautiful?" I asked.

He cocked his head to the side. "No. You'd be the first to say it."

He really was a thing of beauty. Not in the sense a woman or a flower is, but in an ethereal way. His body. That chiseled face. And the wings, as menacing as they were, still managed to take my breath away. The wings flapped, the glowing parts striking orange sparks, and he curled them behind him. He grabbed each of my hips and began that slow rhythm again. I gazed up at the perfect view of him in all his King of the Underworld glory.

I sat up, grabbing onto one of his shoulders. Matching his movements, I rolled my hips against him. He pressed his cheek against the side of my head. I traced my fingers over the bits of black feathers in his wings that weren't on fire or singed. He moaned. With our chests pressed together, the sound vibrated against me. He peeled back, blue flickers of flame igniting in his eyes. He pushed into me, and my head flew back with a gasp.

I gripped onto his arms as his hips bucked, picking up momentum. When the glorious ache pooled between my hips, I grabbed the back of his neck. My insides erupted, and this time I couldn't hold back my cry of pleasure.

As I came down from my climax, he brushed his nose against my cheek, the wolf-teeth idly grazing my skin. "Come undone for me, Stephanie. I sense a tigress in you that's been leashed your entire life. Let me see her."

I dug my nails into the back of his head, my breaths quickening with each passing word from him.

"Let me see her, Steph. It's been far too long since my own caged jackal has wanted to play."

Steph. He called me Steph.

My eyes flew open and a roaring heat shot through me. I grabbed his shoulders and coaxed him to the bed. The wings flared out as I pressed his back against the blackened comforter and moved over top him. Wickedness flashed in his gaze as he gripped my hips, staring up at me. As I straddled him, the sight of the King of the Underworld beneath me sent a shudder through my chest.

I locked eyes with him as I lowered myself on him, letting him fill me inch by inch. As our hips met, I dragged my nails down my throat, groaning at the feel of him throbbing inside me. His pointed nails grazed my skin as an erotic snarl vibrated at the back of his throat. Rocking back and forth on him, I tangled my fingers in my hair. Embers floated from his wings, making the room look like it was lit by fireflies. His stare singed my soul as he beamed up at me. He pressed his fingers against my lower stomach and ever so slowly trailed his hand up, resting it between my breasts.

I collapsed over him, pressing my chest against his and throwing the dark tendrils of my hair over the top of is head. He wrapped an arm around my waist as I continued to roll my hips, keeping us locked together. I slid my lips over his, kissing him, wishing with every brush of my tongue to make him mine. A silent plea that I wasn't even sure could be answered.

Pulling from the kiss, I trailed butterfly kisses over his smooth chin until I reached his ear. "Take us to your throne."

His chest rumbled as he let out a subdued growl, his grip

tightening on my waist. In a flash of smoke and ash we appeared in the throne room. He sat on his throne naked with me straddling his hips. A villainous smile played over his lips as he peered up at me. I trailed my hands over the armrests, fingers grazing over blackened grooves of bones and warped designs. He lifted his hand, making shimmering wisps of fog flutter from his fingers.

False Kings by Poets of the Fall played through the cave as if there were speakers hanging from the sconces.

I bit my lower lip. The same song we'd danced to at the masquerade. "Is this our song now?" My hand took a mind of its own, unabashedly tracing over the hardened muscle of his chest, and trailing over his perfectly sculpted stomach.

"I quite like this song." He sat up, pressing a hand between my shoulder blades, and burying his face between my breasts. "But I'm anything but *false*." He took one breast into his mouth as he encouraged me to roll my hips. As he pulled away, he used his teeth to graze my nipple.

He gripped my hips with both hands and lifted me, switching our positions so I was now the one seated on the throne. His wings flared out, sending bits of ash trickling through my hair only to disappear.

"Let me worship you," he purred before sinking to his knees.

My heart raced at the sight of the King of the Underworld bowing before me and I gripped the armrests. Curling his hands behind my knees, he yanked me forward until my butt teetered on the edge of the throne. His glowing white eyes kept my gaze as he lowered his mouth to me, lapping it once, twice, before devouring me whole. My back arched and I cried out, digging my nails into the twin skulls on each end of the armrests.

His teeth grazed my folds, making me hiss and writhe in pleasure all at once. He slipped my legs over his shoulders, licking me, thrusting his tongue, showing me everything that could be mine. I curled a hand over the back of his head, forcing my eyes open to look down at the ethereal face between my legs. The glowing eyes. The pointed ears. The silken white hair. Those burning wings. I wanted *all* of it.

He pulled away and leaned over me, supporting himself on the armrests as he crashed his lips to mine. I opened my mouth to him, tasting myself on his lips. He plunged into me and my back flopped back to the bed, his frenzied thrusts following as he kissed me so deep my aura burst with radiant pink and orange.

His muscles tensed, and he groaned into my mouth. The fireplace roared, the flames lashing out like an explosion before pulling back in, his wings wrapping around us like a cocoon. I caught one of the burnt feathers on my fingertip, but it turned to ash as soon as it touched my skin.

His finger curled under my chin, lifting my gaze to his. "You *are* a tigress."

"I never knew she was in there." The heat from the fire on his wings warmed my face.

The dimple in his cheek deepened with a smirk, and his wings folded back until they disappeared completely. "I've never had anyone ask me to be *me* during the act."

Our bodies pressed together, and I let locks of his white hair fall through my fingers. "No one? Not even Per—"

"Not even her." He traced his thumb over my cheek before

laying down on his side. He rested his head on his hand, his eyes roaming over my naked satiated body. I too laid on my side, resting my head on my forearm.

"Penny for your thoughts?" I sucked on my lower lip.

He traced one of his black nails down the side of my breast, my ribs, and made lazy circles when he reached my hips. "I'd be lying if I said I wasn't still expecting to wake up tomorrow only to realize this was all a dream."

I rolled onto my stomach, making our faces inches apart. Pressing my elbows into the silken sheets of the bed, I tilted my chin up and kissed him. "Did you feel that?"

His eyelashes fluttered against mine. "Yes."

"Not a dream." I smiled against his lips.

"I'm never going to forget you. Realize that. Thousands of years can pass, and I will never forget the mortal who brightened my heart." He pressed his hand to my cheek.

The taste of salt coated my lips from several tears rolling down my cheeks. I pressed my hand over his. "I could never forget you."

He glanced over his shoulder and kissed my forehead before slipping from the bed. His naked form moved across the room with grace, and I cocked my head from side to side, admiring his perfect backside. He halfway grinned at me and the wings shot out. I traced my finger between my breasts, aching for him all over again.

"That has to be one of the sexiest things I've ever seen," I stammered.

He chuckled. Deep and gravelly. He removed a black box from one of the bookshelves and walked back over, the wings disappearing again. He sat on the edge of the bed and opened the box. Removing a necklace from it, he held it up to the light blazing from the fireplace.

"I want you to have this." He rested it on my palm.

It was a shiny black charm with a serpent wrapped around a cypress tree.

"It's beautiful." I ran my thumb over the branches' detailed grooves.

"May I?" He motioned at the chain.

I nodded, turned my back to him, and lifted my hair from my neck. His fingertips grazed my shoulders as he positioned the necklace and secured its clasp.

"I may not be able to be on the surface, but it doesn't mean we can't at least talk from time to time."

I let my hair fall and looked down at the charm before whipping around to face him. "Are you saying what I think you're saying?"

"You can call on me through the charm. But please don't use it as a paging service." He smirked.

"Paging?" I laughed. "I haven't heard anyone use that word in—no, scratch that. I've only heard it in movies." I felt dizzy, and my eyes fell shut for a moment before I forced them back open.

He frowned. "I need to take you back."

"I know." A deep sigh escaped my lungs.

He touched a fingertip on the charm. "I can't make promises of when, but I *will* be on the surface again."

"I'm unsure which is worse...never seeing you again, or living with the hope I will, but never knowing *when*."

"I hate putting that burden on you." He stood up with a sigh and waved his hands over his body, his gothic, kingly robes, draping over his form.

"It's not a burden. I'm glad I came here, Hades."

He offered a weak grin and splayed his hand over my body. My clothes materialized, and I frowned before sliding off the bed.

"I have to admit, dressing and undressing was not a power I thought the god of the Underworld would possess."

"I'm glad to hear you, too, can be surprised." He slipped his hand into mine and raised his other hand to the ceiling.

I grabbed his forearm, stopping him. "Before I go, can I ask you something?"

"Anything." He lowered his arm.

"Where in the world did you come up with the name Cerberus?" Random. Even for me. But I'd been dying to know.

He rubbed his chin. "Truth be told, it wasn't his original name. Initially, I named him Spot."

I did a slow blink. "Spot?"

"Yes. He has this white spot on the back of his left leg. Sticks out profusely, considering the rest of him is black."

"How in the world did it end up as Cerberus in all the stories?"

"Translations throughout the ages. One being Kerberos, which means spotted."

"Huh. You learn something every day."

"You're stalling, Stephanie." His face softened, and his lip twitched.

"I know," I said with a sigh.

He waved his hand. A portal opened, revealing the green grass and maple trees in a park near my apartment building. I winced and tightened my grip on his hand.

"This isn't goodbye," he said, his tone solemn.

"It could be a decade before I see you again."

He pulled me to him, wrapping his arms around my shoulders. "I wish I could answer you, but know I appreciate all the time you've given me."

My sinuses stung. I kissed him on the cheek before taking a step back. "I'm ready."

Only I wasn't ready. I wanted to be with him. Cure his loneliness. Who would have the power to make mortals into gods? Instinct told me my answer, but I didn't want to believe it.

His brow furrowed, and he nodded before swirling his arm. I appeared in the park, and the Underworld was but a fleeting memory.

NINETEEN

"STEPHANIE," SARA SAID WITH a clipped tone.

I jolted in my chair, smacking my hand into my glasses and making them crooked on my nose. "What?"

"You've been staring out the window. Did you hear anything I said?" She tapped her fingers against her paper coffee cup.

We were on our weekly Sunday morning caffeine date. A month had passed since I was with Hades. I'd tried calling him through the charm, but it didn't work. Ironically, I was somewhat glad for it. Part of me felt like if I heard his voice, it'd make everything that much more difficult. It was bad enough I couldn't talk to anyone about it.

"I didn't." I frowned. "I'm sorry. Repeat it." After jostling on my seat, I leaned forward and clasped my hands around my cup. "I'm all ears."

She narrowed her eyes. "Talk to me, Costas."

I leaned back and played with the charm on my necklace.

"You wouldn't understand."

"Try me." She crossed her arms.

"What if I told you—" I shifted my eyes. "I was considering...
being with Hades? I mean that is—if it were possible."

"You mean—" She leaned forward and I mimicked her.
"Become Queen of the Underworld?" She whispered.

When she put it that way...

"Yes," I squeaked.

"And you'd be married to Hades. A royal godly couple."

"Uh-huh," I whimpered.

"He tells souls where they're to spend their eternal afterlife?
Torture's souls in Tartarus? You're willing to sign up for that?"

"Yes. All of it."

"That's a lot to take in, Steph." She sulked in her chair,
flicking her thumb on the rim of her cup.

"He has wings." I stared out the window, imagining him
floating outside. "But they're not wing wings. They're fiery
and morph into smoke and embers and—" I shut my trap
once I saw one of her eyebrows raise so high, she looked like
The Rock.

"You sound like you have your mind made up."

"This is why I couldn't talk to you about it."

"What did you expect or want me to say?"

I slapped my hand on the table. "I don't know. Call me
crazy and talk sense into me? I don't even know what it all
would entail."

"Steph, I'm your best friend. I care about your happiness.
If that means becoming a goddess and half ruling the
Underworld, well then shit woman, do it."

I opened my mouth but no words followed and I sat back.

"You're so much more yourself around him. I witnessed it firsthand. You both bring something out of each other."

"I don't know when I'll see him again." I wrapped my hand around the necklace. "All I have is this necklace. He gave it to me the last time I saw him."

"You saw him? When?"

"A month ago."

"Wow. You don't tell me everything anymore, do you?"

"I'm sorry. Telling you would've made it even harder."

She clucked her tongue against the inside of her cheek. "There has to be a way to contact him."

My grip tightened on the necklace and I avoided her eyes.

"The necklace. That's how, isn't it?"

Dammit.

"Come on. We're going to call him. You've been a lost puppy dog for long enough." She pushed to her feet.

I looked around at the filled coffee house. "Here? Now? I don't even know if it works. I tried it a couple of weeks ago, and nothing happened."

"Let's go back to your apartment then." She stood and swung her purse onto her shoulder.

I froze in my seat and shook my head like I'd forgotten how to speak.

She picked up my coffee cup and nudged me in the arm. "Come on. You miss him, right?"

I blinked. "Yes."

I felt numb the entire walk back to my apartment building. Sara leaned on the back of my sofa with such nonchalance, there was no indication we were about to summon a Greek god. Would he appear out of thin air? Would it be just his voice like Mufasa in *The Lion King*? Would it still refuse to work?

"Ready?" I asked.

Sara shook her head. "That's the fifth time you've asked. Still ready."

I closed my eyes, rubbed my fingers over the charm, and thought of him. There wasn't anything of note to indicate the necklace worked, no gust of wind or burst of light. Disappointment washed over me. Not again.

"I wasn't expecting an audience," Hades said.

My eyes flew open. He stood in front of me, but as a smokey mirage versus his physical form. I could make out his facial features, white hair, and pointed ears.

Was I the only one who could see him?

Sara's eyes bulged out of her skull, and she gripped onto the couch with both hands.

Clearly not.

"Sorry, Sara insisted—by the way, I tried to contact you weeks ago. It didn't work."

"Ah, yes. Apologies. I was in Tartarus at the time. Figured you'd rather save the conversation for…later."

I widened my eyes. "Forgiven."

"I'll be sure to keep the conversation…PG," he said, his mirage floating closer.

My cheeks warmed as my brain dipped into thoughts of our time together. His head between my legs as I sat on his throne.

"How have you been?" He asked.

"Fine. Fine. And you?"

Awkward personified.

"Lonely," he answered.

Sara appeared beside us and held up two fingers. "Can we pause a moment here? How are you—" She flailed her hand around, speechless.

"A floating smoke monster?" I sidelong grinned at Hades.

"Yes. How are you appearing as a floating smoke monster?"

"He's Hades, Sara," I replied.

He turned to face her, and she stumbled backward, knocking into the end table. "We've met before."

She shook her head. "Not like this, we haven't."

Sara had stared stone-cold killers in the face and frightened them during interrogation. Here she was scared and at a loss for words at the sight of Hades.

She bit down on her lip. "Uh, huh. Uh, huh. I'll uh—let you two have a moment alone while I go and process—" She made circling motions with her hands. "—this." She scampered off, holding her head.

"How are you really doing?" He asked.

I picked at the hem of my dress. "This is harder than I thought it'd be."

"I have a family member who can remove memories if that'd make it easier for you. You shouldn't need to suffer like this, Stephanie." He held his head low.

"No. Absolutely not. I didn't risk my life getting to the Underworld only to have the memory of it ripped away."

He nodded, the smoke of the mirage shifting around his head.

"I'll be fine, Hades. It's hard not to miss you." I gave a weak smile, a single tear rolling down my cheek.

He reached out, his palm cupping my face. "I don't deserve your tears."

"Yes, you do." I sniffled and wiped the tear away. "Let someone miss you, Hades. Truly miss you."

"You're an amazing woman. I count the days until I can return to the surface. To see you again, if you wish to see me."

"I might be an old, silver-haired, wrinkly woman by then, but if you don't stop by when you're in town, I'll never forgive you." I smiled.

"You can count on it." He floated backward. "I'm afraid I must return." He pointed at the charm around my neck. "Please don't hesitate to call on me again."

I bit the inside of my cheek to keep from crying and gave a vigorous nod. "I'll be seeing you," I managed to choke out.

His shoulders hunched forward, and then he was gone.

"Okay, okay. I think I can handle this," Sara said, power-walking into the room.

I slipped my glasses off and rubbed my eyes.

"I—" She frowned, doing several circles, searching. "Where'd he go?"

"Back to the Underworld," I mumbled.

"That's it? I step away for thirty seconds to get my shit together and you wuss out on me?"

"It's not that simple." I fished in my pocket for Tums, but only found an empty wrapper.

"Sure, it is. You say, 'Hades, I want to be with you.' See?" She flopped her hands at her sides.

"God of the Underworld." I slapped my forehead several

times. "I'm such an idiot."

Sara led me to the couch. I sat on the edge and slipped my glasses back on, staring at the paisley patterns of the area rug.

"You're not an idiot. Okay, except for that one guy during your biker phase. What was his name?"

"Snake?"

"Yes, him." She scrunched her nose. "You binge-watched *Sons of Anarchy*, and instead of finding Jax Teller you found— that guy. I'm still in shock."

I smirked and shook my head. "It lasted a week. The moment that fight broke out in the bar, and he smashed a beer bottle over someone's head, I was done."

She sighed and stroked her fingers through the waves in my hair. "How can I help you?"

"You can't. But I appreciate it. I'll be fine. Wounds heal all time, right?" I laid my head on her shoulder.

She chuckled. "Something like that."

She continued to run her fingers through my hair, and I fell asleep.

I gasped, waking up in my bed in the middle of the night in a cold sweat. Pajamas replaced my dress, glasses resting on the nightstand. I didn't remember changing my clothes, let alone crawling into bed. With a groan, I slapped my hand over my face. The universe played a cruel joke bringing a man into my life, a man who called to every fiber of my being. And I had no humanly way possible of being with him.

Human.

Thanatos said only immortals and…gods could survive the Underworld.

The back of my neck tingled, and I sat up, hyperventilating. Could it be possible? Would he accept me? Was I willing to go to those lengths?

I kicked at the blankets, tripping out of bed as I grabbed my glasses. There wasn't enough room to properly pace in my bedroom, so I headed for the living room. Sammy was curled up in his favorite cat bed, and his head shot up like a rocket. My bare feet slapped against the wooden floor as I walked back and forth, chewing my nails.

"You've done a lot of crazy things in your time, Costas, but this would surpass them all," I said to myself.

Sammy followed on my heels, making me stumble several times when he decided to do random figure eights through my legs.

"Just admit it. And stop stalling," I ordered myself.

I'd been mulling it over long enough. I knew what I needed to do to be with Hades, what I *wanted* to do. And who likely I needed to make it happen.

"Zeus," I yelled in my apartment at three o'clock in the morning. The neighbors would get over it.

Silence.

"Zeus, Zeus, Zeus," I repeated over and over like a toddler having a tantrum in a toy store.

A flash of clouds and lightning sent Sammy running and sliding across the floor, hiding behind a planter.

"What?" Zeus roared, standing in a suit, his hands balled into fists, chest pulsing. "Do you have any idea of the heated meeting I had to leave because you won't shut up?" He pointed at me and then dropped his eyes to my—attire.

I crossed my arms over my chest, covered only in a tank top with no bra. He squinted, looking around my apartment, lingering on the doorway to my bedroom.

"I like where you're going with this." A sly grin slid over his lips.

"Do you have the power to turn mortals into gods?" I sputtered.

He put his hands on his hips. "Come again?"

"Can you—" I played with the lace trim of my pajama shorts. "Turn me into a goddess?"

He squinted at me, walking forward. "Are you saying you want to be Queen of the Underworld?"

I gulped. Queen of the Underworld. Yes, yes, that's exactly what I wanted.

"Yes, but—" I started.

"That's all I needed to hear." He snapped his fingers with a malicious grin. "Done."

My heart fell to my feet. "Wait. What? What do you mean 'done'? I wanted to talk to Hades first…"

"Not my problem. I'm an impatient god who's been nothing but patient with you. Believe me." His hand clasped my shoulder, and we stood in Hades' throne room. Hades sulked on his throne and shot to his feet when he noticed us.

"Why did you bring her down here?" Hades boomed.

Zeus pinched the bridge of his nose. "For the love of me. You two are the most difficult project I've had in eons."

My throat tightened. "What are you talking about?"

Hades' wings flapped, and he floated down with a scowl. "What did you do, Zeus?"

Zeus slipped his hands in his pockets with the smugness of the Cheshire Cat. "What I do best, brother. Meddle."

Hades' hands clenched, and the embers on his wings brightened.

"When I found her, I knew she'd be the perfect distraction for you, the easiest to get down here. I put the thought of Corfu into Sara's head because I knew Hades would be there," Zeus said, narrowing his eyes.

"What?" I asked through a shaky breath.

"All it took was a little mental push to get you to talk to him, and remarkably, you did the rest. And then it was a matter of getting you to the Underworld."

My lips parted. "The chains. It was *you*."

"Smart too." Zeus smirked. "Yes. Rupert was so bent on not dying he didn't even question how magical chains appeared in his room. I cast them with magic that would only break in the hands of dear Stephanie here. Did you think you suddenly became Heracles or something?"

I wanted to crawl into a corner and cry.

"I created the perfect opportunity, but Hades sent you right back to the surface." Zeus shook his head. "You've changed, bro. You've changed."

Hades growled, the embers on his wings glowing even brighter.

"Watch it. Or I'll fry those wings so profusely you'll only have two stubs on your back," Zeus said with a snarl.

Everything that happened with Hades was a…lie?

"And then Stephanie called for Thanatos. I couldn't have planned that any better myself, honestly."

"Oh, my God." I slapped a hand over my face.

"Hades had you again. Even jumped in the sack with you, and yet, he still sent you back. Remarkable. You two weren't supposed to fall in love or anything. Quite frankly, I find it disgusting. Who do I look like? Eros?" He shuddered.

I sighed with relief. What I felt for Hades *was* real. At least I had that much despite Zeus' crazy involvement.

"Anyway, you should thank me. You've got your Queen. A willing queen. And she is the only being who has ever existed that can see the *real* you, brother." Zeus narrowed his eyes at Hades. "You're welcome."

"You should've let us decide this, Zeus. It wasn't your place to interfere." Hades' hands shook at his sides.

"Oh, please. You would've let her die as a mortal before asking her. Do you think I'm an idiot? You didn't want the Persephone situation happening all over again."

The corners of Hades' jaw tightened as he glowered at Zeus.

Zeus snapped his fingers. "Here. You'll need to give her this. Can't be Queen of the Underworld for an eternity as a mortal, can she?" Zeus plopped something orange and glowing into Hades' limp hand. "Do whatever you want for her coronation. I got to bolt."

Hades clenched his hand around it so tightly it shook.

Zeus played with the gold pinky ring on his right hand. "By the way, the word in the clouds is that you did Dirty Dancing, brother. Is that true?"

Hades glared. "I thought you were in a hurry," he growled.

"We'll circle back to it," he winked with a grin and disappeared in a flash of blinding white light.

Hades blew out a breath. "Stephanie, I'll talk to him. Get him to reverse this. He can do it. He's just an arrogant prick. He tricked you, he—"

The skin between my eyes wrinkled, and I placed a hand on his forearm. "Hades, he didn't trick me."

He squinted. "What?"

"It caught me off guard happening so quickly because I wanted to talk to you first, to say my goodbyes to Sara, but I *chose* this. Me." I pointed at my chest.

"Really?" His eyes quivered like he was about to cry.

I nodded.

"I…don't know what to say." His gaze dropped to his feet.

I slipped a finger under his chin and met his eyes. "You don't have to say anything, but I'd love to see a smile."

His lips curled back, revealing his pointed teeth and a wide grin spread across his face. The pastel colors of his aura burst through the darkness. A single shimmering tear rolled down his cheek. He pressed his hands on each side of my face and kissed me. Salt from our tears mixed with the taste of smoke and ash.

He peeled away, keeping his hands on my chin. "I'm going to spend the rest of eternity showing you how much I appreciate this, but you need to go back to the surface first. You should've had the chance to say goodbye."

"I can go back? I thought we had to stay here?"

"We do. Zeus seems rather preoccupied at the moment. If he catches wind of where you are, I'll distract him to give you time. You'll have to be quick about it."

My heart thudded against my chest. I cried and wrapped my arms around his neck. "Thank you," I whispered into his ear.

He blew out a breath into my hair. "You do not need to thank me."

"I know you gave it to me as a gift." I stepped back, wiping my tears away, and clutching the charm necklace in my hand. "But, would you mind if I gave this to Sara? So, I can still talk to her?"

He grinned again. His wings were beautiful, but it didn't compare to the brightness of his smile. "That's a great idea. Yes. By all means." He brushed my cheek with his knuckle. "We don't need it anymore."

I beamed up at him.

He waved his hand, producing a portal.

"How do I get back?"

"Simply think about the Underworld and a way will present itself. Make sure you're in an isolated area."

I started to back away.

"Go and say your goodbyes, Stephanie. When you come back, I'll give you the ceremony you deserve."

"I'll be quick. Say my goodbyes and return to you." I smiled.

He grinned back. "Return to you. Those are probably the three most precious words I've ever heard."

"More than the words—I love you?"

He stepped forward, his wings peeking out. "Are you saying you love me?"

"Hades, I wouldn't have done this if I didn't."

He smiled and yanked me forward, kissing me. "I love you too," he responded in a whisper. "Truly."

Was it possible for your heart to grow so large it sprung from your ribcage?

"Go," he said. "I'll be waiting for you."

The portal swallowed me up, and I appeared back in my apartment.

TWENTY

IT WAS STRANGE HOW familiar surroundings now felt foreign. Sammy scampered over, meowing and flicking his tail. Sammy. What was I going to do about him? I picked him up and nuzzled my nose into his fur. Cradling him in the crook of my arm, I grabbed my phone from the nightstand and dialed Sara.

"Stephanie?" Her voice answered in a panic.

A lump formed in my throat. "Hey, Sara. Can you come over? Like, now?"

"Sure, but is everything okay?"

"Yeah, but I'd rather tell you what I need to tell you in person."

"Since when did you get cryptic?"

I pinched my eyes shut. "Please, Sara."

"Be there soon."

I took a tour of my apartment, putting it to memory. What

a stark contrast it was to a kingdom under the ground. A knock sounded at the door, and Sara barged in as soon as I opened it.

"What the hell is going on, Steph?" Dark circles were under her eyes. It looked like she hadn't slept.

I set Sammy on the floor and smoothed out my dress as I stood up. "I'm marrying Hades."

"I want to make sure I heard you right. You're officially doing this with Hades? God of the Underworld?"

"You heard right."

"I encouraged this but now that it's real, I don't know what to say."

"I love him. From the moment we met at the resort, I had this feeling. I can't explain it." I stood still when she started to pace the length of my living room.

"You're going to be a Queen, Steph."

"Yeah, I'm still trying to wrap my head around that part."

She furrowed her brow. "Don't you have to be immortal?"

Whatever Zeus gave to Hades.

I traced my nails down my throat. "Yes."

"You'd never die." Sara's voice went small and distant.

I couldn't look at her and panned my gaze to my feet.

She crossed the room and grabbed my chin, forcing my eyes up. "Don't do that. I don't fear death. Never have. Never will. This should be a happy moment for you, Stephanie. Not a sad one. So, don't get all mopey on me because of me."

I forced back tears. "I can't stay here. Being up here now is defying Zeus."

"Wait. You said you were *going* to be Queen. You're making

it sound like you already are."

I clenched my jaw. "Zeus kind of jumped the gun. I only wanted to ask him if he *could* do it. He took my 'yes' as a concrete answer and literally snapped his fingers. I planned to talk to you first and Hades. Everything's happened so fast."

"And you can never come back?"

"I don't know."

She started to cry, which was a rarity for Sara, and it tugged at my heart.

Removing the necklace, I held it out her. "We can still talk. Whenever we want or need to."

She took it with a sniffle and slipped it over her head.

I fought back the waterworks, not knowing what else to say.

"He cares about you. A lot. It was written all over his face. His actions," she said with a weak smile.

"He does." I hugged her.

She wrapped her arms around me. "I'm happy for you. So, so, happy. You deserve it all."

Tears burst out.

"If you *can* ever come back, you better find me." She peeled back and shoved a finger in my face. "Promise me."

"You know, I will."

She stared at me, her bottom lip trembling before she hugged me again. "God of the Underworld or not, if he hurts you, I will figure out a way to smoke his ass."

I laughed. "Listen, I know you hate cats, but would you please take Sammy?"

Sara narrowed her eyes, looking down at the furball strutting between the two of us. "Fine."

"Thank you. It makes me feel better knowing he'll be with someone he's familiar with." I glanced at the time. "I need to go."

"Already? Is there some midnight clause or something?"

"I have no idea, but I also know that Zeus can be a real ass when he wants to be." I hugged her again, sighing.

She shoved her face into my shoulder. Given our height differences, she had to bend halfway from the waist. "I can't believe this is happening."

Who was she telling? "Trust me. I'm waiting for the morning I wake up next to Hades and have the worst case of impostor syndrome known to man."

She nodded and crossed her arms. "You better get out of here before I hogtie you to the banister."

"Call me on that thing whenever you want. Except if you're in the bathroom. That could be awkward." I grinned.

She laughed. "Go on. Get." She jutted her head, her eyes glistening with tears.

After giving Sammy one last scratch of his head, I slipped out the door before Sara held me to her word. Making up lies to my landlord and job came easier than they ever had. I was ready to walk the only path that didn't make me hesitate—a road that led to Hades, a Queendom, and a place to put my power to good use.

My boss at the state police teared up a little. I couldn't be sure if it were because he genuinely would miss me or miss one of the best civilian examiners they've had. His words. Not mine. A part of me would miss working cases, but considering where I'd be for the rest of my life, there'd be no shortage of mystery. I got to leave with the knowledge of knowing Earnest Fueller after years of searching, of wondering, was officially guilty. It was more than enough to put me at ease.

Standing in a desolate area of Lincoln Park in the middle of the night, trying to figure out a way to 'think' myself back to the Underworld, was new for me. I pinched my eyes shut, touched the side of my head like Professor Xavier, nothing worked.

Underworld.

Underworld go, I need.

Okay, thinking like Yoda didn't work either. I blew out a breath. What if I imagined a *way* to the Underworld? I closed my eyes and thought of the first thing that came to mind. A golden escalator appeared, leading underground. The stairs made the familiar clicking vibration sounds of any run of the mill escalator. I tested it with the tip of my toe before stepping on. Step-by-step, it took me down to the Underworld to an awaiting Hades.

He leaned on a nearby column, a small smirk on his face. "An escalator? Interesting choice."

"It was the first thing that came to mind," I said with a shrug.

"You could've picked a cloud, a Pegasus, a—"

After hopping from the last step, I stood in front of him and tore my glasses away. "I could've come down here on a Pegasus? You've got so much to tell me."

"In due time," he said with a half-smile. "First, I believe a ceremony is in order."

My chest tightened. This was it.

He led us over to his throne, taking both my hands. We

faced each other, and I shivered. I stared up at the god I'd grown to love and regretted nothing. Still didn't mean I wasn't nervous about becoming Queen of the Underworld.

Swirls of smoke, fog, and embers encircled us. We lifted from the ground, floating so high up, we almost touched the cave ceiling. He showed me the glowing orange substance Zeus gave him. It looked like a sugared crystal.

"Ambrosia," he whispered.

He broke a piece off, placing it in his mouth and dipped his head down. His lips smoothed against mine, transitioning the bite of ambrosia. It melted as soon as it hit my tongue. He kissed me, holding me against his him. A blast of white light burst from my chest, a cascading tingle starting from the top of my skull, traveling down to my toes. I didn't dare open my eyes, trusting him, giving into it.

He broke away from the kiss, pressing his lips against my ear. "You need to say it out loud, Stephanie. Zeus made you Queen, but to receive the power that goes with it, you need to claim it."

My eyes fluttered open. "What do I say?"

"I claim the Underworld and its King, as he claims me." A fire roared in his gaze, making my stomach clench.

"I claim the Underworld and its King, as he claims me." The words flowed from my tongue like a practiced melody.

He graced me with another smile, his wings sprouting from his back. He kissed me again with a ferocity that tugged at my inner tigress. I wrapped my arms around his neck. The smoke and fog grew denser. The feel of cloth skirted down my legs, and I broke from the kiss, looking down. A flowy cranberry-colored dress replaced my clothes. I held my left hand up, watching an intricate piece of gold jewelry start as a ring on my finger, attaching to a bracelet, and stopping at an armband.

"What's happening?" I asked through a husky breathy.

He nuzzled his nose against my jaw. "You're becoming the Queen."

My hair stayed its same chocolate tone but grew down to my hips in shimmering waves. My ears itched, and when I pressed my fingertips against them, they came to a point. He turned us so I could look down at his throne. Another raised beside it, white and shimmering in stark contrast to his dark, ghostly one. He lowered us to the ground, leading me over to the throne, my throne.

He moved his hand through the air, and my own reflection stared back at me. He slipped the glasses from my nose. My eyes were glowing and cranberry-colored. He swirled his hand around my head and a crown of two feathers wrapped around my forehead. They sparkled and glowed bright white.

I gasped. "I half expected a flower crown."

"Flowers don't suit you." He places his hands on my shoulders from behind me. "I can't give you wings, but you have such a fascination for them, this was the best I could do."

I beamed.

"Besides, you're allergic to pollen." He winked.

I laughed and stared at my reflection. It was me. I knew it was, but I wanted to cry over how beautiful the image was.

"Do you like it?" He asked.

I turned and cupped his face in my hands. "No words could justify how elated I feel."

He pressed a hand against my back, guiding me to my throne and motioned for me to sit. The armrests felt cool and smooth against my fingers. Carved into the white marble were cypress trees, wings, and a singular serpent.

He smiled down at me. "Welcome to your Kingdom, my Queen."

I sat on my new throne, in my new world, pieces of my hair floating in my peripheral vision. The reality of it all hit me like a backdraft. My heartbeat quickened, and the pace of my breathing followed.

"Stephanie," Hades said, placing a hand on my shoulder.

His white eyes gazed down at me, begging me to confide in him.

"I thought this through, I did, but now that it's real, my brain is trying to catch up. I'm a goddess now. A queen. With responsibilities I'm completely unaware of." I looked up at him, vision blurring with tears.

He frowned and knelt in front of me, taking my trembling hands into his. "Did you think I wouldn't guide you? We'll work through this. Together. You're married to the second most powerful god of Olympus. You're right. Responsibilities come with it. But I promise you. I won't rush you into anything."

I scooted forward, pressing my forehead against his.

"I'd done my duties alone for eons until—" He paused, a crinkle in his brow. "I won't mention her again. The point is, I can handle anything you feel you cannot."

"Like torturing bad guys?"

He looked taken aback. "I would *never* have thought of putting that burden on you." He stood, pulling me up with him. "I wish to give you the Fields if you'd have them."

"What would I do?"

He slipped his arm through mine, patting my hand that rested on his bicep. He led me to an entry in the cave I had yet to see. "You'd guide souls to their eternal paradise. Something tells me they'd be more at ease seeing your face over mine." He half-smiled. "You could read them. See who they are beyond the surface. It will keep the Elysian Fields a paradise without the risk of a few bad apples sneaking in."

We stopped at a black entrance covered with fog.

I closed my eyes, imagining the serene looks on their faces when they realized death might not have been so bad after all. "I'd be honored to have the Fields."

He waved his hand over the entrance. Bright blue skies, lush green fields, flowers, waterfalls. Pure paradise. My heart soared.

He dipped his lips to my ear. "You have the power to visit someone here if you wish. But only once."

I turned to face him and my throat constricted. Mom. "How do I change myself to look normal? She hasn't seen me since I was a kid. She'd barely recognize me as an adult, let alone like this."

He caressed my temple. "Simply think it, and it will be."

I closed my eyes, a tingle starting from my hairline traveled down to my toes.

Hades smiled down at me and slipped my glasses on. "You don't need them anymore, but they suit you."

Out of habit, I adjusted them and then did a turn for his perusal. "How do I look?"

"Like a goddess." He brushed my bangs away from my eyes and gestured at the Fields. "Go take a look at your new realm. And talk to her. She'll be pleased to see you."

I bit down on my lip with a nod, feeling those excited jitters I felt when I was about to do public speaking. The grass felt soft under the weight of my ballet flats, hugging my feet like a cloud with each step. Birds chirped from tree branches, and bubbling brooks streamed over rocks in a nearby river. Where was everyone?

A couple trotted out from a thicket, dressed in white linen, holding hands. A young couple. They couldn't have been any older than early twenties. They looked as carefree as children. Before the world influences you and the harsh realities settle in. A calm pooled in my abdomen that I couldn't remember the last time I'd felt. The Fields were mine to oversee now.

Further in, houses sat on hills overlooking the water. Dozens of more people crossed my path of all ages, genders, and races. No one frowned, or cried, or yelled. It was never-ending; the edges of the horizon blurring against the sky. How was I supposed to find her? Hades said to think it, and it will be. I closed my eyes and imagined my mother's face. When I opened them, she sat on a bench underneath a cypress tree.

I knew she wouldn't recognize me right away, but hoped deep down she'd know it was me. I clasped my hands behind my back and walked up to her.

"Marianne?" I asked, dipping my head to meet her gaze.

She looked over her shoulder, squinting at me. She rose to her feet, eyes narrowing to slits.

I stepped closer and took a deep breath. "It's me. Stephanie."

She searched my face and, gradually, the widest smile I'd ever seen on her brightened her eyes. She leaped from the bench, hugging me tightly and weeping. "Stephanie? Is it really you?"

I suppressed tears, hugging her back. The smell of her shampoo still clung to her brown hair, and hundreds of memories flooded my thoughts. "Yes, Mom. It's me. I can't believe you recognized me."

She peeled back, pressing her hands to my cheeks. "It took me a moment, but I can see that little girl in your eyes. You've grown into such a beautiful woman, Steph, my word." She played with my hair that matched hers and ran a finger down my nose that resembled Dad's.

"Are you happy here, Mom?"

"How could I not be?" She smiled, but then it morphed into a frown. "Wait—if you're here that means you're—"

I grabbed her hands. "No. I'm not."

"Then, how?" Her eyes blinked with the speed of a hummingbird.

I took a deep breath. "Let's go for a walk." After slipping my arm through hers, I walked her to the lakeshore. She'd always had a deep love for life on the water. Part of me wondered if it was why Dad ended up in a lake house in Alaska. To be reminded of her.

"After the fire, I struggled for years, not blaming myself. The arsonist. It was his fault, but I kept circling back to: if I'd only been there." I stared at the small fish bobbing underwater for the tiny gnats floating on the surface.

"Oh, Stephanie," she said, resting a hand on my face. "You

couldn't have done anything. You were a child. I'm glad you weren't there."

"Do you remember Grandma saying she thought I could see people's auras?"

She nodded. "I loved my mother and always thought she said such absurd things. And now here I am in the Underworld." She chuckled, picking up a rock and throwing it in the water.

"She was right." I couldn't blink, watching the ripples from the rock cascade in expanding circles.

"What do you mean?"

"The colors I see in most people have some form of vibrance yearning to push through, but the arsonist...pure black." I took my glasses off, letting the stem roll between my fingers. "It's something I've always been able to do. Search for that good in humanity. He was the first one I couldn't see it. It drove me to keep that hope alive. It's what led me to my... husband." One step at a time. Telling her flat out, I was Queen of the Underworld, might have been a bit jarring.

Her eyes teared up, and she pulled me into a side hug. "Who is he? What's his name? Where'd you meet?"

"A few months ago, I went on vacation to Greece. We met at the resort."

"Greece. How romantic," the beaming in her brown eyes made my heart melt. It'd been so long seeing the expression of a proud parent.

I licked my lips. "His name is Hades."

"Hades? The same as—" She looked off into the distance.

I couldn't drag it on any longer. "Mom, I married the god of the Underworld. *This* Underworld."

She made a small 'o' shape with her mouth, staring at the water before smiling. "My daughter is Queen of the Underworld?"

I leaned back. "How are you taking this so well?"

"Come here," she said, leading me to the water's edge.

She slipped off her sandals and rolled her pant legs, dipping her bare feet in the lake. I did the same and sat next to her.

"I know all of this exists because I'm here. You were always so special. Your grandma's intuitions frightened me. She always told me you were destined for great things. Things beyond this known world. And here I thought she met you'd travel the universe as an astronaut or something." She half smiled, swirling her toes. "So, it doesn't surprise me that my daughter, the little girl who once gave a cookie to a man yelling at a waiter because she could tell he was having a bad day, would end up in such a position."

"The position of a fated eternity in the Underworld?"

She shook her head, resting her hand on my shoulder. "You spent your life always seeing the good in people, only to now be the first thing a good soul sees when being led to their afterlife."

Mom had a way of putting things into perspective. "I miss you."

She hugged me, stroking her hand over my hair. "And I, you. But I'm so glad to hear you did alright without me. I knew you'd be fine. Hades. He treats you well?"

"He goes above and beyond. Better than any human guy I've ever dated." I bit my lower lip. "I feel calm when I'm with him. Like I finally have nothing to worry about it."

She continued to smooth my hair as we both stared at the

still water. I knew our time together needed to wrap up.

"I have to go, Mama." I hadn't called her that since I was four, but sitting here with her as she played with my hair made me revert to my youth.

"I know. I'm glad we got to see each other one last time."

I leaned back, sniffling. "You know this could only happen once?"

She nodded, brushing her fingers through my bangs. "We all know. The departed must move on."

The departed. A fate I no longer had.

"You'll be good for this place. Far better than the other woman."

I cocked an eyebrow. "Other woman? You mean Persephone?"

"Yes. She grew to be a tyrant. Rushing people here. Not giving them time to let the idea of them being dead sink in. She didn't care."

When Persephone had said this place turned her into something she hadn't wished to become...

But I chose this. It wouldn't be the same for me and I knew it.

"I'll be different."

"I know. And you *willingly* married Hades. For love. You are special, Stephanie. Don't ever forget it." She kissed my forehead.

"Goodbye," I said, barely above a whisper.

She disappeared into golden shimmers, the wind carrying it away. I sat motionless with my hands in my lap before closing my eyes. When I opened them, I was back in the throne room. Hades sat up when I appeared. The sight of his face warmed me. Like he'd been holding his breath the mere minutes I was gone, unsure if I'd return.

"Did it go well?" He asked.

I nodded. "I missed her. It was nice to be able to say goodbye. Thank you."

"Steph, again, there's absolutely no need for you to thank *me*."

He spoke the truth, as he always had, and it made my stomach flutter. I pushed my glasses further up my nose and realized I'd forgotten to transform myself back.

He patted my throne, motioning for me to sit. "I have some news for you."

His robes shifted, falling over his form in perfect folds as he turned to face me. "While you were gone, I had a talk with Zeus—and Thanatos."

I crossed my legs, leaning in. "Oh?"

"We made a deal, that once a year, you and I will be allowed time on the surface for no longer than two weeks." His glowing eyes pierced mine.

"We can—we can go to the surface?" I tried to hold it back. I really did. The excitement was too much to contain, and I let out a high-pitched shriek, leaping over the armrest of my throne to hug him.

He grunted as my shoulder shoved into his chest, and he slipped an arm around me. "I knew you'd be pleased..." He let his last word trail off.

I peeled back. "There's a catch, isn't there?"

"I'll be duty-bound to uphold Thanatos' role while on the surface. So he too can take a break. Only me, though. Not you. Not ever you."

I kissed him and trailed my fingers through his hair. Every minute spent with him reminded me why I chose to do it all in the first place.

He pulled away. "There's one more thing."

"Let me guess." I slumped back. "Zeus?"

"You know him so well already."

I flicked the air. "I knew one like him in high school."

"He requested a yearly performance from us. A dance. In front of—the entire family." Hades pinched the bridge of his nose with a grimace.

"Is this his way of trying to humiliate you?"

He dragged his hand down his face. "At every turn."

"Doesn't seem so bad—the *entire* family? How many gods and goddesses is that?" My heart leaped to my throat, choking me.

He blinked. "I've lost count."

I went silent.

"Steph? Are you okay? You have that same look on your face right before you passed out."

I slunk further into the throne, dreading the thought of thousands of people watching me.

He kneeled in front of me, resting his hands on my knees. His touch sent a wave of calm like a gust of wind at the beach.

"You'll be fine. If the god of the Underworld, known for his brood and menace, can find his inner Patrick Swayze, you should have no problem dancing with him in front of family."

I smiled, morphing myself into my Underworld form. His face brightened, a harsh breath escaping his nostrils. "You're right. A small price to pay to be able to go to the surface. Besides, I can't wait to see the look on Zeus' face when we *own* that shit."

He chuckled, running his finger over the point of my ear. The touch made my toes curl. "Are you certain you can be happy down here? Truly happy? With me?"

I moved forward until my knees brushed against his ribs, sliding him between my legs. "Low self-esteem doesn't suit you, Hades. I hope to change that. See the version of you before you became battered and torn."

He gripped the back of my neck and kissed me, swallowing any other words I might've said.

Once we came up for air, I narrowed my eyes. "Cerberus doesn't sleep in the bedroom, does he?"

Hades stared at me wide-eyed before letting out a hearty chuckle. "No. And I don't plan to start."

"Worship me, Hades," I whispered before a wicked grin tugged at my lips.

He smiled back, villainous and beautiful. Smoke, embers, and burnt feathers flittered the air as his wings escaped.

EPILOGUE

ONE YEAR LATER...

MY EYES FLUTTERED OPEN, and I turned on my side. It shouldn't have surprised me. The bed was empty except for me, but it didn't disappoint me any less. I smoothed my hand over the black silk sheets where Hades' imprint was with a sigh. There was a devastating volcanic eruption in Indonesia, which meant he and I worked overtime.

I slipped from the bed, swirling my hand around myself. The satin nightgown clinging to my body morphed into the Queenly attire.

I tried to convince Hades to let me pick up some of the slack when the Underworld got overly busy such as it was now. He insisted he'd rather be the one losing sleep, not me. The man could be so sweet sometimes it made my teeth ache.

I took a seat at my desk, smiling to myself as I grabbed a piece of parchment. Hades had taught me how to write in calligraphy. Though I could communicate to him in any way I chose, old-fashioned note passing continued to be my favorite. After scrolling what I wanted to say, I held it up. The paper burnt away in floating bits of embers and smoke before disappearing entirely.

My pet scurried from the other room, slipping on the floor several times as it tried to gain traction. Pluto looked like a mix between a Pomeranian and the Cheshire Cat. Wide mouth, with an elongated tongue. Poofy blue striped fur. It was the kind of ugly you couldn't help but find adorable. Hades created him for me when he realized how much I missed Sammy, knowing I couldn't bring him down here. The mortal clause applied to human and animals alike.

"Good morning, boy. Ready for breakfast?" I scratched the top of his head.

His tongue fell out onto the floor, caking it with drool, and his forked tail whipped back and forth. I conjured a bowl of kibble, and he shoved his entire head in it.

I made my way to the hallway, scooping my steaming coffee cup from the maker I'd created for myself. The smell of vanilla and cinnamon wafted through the air. The caffeine in coffee would do nothing for me anymore, but it was a simplistic normalcy I wanted to keep around. I made a bone the size of my arm appear in my hand, and whistled down the hall, the high-pitched sound echoing off the walls. Cerberus came barreling around the corner, and I tossed the bone. He charged past me, all three of his heads snapping excitedly.

A tingle traveled down my spine, and I closed my eyes. The sensation meant another soul required guidance to the Fields. I swirled my hand around my head, producing my winged crown. When I appeared at the hidden entrance to the Fields, a young woman with auburn hair stood there shivering. I touched her shoulder with the gentleness of a passing cloud.

She gasped and turned around. Her widened eyes and trembling lips melted from her expression upon seeing me. I smiled and waved my hand, producing a portal window. The woman's lips parted, the sun from the Fields illuminating her face. Her aura sparkled with shimmering waves of yellow and beige. There was no where else she was meant to be. The perfect candidate for the Fields.

"It's so beautiful I almost forgot I died," the woman muttered.

I held my hand out, beckoning her to follow me. "Death only of the mortal sense. *This* is your new home. Your new life."

She let me lead her onto the green grass. It didn't take long for me to sense her comfort, her contentment. My job was done. They weren't all as easy. Sometimes I'd spend hours soothing them before I felt confident enough to leave them alone. The woman ran to a nearby stream, dipping her hands into the sparkling water. I backed away, slipping back through the portal.

Hades and I spent most of the day apart taking care of our realms, but would always come together at the same time to spend the rest of the evening together. And that time was right about—

His presence loomed behind me with the scent of burning wood. He traced his fingers down my neck, and I purred.

His lips brushed my ear, making my heart race. "I got your note," he said, making the note appear in a burst of flame.

"Florida," Hades said monotone. "Our first time back on the surface. You could choose anywhere in the known world, and you choose…Florida?"

I held my cup of cold coffee out to him with a wide grin, wiggling it back and forth.

He touched the side of it with a single orange glowing finger and the cup steamed back to life. "And you do realize we still have months before we get to go back?"

I waved my hand through the note, making it disappear. "I'm a planner. You know that." Was it insane how much I missed him even though it'd only been hours apart? I beamed up at him and said, "Besides, what's wrong with Florida? It's sunny, has Disney—"

"Surrounded on nearly all sides by water," Hades mumbled.

I grinned and sauntered forward, curling his hair around my finger. "And then after that, I was thinking—Alaska."

His eyes narrowed. "Water *and* cold," he grumbled. "I think there are souls who need torturing," he joked, pretending to turn away.

I laughed and yanked on his arm. He looked down at me with a smile.

"Lucky for me, you're excellent at putting on a brave face," I teased, running my finger over the part of his chest that poked out from his robes.

He wrapped his arm around me, pushing his palm into my lower back. "Mm and lucky for me darlin', I married an enchantress."

Normally, he saved the southern drawl for his mortal guise, but he surprised me with it every once and awhile because he knew it drove me wild.

"Has Tartarus slowed down at all?"

"I've spent this time away to ensure it wouldn't become overrun in my absence. Though the volcano was an unwanted surprise." His finger drew absent circles over my exposed back. "But now you get me all to yourself for the rest of the night." His voice grew husky.

I grinned. "And what should we do with our night?"

"Do you remember what you said when I asked what you missed most about life on Earth?"

I squinted and tapped my finger against my lip. "Me and Sara's Friday the thirteenth movie ritual?"

He nodded. "Not sure if you've been keeping track of Earth calendar days, but today…is Friday the thirteenth."

"What are you saying?"

He waved his arm, and we appeared in a small room with a red love seat and big screen TV. He transformed himself into his mortal guise and touched a hand to my shoulder, changing me as well.

His dimple deepened as he gave a lopsided grin, staring down at me.

"Why are you looking at me like that?" I asked.

"The Underworld version of you is my Queen and beautiful beyond what I could imagine, but *this* you," he traced the back of his hand down my arm. "Was my salvation." Those wisps of hair fell over his eyes as he dipped his chin, and my stomach flipped.

I leaped up, wrapping my arms around his neck. He caught me, his forearms supporting under my rump. I kissed his lips and then pecked all over his cheeks and nose. He laughed, wincing like one of my kisses would take an eye out.

He lowered me to the ground. "Tonight, let's simply be a normal couple, having a normal movie night." He slipped my glasses on my nose with a snarky grin.

I bit down on my lower lip. "I wasn't sure if it was possible to love you anymore. I was wrong."

He conjured a pan of Jiffy Pop and held his hand under it. A burst of flame popped the corn in an instant.

I folded my arms. "What happened to normal?"

"Except for that. It takes too long, and I don't feel like creating a stove." He winked and flopped onto the couch. "Pick whatever you want, sweetheart."

I sat down and patted my thighs. "Well, I think we start a new tradition. Instead of *Dirty Dancing* like Sara and I watched, we'll watch…eighties horror movies." I grinned.

He paused with popcorn in his mouth, turning to cock an eyebrow at me. Pluto trotted past us, sliding on the floor before leaping to my lap. He panted and looked between us, one of his eyes squinting.

"I still can't believe you named your pet after me," Hades deadpanned.

"Hey, I can't help your Roman name also happens to be a beloved Disney dog."

Hades grimaced at the dog. "I can make him look… different, you know?"

I gasped and held Pluto in his face, waving him back and

forth. "He is adorable just the way he is."

Hades leaned past the dog with a cock of his brow.

I re-emphasized Pluto's said cuteness by wiggling him again. Pluto licked Hades' cheek and panted.

"Fine." Hades wiped his face with a shirt sleeve. "He's not…repulsive."

I nodded once and set Pluto back on my lap, scratching his ears, and making his back leg bounce. "Alright, first up." I waved my hand at the TV. "*Evil Dead.*"

"Sounds like something I'm not going to like," he grumbled.

"No brooding on movie night." I nuzzled against him and threw some popcorn in my mouth.

Pluto did several circles before nuzzling into my lap and shutting his eyes.

Hades was reasonably quiet for the entire movie, only making the occasional scowl. It was after the third deadite soul took over a living mortal he felt compelled to express his opinion.

"Okay, this is ridiculous. Are they trying to say the evil dead can escape Tartarus and take over a living mortal just because some words were spoken in a made-up language? They'd never make it past Cerberus, let alone up to the surface."

I slipped a hand over his mouth. "You're missing all the best Ash one-liners."

"Ash?" he asked into my palm.

I laughed and pulled my hand away. "Bruce Campbell. Ash. The guy in the blue shirt with the chain saw? The *main* guy?"

"Right," he clipped.

We spent the rest of the movie eating endless popcorn and

cuddling. He even chuckled a time or two.

When it was over, I turned to face him. "Was it as torturous as Tartarus?"

"Not at all. I quite enjoyed it after I stopped comparing it to the *true* way death works." He smiled.

I threw popcorn at him. Pluto yipped and jumped to the floor.

His smile faded, and he narrowed his eyes before throwing some back. Several pieces landed in my hair. My jaw dropped. A sly grin slowly spread across his lips.

"Hey!" I protested through a giggle.

He tackled me onto the couch, hovering above me on his forearms. He rolled his hips against me. "Are you happy, Steph?"

"Very," I cooed.

"Did this night of normalcy help your homesickness?"

I smiled. "Very. But I have a favor to ask."

"Anything." He lowered his head and brushed his lips over my nose.

"Next time, use your wings to heat the popcorn. Because let's face it, sweetie, this *is* my new normal."

He kissed me and grinned against my mouth. "As you wish, darlin'."

THE
CONTEMPORARY MYTHOS
WILL CONTINUE

APOLLO

Available on Amazon

EXCERPT FROM

A P O L L O

NEXT IN THE
CONTEMPORARY MYTHOS
SERIES:

THE LIGHTS DIMMED, AND I sat up straight. Kate wasn't back yet. Fog flowed over the stage, and the audience went wild. Whistles, whoops, and screams flooded my ears. Everyone around me stood up, but I remained in my seat, slouching down as far as possible. The drummer appeared first, starting a steady rhythm that reminded me of wrestling entrance music. The crowd's rowdiness increased.

Where was Kate? She was going to kill me. Stupid nachos.

The lead guitarist walked on stage next. He had black hair down to his hips, a black t-shirt with a Punisher skull, and a baggy pair of shorts. He stuck his tongue out and raised his fists in two rock symbols. The crowd answered him by throwing their fists in the air. I wanted to curl the jacket over my head.

The bassist did a front flip onto the stage, with the bass guitar strapped to his chest. He had spiky short brown hair and enough charcoal around his eyes to put Jack Sparrow to shame. The drummer picked up speed, his arms flailing from one side to the other. A sun appeared on the farthest left jumbo screen behind the stage and transitioned to the middle one. The crowd screamed so loudly, I winced.

Ace appeared in the middle of the stage within a burst of flames. His guitar was strapped to his back, and he kept his head held low. A retro unidirectional microphone on a stand rose from the floor. He wrapped a tanned hand around it. The drums came to a stop, and the lights went out.

I gripped my armrests, not being able to see my hand in front of my face. A shimmery orange bow and arrow floated on stage. The arrow pulled back and shot into the audience, before exploding in a spray of orange glitter. I held my hand out, expecting it to collect in my hand, but instead, it disappeared as if it never existed. The lights blared back on, and I squinted my eyes as they adjusted.

Ace lifted his head and threw a fist into the air. "How are we doing tonight, Buffalo?"

Why did he have to be so disgustingly attractive?

He had pale blonde hair that fell just past his collar bone, bright blue eyes, and an insanely strong clean-shaven jawline. He wore golden skintight pants and a golden vest, giving a clear view of his upper half. Tanned. Muscular. Cut.

He smiled. I could've sworn the stage lights glinted off his teeth they were so white. And then his gaze dropped—to me. I shifted my eyes. How the hell did he even see me within my hole of standing fans? He kept his electric grin but squinted his eyes as if taken aback at my lack of enthusiasm for being in the first row.

"The line was insane. Oh my—how much did I miss?" Kate said, scooting past several people and thankfully—blocking my view.

"Not much. He just appeared in a burst of flames after shooting a glittery bow and arrow into the audience," I said monotone.

She shoved the nachos in my face. The smell of liquid cheese and jalapenos wafted through the air.

"He did what? Oh, man," she pouted, but quickly recovered when Ace started to sing.

I remained seated, eating as many nachos that I figured would appease Kate before shoving the remainder under my chair.

Ace swung the guitar from his back to his front, sliding his left hand down the neck of it like caressing an arm. It was white pearlescent with chrome accents and down the length of the neck, underneath the strings, were glowing orange suns. He dragged a hand through his hair, which had just enough greasiness to maintain sexy versus gross. He stood in front of the mic, strumming the guitar as he sang. His eyes never left the audience, moving from one person to the next.

He sang about being born from the sun and something about sharing the warmth. It should've come as no surprise the lyrics were as if he thought he truly *was* a god. Kate grabbed my arm and hoisted me up.

"At least pretend like you're having a good time," she said with a snicker.

Ace swung the guitar to his back and removed the mic from the stand. He started at the end of the stage farthest from us, holding his hand out for anyone who wanted the privilege of touching his clammy fingers. Kate leaned forward, her chin barely above the stage. She waved her arms, stretching her fingers as far as they'd go. I folded my arms.

When he got to us, he brushed Kate's fingers, and I thought she'd pass out on the spot. He continued to sing, squinting at me again as he passed. Why did he keep looking at me? Move along rockstar. He moved back to the stand, repositioning the mic on it. He took his guitar off, resting it on the floor and stepped to the edge of the stage.

Kate had the hand he touched up in the air like she was a prepping surgeon.

"Please tell me you intend on washing that hand again," I yelled over the music.

She shrugged. "I honestly couldn't tell you."

Ace pumped his leg in beat with the music, biting down on his lower lip. He grabbed both sides of his vest and raised his brows.

Women in the crowd yelled with such high-pitched shrills it could shatter glass. One woman next to us shouted, "Take it off!"

Ace slid one side of the vest over his shoulder, followed by the other, and let it slide down his forearms until it was in his hand. He swung it around several times before throwing it into the audience. One woman caught it, but another near her latched onto it, and a catfight ensued.

My God. Was I even on planet Earth anymore?

He stood in all his bronzed skin, shirtless glory, the lights casting the perfect shadows over every piece of taut muscle. Did he plan it that way?

He scooped the guitar up, throwing the strap over his head. Not missing a beat, he played with the interlude, and my head started to nod. I couldn't help it. The song had a nice beat to it, and rhythm was ingrained in my very soul. The nod turned into a full-on head bob.

Ace walked in front of us and dropped to his knees. He held the guitar vertical, and his fingers flew feverishly over the strings. His muscles twitched and flexed, and veins popped out over his forearms. I gulped.

"Oh my, God!" Kate squealed, jumping up and down, and clamping her hands over her mouth.

The concert went on for another hour, and the audience persuaded them to play not only one, but two encores. Something told me Ace had no issue with it. He didn't even seem out of breath. He made eye contact with me five more times throughout the performance and did his shirtless guitar playing in front of us another three times. No exaggeration. I counted.

Once they said their goodbyes and the clapping and screaming finally started to die down, they walked off stage, and a security guard appeared in front of us.

"You two ready?" He asked.

"For what?" I asked back.

He cocked a bushy eyebrow. "You have backstage passes."

"Don't mind her," Kate said, shoving me to the aisle. "We're *so* ready."

The closer we got to the stairs leading backstage, my heart beat faster. Sweat soaked the back of my neck, and I wanted to turn away, but Kate had me trapped in her damn arm curl.

Ace stood in the distance, chatting it up and laughing with the bassist. A female fan with a bosom twice the size of her head bounced in front of them. She handed Ace a sharpie, and he gave a lopsided grin. Without batting an eyelash, he signed her cleavage. He was still very shirtless.

"These are the two backstage pass winners, guys," the security guard said, holding his hand out for us to approach them. He motioned for the buxom woman. She frowned, and he led her off stage.

I dug my heels into the ground, but Kate pulled me right along. For such a tiny woman, she had the strength of a rhino.

Ace glanced at Kate, but concentrated on me, flashing one of his trademark grins. "Ah, the two beauties from the front row."

I looked at the rafters, the ground, the roadie bent over and showing his butt crack, anywhere but at him.

Kate giggled, draping a hand over her mouth. "You all put on an amazing show. And those pyrotechnics? They looked *so* real."

"We have an amazing crew," Ace said.

Kate gasped. "Oh my God, the drummer. I'll be right back, Laurel." She ran off, the little traitor.

The bassist looked between us and then snapped his fingers. "I'm going to go—over here," he mumbled before walking away.

"Your name is Laurel?" He asked with a twinkle in his eye.

"Yes. Do you have a problem with that name?" I finally found the will to look at him, but tried not to stare at his nipples.

He smirked, and his pecs bounced. "Not at all. Did you enjoy the show?"

"It was alright," I lied.

He laughed, and his damn pecs danced again. "I saw your head bobbing. You were into it."

"Music is music." I turned my head away.

He dropped his face to look at mine. "Why can't you look at me?"

"You're standing here half-naked."

He dragged his hands over his chest and abdomen.

My stomach flipped.

"Does this bother you?"

I didn't answer.

"Wait. Are you a lesbian? Not that there's anything—"

"No. I'm not a lesbian. You're so arrogant. It truly astounds me." I crossed my arms in a huff.

He put one hand on his hip and pointed at me with the other. "And you're snooty."

My jaw dropped. "Why? Because I didn't drop my pants at first sight of you?"

"Amongst other things." He rubbed his hand over his chin, eyeing me like one would eye up pieces of a jigsaw puzzle.

"Not used to having your ego bruised, are you?"

He chuckled. "You think you're bruising my ego?" His golden hair fell in a perfect frame over his face.

"Definitely." I pulled my shoulders back.

He pointed at my shirt. "What's the cartoon supposed to be?"

"Hades."

He narrowed his eyes and smirked. "Real cute."

"I thought so."

Kate, my unsung hero, appeared beside me. "They're saying we have to go," she groaned.

"Have to go already?" He leaned toward me. "Such a shame," he said, sarcasm lacing his tone.

Was it horrible I felt the urge to stick my tongue out at him? Instead, I lifted my chin in the air and grabbed the crook of Kate's elbow.

"Come on, Kate. It's getting *stuffy* in here." I glared at him over my shoulder.

She whined. "But I don't want to go."

"Would ice cream help?" I asked.

She perked up. "Soft serve?"

"Is there any other kind?"

Her pace quickened, and I stopped at the stairs to risk a look back. Ace stood in the same spot we'd left him, rubbing his smooth chin. He stared at the ground before catching my gaze. He made a 'shoo' gesture with his hands. It took every ounce of my willpower to not throw one of the nearby stage lights at him. Not that I could throw it that far anyway. I blew air out of my nostrils like a bull and clamored down the stairs.

"So, you and Ace were alone," Kate said, nudging me in the rib with her elbow.

"I don't like him. He doesn't like me. So, stop whatever fantasy is rolling around in that crazy brain of yours pronto."

Her grin widened into a maniacal one.

"Why do you have that look on your face?" I asked, leaning away.

"Because all the best romances start that way." She raised on the balls of her feet and skipped toward the parking lot.

STAY TUNED!

WWW.CARLYSPADE.COM

ACKNOWLEDGEMENTS

FIRST, TO MY HUSBAND, you gave me so many unique ideas to flesh out Hades' character, and as always, I appreciate your support and continued willingness to hear my thoughts.

To my critique partner: Sarah. I can't thank you enough for the honesty you always give, and with this book in particular, it needed those harsh truths. Thank you for making it better.

To my beta readers, your feedback made this story bigger, better, and totally badass. I can't thank you all enough for taking the time to read and comment, all the while being honest and enthusiastic.

Meghan and Brittany AKA "Miss Poopy Pants", you both read Hades not once, but twice as I made revisions. You're both my heroes, and I couldn't ask for better cheerleaders in my corner.

Matt, thank you for being my go-to with anything law enforcement related. I couldn't have come up with such a plausible case and I appreciated your help and input.

A special thanks to the creators of the nineties shows *Hercules: The Legendary Journeys* and *Xena: Warrior Princess*. Those shows shaped my childhood and made me the Greek mythology fiend I am today.

To the readers, I know there are so many Greek myth retellings out there, and I thank you for taking the chance on yet another series. Greek mythology has been a passion of mine for over twenty years, and it was only a matter of time before it seeped into my writing. I hope this series will remain unique from what you've read and continue to feed into your hunger for more Greek god and goddess goodies!

ABOUT THE AUTHOR

CARLY SPADE is an adult romance writer who has been writing since she could pick up a pencil. After the insanity of obtaining a bachelor's and master's degree in cybersecurity, creating worlds to escape to still ate at her very soul. She started writing FanFiction (which can still be found if you scour the internet), and soon felt the need to get her original ideas on paper. And so the adventure began.

She lives in Colorado with her husband and two fur babies, and revels in an enemies to lovers trope with a slow burn.

Find her online:

WWW.CARLYSPADE.COM

Printed in Great Britain
by Amazon